Vladimir

Vladimir

Julia May Jonas

PICADOR

First published 2022 by Avid Reader Press
An imprint of Simon & Schuster, Inc.
1230 Avenue of the Americas, New York, NY 10020

First published in paperback in the UK 2022 by Picador

This edition published 2022 by Picador
an imprint of Pan Macmillan
The Smithson, 6 Briset Street, London ECIM 5NR
EU representative: Macmillan Publishers Ireland Ltd,
1st Floor, The Liffey Trust Centre,
117–126 Sheriff Street Upper, Dublin 1, DOI YC43
Associated companies throughout the world
www.panmacmillan.com

ISBN 978-1-5290-8044-5

1 3 5 7 9 8 6 4 2

A CIP catalogue record for this book is available from the British Library.

Printed and bound by CPI Group (UK) Ltd, Croydon, CRO 4YY

Visit **www.picador.com** to read more about all our books
and to buy them. You will also find features, author interviews and
news of any author events, and you can sign up for e-newsletters
so that you're always first to hear about our new releases.

For Adam

I ask this one thing:
let me go mad in my own way.

—SOPHOKLES, *ELEKTRA*

Vladimir

Prologue

When I was a child, I loved old men, and I could tell that they also loved me. They loved how eager I was to please them, how much I wanted them to think well of me. They would wink at me, and find me precocious. I would encounter them at church, and at family gatherings, and as friends of my friends' parents. They were the husbands of my dance instructors, or my science or history teachers.

Their approval filled me with pleasure. When I remember my childhood I am wearing a white dress with a blue accent. *Girls in white dresses*—a song written by an old man. This is not what I wore but it is what I remember myself wearing, especially when I interacted with old men. I remember feeling like a classic young girl, and thinking that my goodness shone out of me. Goodness and intelligence radiated from my eyes, and the men recognized it, even the oldest and most cantankerous.

I still like many of the things old men tend to enjoy. Jazz music, folk music, the blues, guitar virtuosity. Long, well-researched histories. Existentialists and muscular writers. Depravity, and funny, violent criminals. Emotional rock 'n' roll. Meanness. I like folksy stories of city life, or country life, or anecdotes about political history. I like clever jokes, and talking about the mechanics of jokes, and turns of phrase, and card games, and war stories.

What I like most about old men now, however, and the reason I often feel that perhaps I *am* an old man more than I am an oldish white woman in her late fifties (the identity I am burdened with publicly presenting, to my general embarrassment), is that old men are composed of desire. Everything about them is wanting. They have appetites for food, boats, vacations, entertainment. They want to be stimulated. They want to sleep. They are guided by desire—their world is made up of their desires. For the old men who I am thinking of (and perhaps I mean a certain kind of old man that I encountered and that has enshrined itself in my mind from youth), they do not know or cannot imagine a kind of world that is not completely and totally guided by a sense of wanting and getting. And of course, they desire the adoration of a sexual partner, even if only in their imaginations, through the blue light of their television screens.

I wrote the above words while looking at Vladimir and his tawny, well-formed head leaning against the wooden chair. His bold—you could call it protruding—forehead catches the light, illuminating the drum-tight skin atop the manly cranial bulges. At forty, he is the kind of man whose face will grow tighter before it softens. His grayish-blond hair rests like mussed hay, plentiful now, but with the threat of translucence and eventual absence in years to come. He is asleep in the chair, and the hair on his left arm (the one that I have not shackled) glows in the late-afternoon sun. The sight of that arm hair, ablaze in the sun, sends a sob down my spine. I run my fingers over its springy softness, as lightly as a tiny, courteous insect.

The chair is big, medieval-style, made of dark brown pine, the finish soft with use. It came from a junk shop, and before that a beer hall on Route 9 that went out of business. The wood is covered with gummy black carvings of names and initials, some pairings encircled by hearts, some with dates. When I'm trying to find inspiration, I will zero in on a set of initials: J. S. + R. B. 1987. I will make up names for the initials: Jehan Soon and Robert Black, let's say, a gay couple who moved upstate from New York City, fleeing the horror of the AIDS crisis—architects, both of them—Jehan the son of immigrant Korean parents, born and raised in Flushing, Queens, and Robert Black, son of a *Mayflower* family, a blue-blooded black sheep, pun lightly intended. They buy a rambling Victorian and decorate it in obsessive style, finding antiques and oddities possible only in the age before the internet, before everyone understood what everything was worth, from Eames chairs to vintage sixties kitsch figurines. One night they venture out in their new town and stumble across a beer hall. It is a warm spring and they sit outside, romantically, beneath trees that are heavy and dripping with flower petals. Jehan becomes tipsy and affectionate, and Robert, frightened of the upstate town and the chunky groups of chunky men who, if not members of, at least draw aesthetic inspiration from Hells Angels, pushes him away. They quarrel, badly, and go home angry—Jehan feeling humiliated, Robert feeling helpless. Much later, after they have made up, Robert, on his own, comes to the beer hall and carves their initials into the chair and, on the first anniversary of their life in this upstate town, brings Jehan to sit in that chair and shows him the carving.

Then they spontaneously combust.

For example.

Vladimir snores lightly, a soft, soothing purr of a snore. It's a sweet, even sound. If I lived with him, if I were his little wife, I would wrap myself around him and let that snore lull me to sleep, like the sound of a rushing ocean.

I could tidy the cabin—the limes from our drinks are squashed on the counter, our shoes in the mudroom point every which way. I could write more, work on my book, but instead I want to sit and stare at the light as it moves across him. I am aware of this moment as a perfect example of liminality. I am living in the reality before Vladimir wakes. I wish some of my students, who have a postadolescent passion for literary terms, were here. I am sure if they were, they could feel it. The no-place-ness and no-time-ness of now. The pulsing presence of this moment between moments.

I.

Although I had seen and heard Vladimir speak during the master class, the candidates luncheon, and the faculty retreat, I had not had the chance to say more than a few words directly to him until the fall semester. When I first met him, in the spring after he'd been hired as a full-time junior professor, I was coming late to and leaving early from all full-faculty events to avoid having to talk with any of my colleagues. Even sitting three chairs away from Florence was almost too much for me to bear—lightning bolts of anger shot from my vagina to my extremities. I've always felt the origin of anger in my vagina and am surprised it is not mentioned more in literature.

On an early September evening, the first week of the semester, he visited me at my home, and that is when we had our first real conversation. I was enjoying the cool breeze in the sitting room of our town house, drinking mineral water—my rule is that if I am alone I do not drink alcohol until 9 p.m. (a practical tactic to keep my weight down)—and reading a history of witches in America, when he rang the bell. Since the allegations had been brought against my husband, I felt unable to read fiction. Usually I eagerly set about a reading project each summer to find at least one or two new short stories or novel excerpts to read with my classes. It was important for them and me to always keep acquainted with the contemporary voice. This summer, however, my eyes felt as though they could not focus on the words. The invented worlds, all the made-up-ness and stolen-ness of fiction, all the characters—they felt like a meager and pitiful offering. I needed dates, facts, numbers, and statistics. Weapons. This is our world and this is what happened in it. In the first class of my survey courses I was accustomed to reading a section of *Poetics* aloud. In it Aristotle discusses the difference between history and poetry and why poetry, being crafted and theoretical, is a superior representation of humanity. This year I skipped it. This year I skipped my whole introductory lecture—usually a litany of references and quotations that I prepped and practiced for well in advance—designed to cow and delight my students. This year, instead, I asked them to speak about themselves and their experiences. While I wish I could say that this decision came from a desire to get to know them, it did not. On my notes for the class I wrote: "Have them talk! (They're only interested in what they think, anyway.)"

I heard a car pull into the drive, and then listened for a while as someone paced around the property, wondering which door to approach. In our town, there's a general custom of entering through the back porch, which, if the house has not been completely remodeled, opens to the kitchen, from a time when in-house help was more prevalent, and domestic labor less of a performance displaying taste, choice, and skill.

Vladimir, however, being new, rang the entrance at the front of the house—which opened to a cold little corridor that we used only as a pass-through to the upstairs. When I opened the door he stood spotlit by the porch light, and immediately put his free hand in his pocket, as though he had been adjusting his hair. He seemed abashed. I remembered my thirties, as a young mother, meeting young fathers, talking about where their sons or daughters were going to elementary school, or whether they were going to try out karate, and how thrilled it made me to see them adjusting their hair or clothing subconsciously: a nervous nod to the powers of attraction I possessed at the time.

He held a bottle of red wine in his other hand and a book tucked into his armpit. When I opened the door he awkwardly switched the two—moving the wine underneath his opposite arm, so it lay against his side like a violin at rest. He wore a knit tie with an engraved tie bar over a checked shirt with rolled-up sleeves, well-cut pants, and good-quality

6

leather boots with thick white soles. Clearly a transplant from the city—no heterosexual man who'd spent much time here would look like that. Even my husband, a vain man with a taste for expensive Irish knit sweaters, had forgotten the specificity and light irony of urban style. My husband wore what he wore because he believed in it—he had lost the sense of costuming and presentation that well-dressed city dwellers naturally possessed. That perambulating sense of always being on display.

Vladimir held out the slim book, chalkboard green with sans serif lettering. "I was going to say I was in the neighborhood but I wasn't—I came from the college—I wanted to give—John and I had spoken earlier—I wanted to bring him—and you, *you*—this.

"And this," he said, holding up the wine. "I wouldn't presume that bringing only my book was enough to justify a visit."

I ignored the wine and put on my act of matronly fandom that these days I used more and more with my students and the young people around me. My Big Mom Energy, as they say. "*negligible generalities* by Vladimir Vladinski," I read. "Your book. I'm so excited, please come in."

After some negotiation with the clunky door that involved his tie being caught, he followed me into the sitting room. As I led him though the corridor, I grabbed a pashmina to wrap around my neck. I prefer to conceal my neck.

"John is out, actually, but can I invite you to have a drink with me? Since you weren't in the neighborhood?"

He agreed after looking at his watch, a gesture to let me know his time was limited.

"Come with me to the kitchen. You can have your wine or beer or a martini."

I am naturally a busy host, and I like busy hosts, though some do not. When someone comes into my house, for a good portion of time I do not stop moving—tidying, making coffee, cleaning. My mother never sat still unless she was reading, typing, paying bills, or asleep, and I share this quality. When I go into someone's house and they are doing many

7

chores, and their attention is divided, and they are packing a suitcase or mopping their floors while I linger about, I feel distinctly at ease. I have always liked the feeling of hanging around, and a host who gives me too much of their attention makes me feel unnerved.

When I had a little affair, back in the city, when I was an all-but-dissertation TA, it was with a very slow-moving young man who made intense and lasting eye contact. He was in my section of the Women in Literature seminar, and his gaze upon me, when he would offer a thought about Woolf or Eliot or Aphra Behn, felt so penetrating and impertinent I didn't know how to take it. I thought it was funny at the beginning, a kind of affectation. As he spent more and more time in my office I became addicted to the eye contact and would try to blink as slowly as possible when we were speaking, so that I could get a sense of leaving and coming back to that warm bath of his ocular attention. When we finally consummated our flirtation, I was devastated to find (though I shouldn't have been surprised) that he could not maintain this communication while making love and turned as screwed-eyed and internal as any other twenty-one-year-old boy. (Lest you be too horrified, I was only twenty-eight.) Once the affair dissolved, I started to find his eye contact irritating, then enraging, and finally simply cow-eyed and insipid. I had to move through all these points of perception. He is "in business" now, and Republican, I think.

"I mean, a martini, now, why not," said Vladimir, sounding titillated by the prospect.

"I make them with vodka so you know. They are suburban martinis. Dirty, and wet, with lots of olive juice and vermouth."

He assured me that was fine, lovely, how he liked them. I opened the bottom cupboard to stand on its ledge so I could reach the glasses on a higher shelf. I am a short woman. This anatomical fact feels at odds with my personality. All my adult life, people, when they find out my height, marvel that I am only five foot three inches tall. They think me to be at least five foot six or even seven. In pictures I am often surprised to see how little I am in comparison to my husband. In my mind, he and I are the same.

I pulled the glasses out of the cupboard. I felt as though Vladimir was standing very close to me, and in fact, when I turned around to hand him the glasses I almost placed them on his chest.

"Sorry," we both said.

"Jinx," I said.

When the drinks were fixed, I led him out to the living room. He sat on the loveseat across from me and spread out in an appealingly masculine way, with a big, wide cross of one leg over the other, ankle to knee. He told me that he had a young child at home, three years old (Philomena, but they called her Phee), and that his wife (a person of great fascination to the department who would be teaching a memoir-writing class for us, a beautiful woman I had seen at faculty events but not yet spoken to) was not adjusting well to the change to the country from the city. He asked where my husband was and seemed surprised when I told him that he was out getting a drink with a former student.

"A student?"

I clarified that it was a male student, which relaxed him.

My husband, John, is the chair of our small English Department in our small upstate New York college, population less than 2,200 students. At the start of the spring semester (last January), our department was handed a petition, with more than three hundred signatures, requesting his removal. Attached to the petition were affidavits by seven women, now of various ages, former students at the college, who, over the course of his twenty-eight years of teaching here, had engaged with him sexually. None, mind you, in the past five years, after teacher/student relationships were explicitly banned. At one point we would have called these affairs consensual, for they were, and were conducted with my vague understanding that they were happening. Now, however, young women have apparently lost all agency in romantic entanglements. Now my husband was abusing his power, never mind that power is the reason they desired him in the first place. Whatever the current state of my marriage may be, I still can't think about it all without my blood boiling. My anger is not so much directed toward the accusations as it is toward the lack of self-regard these women have— the lack of their own confidence. I wish they could see themselves not as little leaves swirled around by the wind of a world that does not belong to them, but as powerful, sexual women interested in engaging in a little bit of danger, a little bit of taboo, a little bit of fun. With the general, highly objectionable move toward a populist insistence of morality in art, I find this post hoc prudery offensive, as a fellow female. I am depressed that they feel so guilty about their encounters with my husband that they have decided he was taking advantage of them. I want to throw them all a Slut Walk and let them know that when they're sad, it's probably not because of the sex they had, and more because they spend too much time on the internet, wondering what people think of them.

Vladimir Vladinski, the young, new professor, who I imagined would work his way up to chair of the department in his tenure, if he receives tenure (which he will, given his adroitness, his literary reputation, his youth, his clear ambition), looked around my living room. I followed his eyes as they rested on the marquee-sized poster of Buñuel's *Belle de Jour*, bought as part of a Film Forum fundraiser when they were liquidating their poster stock, and the series of framed prints from the homes of great American writers, put together after the cross-country adventure we took when my daughter, Sidney, was eight, and we mapped the trip by visiting the hometowns of important American novelists, from Hemingway to Faulkner to O'Connor to Morrison to Wright to Cather to Didion in Los Angeles. To his left, on the wall, backed and hung, were our brochures of the Dostoevsky museum, the Tolstoy museum, and the Turgenev museum from our trip to Russia. On the shelf below the coffee table, piled high, were the programs of the theater we'd seen in our yearly week in New York City. There was nearly an entire wall devoted to representations of Don Quixote, and a large map of Spain, upon which his journey was tracked with pins and coasters from cafés in those towns. A shrine to our far-flung travel stood in a corner of the room, a collection that included an authentic Noh theater Shiite mask, several little statues purchased in the Ariaria Market in Nigeria, Norwegian-carved bookends, a Swedish antique coffeepot, a sitar from India, and a Moroccan wall hanging.

"Your house is amazing," he said, picking up a program of Frida Kahlo's home in Mexico and turning it over in his hands.

"Well, it's a document. Of time passed and things seen." I carefully set my martini down on the antique ashtray stand we used as a drink table. "Sometimes I look at it as a life well-lived. Sometimes I want to burn it all to the ground and become a minimalist."

He shook his head. "But this is the best kind of clutter—this looks like a museum—it's not chain store junk, plastic containers, remote controls."

"Those are more hidden. I have my bags of bags of bags. But does one always want to be surrounded by so much culture? There's something exhausting about being constantly bombarded by everyone's best efforts," I said.

"I don't believe you think that. If you're exhausted by that, you wouldn't be able to survive academia," he said. He was, to my great delight, sparring with me.

"Well, who says I have?" I raised my eyebrows and pursed my lips in what I hoped looked like a knowing nod at the Human Comedy.

He took a large drink from his glass and spilled several drops on his chinos, right at the tip of the crotch of his pants that stretched tight like a trampoline between his crossed legs. "I'm surprised he's allowed out."

He looked toward the window, black and reflective with the night behind it. From the angle we were both sitting, we could see each other in the reflection, but not ourselves. Without trying, we caught each other's gaze. We each smiled, close-lipped, shyly. He averted his eyes.

In the days and nights that followed, it was that image of him in the black glass of the window that haunted and warmed me. His arm extended across the sofa cushion, the cross of his leg revealing the stripe of his sock, his head turned over his shoulder, the gesture of his eyes casting down, like an old-fashioned stage actress looking bashfully at a bouquet.

I usually demurred from frankly addressing details about my marriage, and I sometimes wonder why I chose to be so forthright with Vladimir Vladinski, experimental novelist and junior professor of literature at our small college. But of course I immediately answer myself. I wanted to be intimate with him, so deeply intimate, from that moment I saw him with his legs crossed in the reflection of the window. It was as if an entirely new world had opened up for me, or if not a world, a pit, with no bottom—a continual experience of the exhilarating delirium of falling.

And so I divulged everything. How my husband and I had a tacit agreement that we would be as sexually free as we liked during our marriage. No asking, no telling, mostly communicated through off-handed comments and nods. We didn't discuss it, good lord, who wanted to take the time to discuss such things? Embarrassing, pedestrian, and truly, not our style. I enjoyed the idea of his virility, and I enjoyed the space that his affairs gave me. I was a professor of literature, a mother to Sidney, and a writer. What did I want with a husband who wanted my attention? I wanted to avoid, and I wanted to be avoided. As to the age of the women, I felt too connected to my experience of myself when I was in college to protest. When I was in college, the lust I felt for my professors was overwhelming. It did not matter if they were men or women, attractive or unattractive, brilliant or average, I desired them deeply. I desired them because I thought they had the power to tell me about myself. If I had a shred of brazenness, or even confidence, at the time, I'm sure I would have walked into one of their offices and thrown myself at them. I did not. But if one of them had whistled, I surely would have come running.

And my husband was weak. He wanted to be desired, he lived off it, it was his sunlight and water and oxygen. And every fall a new, fresh group of young and fervent women flooded in, their skin more luminous and beautiful each year, especially in comparison to our own, which seemed to fade and chap the longer we stayed in that upstate town that was cold from October through June.

In my twenties and thirties I had my affairs too. There was the one with the student that I mentioned (though he was the only student—I found that even at the age of twenty-eight I was self-conscious about the aging of my body in comparison to the young, springy women that my young lover would have been most intimately familiar with), and there were men from the area—Thomas, the contractor who renovated our upstairs bath; Robert, a professor from the business department; and Boris, a painter who lived several towns away who hosted me in his large converted barn/studio space (the most cinematic).

Toward the end of my thirties I made the mistake of mingling with someone in my department. It ended badly, with tears and threats and phone calls with hang-ups and hurt feelings. My daughter was nine, and increasingly aware of the world around her. It was complicated and exhausting. I decided to embrace abstinence, to pull myself from the game. I would focus on my work, my home, my writing. The distraction of my colleague, as intriguing as it was, had made me feel ridiculous and undignified; desperate, weak, and grasping. I would pursue dignity, elegance, erudition. I abandoned lust and desire. I authored several essays on form and structure. I published my second novel.

After I told Vlad all this, he looked pained. I think he had expected me to protest that my husband was innocent, that it was some sort of campaign to besmirch his name—to rid the college of the old white men, that sort of thing. He emptied his martini in a few minutes.

He sucked on an olive pit as he asked me questions. "So you knew that your husband had multiple affairs with students?"

I widened my eyes to prevent them from visibly rolling. "Multiple affairs. What silly wording. He fucked them, and they fucked him. He fucked their shining skin and their panties got wet from his approval. They liked it and he couldn't help it."

He winced. Prude. "Couldn't help it. I don't believe that. I don't believe it's possible to simply fall."

"What, in love?" I asked. "Or in lust?"

"Both. There's always a part of you that you let go slack. You don't have to do it if you don't want to."

He was red in the face, and perturbed. He reminded me of some New England preacher from the nineteenth century—a transcendentalist Unitarian with strict principles. He seemed vegan. I liked it. I liked his arrogant anger.

I folded my hands in my lap. "I feel like I've upset you."

"It doesn't matter." He looked like a perturbed teenager. (Not Fair!) "It's why you should never admire people. They'll only disappoint you."

"You can still admire my husband without condoning what he did," I said. Though it's not up to you to condone, I thought.

"I wish I could. Maybe I can. I'm sorry. I didn't eat enough before I drank this."

We changed subjects after that—we talked about a new novel that had come out from a substantial writer, a play we had both seen in New York and whether it was a feminist retelling of a classic work or patriarchal pandering. I pressed some cheese and bread on him, and some water. We spoke about the differences between the sophomore and junior classes (the juniors were dim, the sophomores were keen). I told him, to the best of my memory, about child-friendly activities in the area for his three-year-old.

We parted in the pitch-black darkness. I let him know once more how much I looked forward to reading his book. He seemed remiss when he said goodbye and told me he "really would" love to hear what both of us thought, especially me. After his car pulled from the drive, I sat out back in a Muskoka chair on the side of our pool. I leaned my head back and looked at the stars. I had a craving for a cigarette, though I hadn't had one for twenty years. I felt a growing excitement and wildness creep up into my nervous system—a prickly awareness that started in my bones and radiated outward. I thought of Vladimir Vladinski using his large, rough hands to hold my hair back from my face. On the far side of our property, behind the chain-link fence that enclosed the yard, the eyes of a stray cat or a fox reflected the porch light. They glowed like the eyes of a demon.

II.

I read his book the following week. I took it to the campus library and sat in one of the armchairs in a glass alcove on the silent floor. The librarians had printed out signs of the Brontës and Jane Austen with fingers to their mouths and pasted them at the ends of the stacks. Shhh! From my perch in the alcove, I could look down and see a grassy part of the campus, four floors below me. It was 8 a.m., and I watched sleepy students in sweats or pajamas stumbling past on their way to early morning classes. A few male athletes ran in a superior manner; a few female athletes ran as if to punish themselves. A few young women wore elaborate outfits and full faces of makeup, their eyes darting to and fro to see who noticed them. A few misguided young business students wore badly cut suits, having internalized some inaccurate message about dressing for success.

I didn't want to sit in my office where I could be disturbed at any moment by coworkers or students. I typically had a good relationship with my students—our college is a student-oriented college, not an R1 school, and, until everything happened with John, I liked talking to them and getting to know about their passions and dreams. I liked giving life advice just as much as I liked giving advice about essays or books, and I liked that a few, who possessed a boldness I had never felt with any authority figure in my life, would flop onto the sofa across from my desk and allow me to witness them amid their tortured confusion.

I tended to read manuscripts, however, in the library. Even at fifty-eight, even at this college where I have taught for nearly thirty years, I still feel the thrill of excitement in a university library. I still feel the potentiality—the students working toward becoming *something*, the stretching, searching minds, the curiosities of what will become of oneself buzzing at the study tables and between the rows of books. I find being among all that to be far more energizing than an enclosed and solitary space. Here I feel as though I'm engaged in the knowledge project. In my office I'm engaged in the knowing project. In my office I am of college life but not in it. In the library I am in but not of it. I like feeling the thrum of the students' brains and hearts, uncensored by the classroom setting. In the library their lives swirl around me—I'm aware of their romantic entanglements, their grudges, hatreds, obsessions, all vibrating at a frequency I won't ever feel again. Never will I love as they love, or hate as they hate, or want what they want with such strong and solidified identification.

Our last meeting had such an effect on me that I decided to wait a few days to read Vladimir's book. Not that he would care, but it was unlike me. Usually I was so sensitive to the anxieties that possessed someone who sent a manuscript that I read it right away. I remember, with my early fiction, how nervous I was to hear what someone thought, and how much umbrage I would take if I felt as though someone had not responded promptly to a piece of writing I sent them. I dealt with young writers frequently (along with my academic courses I taught a creative-writing course every spring), and normally, if I did not read something right away due to workloads or faculty responsibilities, I would let them know that as soon as I started reading I would contact them, so that they could manage when to expect a response. But I found that I couldn't treat Vladimir with the same courtesy.

Of course it was different. His book was already published by a major publishing house. It existed in the world and did not require my reflections or feedback—it was impervious to it. We had read the reviews and the accolades, we had seen it in the "Best of" lists when it came out. It wasn't reviewed in the *Times*, but it got a review in the *Washington Post*, a mention in the *New Yorker*'s "Briefly Noted" book column, and a starred review in *Booklist* and *Kirkus*. When the first wave of allegations came against John and he was asked to leave the hiring committee, I was told I could stay on but I requested I be released. I knew the words that would be volleyed back and forth when I left the room, I knew that they would feel constrained by my presence because they couldn't talk freely about hiring the kind of person who would never tarnish the department in the same way again. I was sure they wouldn't hire a straight white man, but Vladimir had a better reputation than the writers that the college was accustomed to receiving applications from. With the splash that his first novel made in the literary world, if not the commercial one, he might have gone to many colleges closer to an urban area and still been competitive. And his interview, in which he apparently (again, I was not there) revealed some disturbing domestic details (of which I had heard), had been deemed extraordinarily compelling.

Which is all to say that until he brought his book by, I hadn't read it out of spite and willful ignorance. And if he hadn't brought it that night, and if I hadn't caught his gaze in the reflection of the darkened window, and if he hadn't dropped his eyes in tender and exposed self-consciousness, I don't know if I ever would have.

I read all morning, until I had to hurry to my eleven thirty class. I had thought I would get a cup of coffee midway through but I didn't, and I was so absorbed that I arrived to the classroom slightly late, disoriented, and had to spend some time asking the students about how they were faring before I could organize my thoughts enough to remember what we were covering that day. Luckily, all my students love nothing more than to speak about their psychological wellness, so my buying of time was met with some eager stories about medication, campus counseling, time management, and ADHD, told with wry self-awareness while I settled myself.

After class I drifted up to my office and was met there by Edwina, a devotee of mine asking about recommendation letters. Edwina wanted to complete two programs this summer—an internship with a Black, female-run film-production company whose last feature won the Palme d'Or at Cannes, and a summer course in art semiotics at Brown. She wanted to be a producer, she told me, but a respected one, one who could bring about cultural change. She told me that when she had worked as an intern at another film company last summer there was this woman, one of the more powerful executive producers, who had her PhD in classics from Harvard. Every time she left a room her degree was mentioned in hushed and reverential tones. Edwina's goal was to be like her: a cloud sweeper, weather controller, "bone-bringer," as well as a revered mind with an impressive degree.

After agreeing to write them (I do believe that anyone who does not write recommendation letters if asked is monstrous, and even though I am the most selfish human being I know, I write them, and write them from scratch without asking the requestor to write a draft of them first) and dispensing with some quick advice, I urged her out. I could tell she was disappointed at not speaking more—I did quite like her and liked to see what she was reading and give her recommendations and hear her gossip about her other classes and classmates and professors, but I could not give her my full attention. All I could think about was Vladimir's book. I didn't pick it up to read it again—to do so in my office would be humiliating—but I wanted to see if I could think about it and re-create the passages in my mind.

When I was reading in the library, I was overwhelmed with a mixture of genuine admiration and seething jealousy. The book was funny, clear, awake, vivid. The prose was spare but the voice was not sacrificed in his exact word choice. It felt both like life and beyond life. He was a truly great writer, and though this book, an epigrammatic roman à clef, might not have catapulted him into fame, I had no doubt, reading it, that he would have it all—the bestseller; the interviews; the columns; the articles not only about his writing but about the decoration of his home, his fitness routines, his office, his food consumption, his work habits and sleep habits and opinions on politics.

For context, I have published two novels—my last one at forty-three years old. I have since then published mostly nonfiction work about literature for academic journals and occasionally, at more desperate times, written book reviews for our local newspaper. My first novel was deemed to hold promise; my second novel was deemed a disaster. The first I felt was a complete and utter lie, the second meant something to me but was roundly dismissed for being solipsistic. Since that time, for the past fifteen years, I have been trying to balance the important with the truthful. This has meant endless false starts, long projects of research that have been abandoned, mornings when I have woken up at five and prayed for an urgency of voice to come to me only to be disappointed. I have watched writing the female experience—particularly the motherhood experience (the subject of my second book) rise and reach praise and prominence in the past decade. I do not think I was ahead of my time; I think I wasn't as unapologetic as this new crop of writers are. These new young mothers write with force and wit and humor. They embrace the I I I with fervor. They don't shy away from talking about the banality of existence that comes with being a mother—the lunches in rest stops, the weariness of the body, the bad and mortifying toys and food and games and lackluster vacations and compromises that fall like an avalanche over the false totem of one's own self-regard. I suppose I had always been too shy to address that banality head-on. My second book was a discussion of three women—a career woman, a mother, an artist. They begin in their own worlds, full chapters apiece. Then the narratives begin to intercut. Over the course of the book, it is revealed they are, in fact, one person. The response of critics at the time—some male, mostly female, boiled down to "who gives a fuck." I won't say I was undervalued, because I don't believe that. Alice Munro was winning every award at the time, with her gentle, insightful stories of women's lives. Generosity. Margaret Atwood wrote exciting books that practically lived inside of a uterus. Be a Fan. There were the others—Lorrie Moore, Joy Williams, Joyce Carol Oates, Barbara Kingsolver—the list is long—who wrote my kind of female experience. No, my work was simply not *enough*—not loud enough, not forceful enough, not realistic enough, not poetic enough, not funny enough, not speculative enough, not good enough.

When I was in my PhD program, I had lunch with one of the university's writers in residence. I was a messy and distended twenty-seven-year-old with yellow teeth and bad clothing who smoked incessantly, but I remember believing that there was a flirtation to the lunch. And perhaps there was: when I look at my female students now, even the messiest, the sloppiest, the ones who drink Pepsi Max at 9 a.m., I see in them the beauty of youth—the beauty of their plumpness, their half-formed-ness, that skin that's lit from underneath. At this lunch I was supposed to be asking questions about melding creative work with an academic life. I was in the English lit department and the lunch came about because I had attended one of his classes and mentioned that I wished to write fiction, and he, who had taken the same path of academia and literature, extended an offer of advice. We had lunch in a spot he suggested, which felt like the pinnacle of elegance—not fussily fancy, not achingly hip, a place that was refined, classic, the kind of place I could never imagine picking. John and I were engaged to be married at the end of the year. There was a moment at this lunch when the writer in residence (whose career I thought at the time was enviable, but now I realize was probably an ongoing series of disappointments and slights) reached for my hand and I pulled mine away as if from a hot stove.

I still, to this day, do not know if he was truly reaching for my hand or if I misconstrued the gesture—he could have been reaching for the salt. The moment sticks in my mind mostly because it reminds me of how timid I have always been (God, you are a pussy, Sidney used to scream at me during her teenage rampages). I had lusted after this writer in residence, constructed elaborate fantasies about us meeting in darkened hallways or him sitting alone in a classroom and me straddling him on the chair from where he taught. But when he moved his hand toward mine it was as if I was as limited and repressed as an Edith Wharton heroine. A swirl of fear and morality welled as I jerked my hand from the table back into my lap. We continued speaking as if nothing had happened (and again, perhaps nothing had). I remember one thing he said about writing at the time, which enraged me with its cliché. I had asked him, in a pretentious way, I'm sure, if he had any credo about writing—anything he truly lived by. He said, "I only write if I have something to say."

I remember feeling so angry about this bland statement—about how hokey the advice was, how banal and corny. But there was a deeper rage as well—the rage of embarrassment. I was a working-class girl who, despite a parental divorce and some suffering in my adolescence, had gone to a decent university. I had become energized in the academic setting and got myself into a well-regarded graduate program. There I had met my future husband. I would never have anything to say. I knew theoretically that everything was happening all the time and that I only needed to sit and look closely and I would find a story worth telling. I didn't yet know that many writers find what they want to say in the writing. After I left the lunch I avoided the writer in residence. He called several times to discuss a short story I sent him and I never called him back. I saw him at a conference many years later—we were waiting for the same elevator. I said hello and he deliberately ignored me, almost comically so, for the entire week.

Reflecting on Vladimir's book I was struck that I was in the literary presence of someone who, for whatever reason, had something to say, and a way to say it. I researched his backstory. He was the son of Russian émigrés, obviously, and grew up in Florida. He attended an Ivy League, then volunteered for the Peace Corps and spent time in Africa like his hero, Norman Rush, had done. When he returned, he was accepted to and enrolled in what is widely considered the best writing MFA program in the country. Then he stalled. I assume he was unable to sell his thesis book after graduation. He and Cynthia, a fellow MFAer, were married. He took several adjunct positions at scattered colleges in and around New York City. Eventually his work began to appear in literary journals, and then the sale of his first book was announced. He was thirty-eight when it was sold and is now forty years old. Cynthia has a book deal with HarperCollins for a memoir that has not yet been completed. She is thirty-two.

From the window of my office I could see a young girl leaning against a tree with her hands behind her back. A freshman—I met her at an orientation event this year. Her body is the kind that could only belong to eighteen- or nineteen-year-old women—pencil legs, rounded hips, a lean flat stomach, an impossibly small waist supporting immense breasts. Even in one year, that body, despite all her stubborn urgings and attempts, would thicken in the waist and haunches to support the load of her curves. Her hair had been bleached blond and grown out at some point; it extended to her waist, half-yellow, half–walnut brown. She wore circular sunglasses, tiny cutoff shorts, and a sweatshirt that was cut to reveal her shrunken midriff. If I remembered, she had poor skin, though I couldn't see from out my window. A skinny, ugly senior boy held his hand at the right side of her hip, tentatively. He was clearly out of his mind with desire and trying to hide his inexperience. He held a SoBe Green Tea bottle between two fingers in the hand that was not touching her. The girl's pose was both eager and deflective—the desire for admiration trumping the lurking suspicion that this homely boy was able to be so forward with her only because of the disparities in their ages. He leaned in to kiss her with an odd, wide mouth. Even from fifty feet away I could see the laboriousness of this activity between the two of them—a smashing motion that brought neither pleasure.

Vladimir was eight years older than his wife.

Well.

The age difference shouldn't have bothered me: I was five years younger than my husband. Eight years is not such a great difference. And yet all women recoil a bit when a male chooses a younger woman as a life partner, even if everyone is a consenting adult and a power dynamic does not seem to be present. We know that the younger woman perhaps feels chosen, and the older man perhaps feels lucky. We know there's a sense of promise in the younger woman from the perspective of the man, and a sense of reverence for experience from the perspective of the woman.

Plus, even though I was not yet ready to admit to myself the depth of my attraction for Vladimir, or how competitive I was with Cynthia Tong, his first-generation Chinese-American wife with her credentials, her style, her ability to wear flat shoes and look graceful rather than stubby-legged, her what I assumed was effortless thinness, her buckets of potential, and her book deal based on her traumatic history that I knew a bit about from departmental rumors, I still felt the sting of their youth in the face of my age. At fifty-eight, I felt past the point of establishing myself as a literary writer. I was just as old as Penelope Fitzgerald had been when she had published her first novel, and I didn't know another serious female author who'd begun a career this late. It seemed whenever I looked up the ages of writers who were reputed to have started older, they turned out to be decades younger than me. Yes, I had published two novels, but that was nearly twenty years ago, and it wasn't as though they were highly lauded and enshrined and the public was waiting for my next offering. No, they had done so poorly that a new offering from me would be the same as a debut. At best, if I kept trying, if I "broke through," I might have one or two meaningful books. My name, though, if I cared about it, was sure to be lost to time.

Lest you think I haven't evolved at all over the course of my fifty-eight years, and that I have been simply sitting here hoping to be famous like some imbecilic ingenue, I want to say that the urge to make a mark has only recently renewed in me. In fits and starts my ambition has ebbed and swelled. After my second book, for many years, I was content to write for myself. Content to tinker. I kept a truth journal, collecting little observations and metaphors in a notebook. I practiced writing like practicing the piano—I wanted to be absorbed and taken away by it—I didn't mind if it ever met an audience. I had many years of peace. I loved to read and be engaged and surprised by new voices. I wanted to be an admirer. When Sidney was an older child I wanted to model being an admirer for her. I thought she would suffer unless she learned a certain level of contentment with one's life, a certain holding of oneself in deference to the world.

And unfortunately, and unflatteringly, when I examine the suppression of my ambition most thoroughly, I also wanted to be content and without ambition for John, who had given up writing before we met, but nearly had a nervous breakdown when I published my first novel, and hit me (the only time, and very drunk) while we were discussing the logistics of a minor book tour for my second.

Now that Sidney was not only out of the house but out in the workforce doing good, meaningful, and often righteous work as a lawyer for a nonprofit and living with a woman and becoming more and more a separate person from me, with eyes that watched and judged me, and now that John had been publicly shamed as a lecherous pervert, my perspective on my ambition had shifted.

The boy and girl outside were still kissing, he was now scooping his pelvis in and up toward her, his skinny rear visibly clenching and releasing in his tight jeans. One of her hands was outstretched awkwardly—like she was trying to get someone's attention to come rescue her, or she didn't know exactly where to put it.

"Where are you?" I heard, and turned to see my husband at my office doorway, holding his gym bag, wearing salmon-colored shorts that revealed his lanky calves (his long, slim legs and hips are his best feature) and a button-down, snug at his belly. He came over to my desk, sat on the edge, and leaned down close so he could see from my perspective. He smelled like John, nice, he always smelled nice, aftershave and detergent and tea tree oil and coffee. I was lucky in that other than the time I was pregnant, when John's smell was distressingly repulsive to me, his scent was always comforting and attracting. "Ugh," he said, looking at the couple beneath the tree.

I smiled and shrugged, and checked my computer screen quickly to make sure that I had minimized anything relating to Vladimir or his book.

Since the accusations had come out, John had been suspended from teaching and interacting with students until an as-yet-undisclosed date in October, when he would have his dismissal hearing in front of the Title IX committee. He had been allowed to keep his office and other campus privileges like going to the library (which he never used) and the gym (which he went to every day), and he was still on the budget committee. They needed him: he had been chair for six years, nobody else knew the intricacies of where the department's money went, or how to craft a budget that would get approval from the dean's office.

Separate from the scandal, for several years now John and I maintained a distant relationship when we were at home—more of a sharing space than a true living together, more roommates than spouses. It was something we had fallen into—like we each kept choosing different turns inside a labyrinth until, without intending to, we ended up on opposite sides of the kingdom. I slept in the guest room in our house because of John's snoring. We were away from each other most nights of the week—I went to exercise classes and out to drinks with friends and down to Albany to see art house films and to a weekly music night at a pub that functioned as a kind of salon for local artists. On the occasions that we were home together, I either disappeared to my office to work or gardened outside or read by the pool if it was warm. Sometimes we watched a movie together, but I tended to sit in a chair rather than on the couch with him, citing my back.

I stopped making dinner when Sidney left the house for college ten years ago, unless we were having people over or I was struck with some urge. The end to cooking had been a relief to both of us—I had certainly resented the endless tick in the back of my mind, what will we have for dinner, that would start up at noon each day, and John had resented my resentment. After John and I had dropped her off at Wellesley and driven back, and I spent a tear-drenched twenty-four hours in bed, I announced the end of my culinary career. Instead, I tried to keep a well-stocked pantry and fridge—roast chickens and eggs and vegetables and sausages and salami and lentils and olives and smoked salmon and whitefish and fruits and yogurts and cheeses and grains and breads and nuts. Salads from delis—all the things one likes to eat that can be easily assembled. Which is to say we didn't eat together. We used to gather breakfast and meet on the porch, but when I was trying to reestablish my morning writing practice I started taking my food upstairs with me. We used to have a cocktail hour around 6 p.m. to check in with each other, but a few years ago I found it hard to maintain my ideal weight unless I curtailed my daily drinking.

We traveled (still very well) as a couple, and, of course, we saw each other at work. Our offices were on the same floor in our small department at our small college—the walk from his to mine was less than ten loping paces. And it was at work, when we could pretend that the personal didn't exist between us, where I would feel my resistance to him, so stubborn at home, slide off. Here, we dealt with the common enemy. Here, I could be his ally. It was like the early days between us. If we were ever feeling at emotional odds with each other, distant or angry, we knew that the only thing we would need to do was go visit his parents. After less than eight hours of his father's Marine-style barking and his mother's glazed disassociation we would fall into each other's arms with relief and unity, so glad to be who we were, together.

He rubbed his forehead back and forth in my hair. I pushed him away. Clearly, he was restless today, eager for someone's companionship. "What do you want?" I asked him. He looked at me chastened. All this drama at the college had brought out his neediness—more and more these days he played the part of the old dog that has done something wrong coming to look for the approval of its master, all contrite sweetness. More and more I played the part of the angry owner, pushing the dog away, knowing it would always return. It was bad behavior on both our parts, the patterns were dangerous. John was not a happy fool, and he was not content to sidle up to me day after day only to be rejected over and over again. At some point he would decide he had been mishandled too many times, and he would bite back hard.

What I had said to Vladimir the other night, when he visited, had been true. I had known about the affairs, the existence of them. I had known they were with students. But I hadn't known the details about the behavior, which, as such details have been revealed, are more unsettling than I cared to admit. For example, there are records of 1,183 text messages exchanged between John, fifty-five at the time, and Frannie Thompson, twenty-two. I find the mental image of my husband with his fat thumbs on his phone, texting back and forth with this young woman—who, as far as I knew, had a certain transplant-from-the-city élan and nice and shiny hair, but no real humor—very undignified. When I think of his little excitements at his own quips, the amount of time he spent caressing that device with quivery anticipation when he could have been doing something worthwhile, it all feels grotesque.

I also had not expected that I would be caught in the fray. The tide had been shifting away from his behavior being acceptable since even before we received our PhDs, I knew that. There were always whispers about him, and occasionally a new and drunk colleague would, with righteousness, confess to me that they knew about one of his indiscretions, and I would have to explain to them our arrangement. But because he was a general advocate of women in academia and women writers, and was committed to all sorts of social justice and diversity initiatives in the college—because, in effect, his politics were not only impeccable but admirable—I, not as his wife, but as a professional, along with the rest of the college, had collectively decided to look the other way. These women were of age. The whispers remained whispers and nothing more. That's the way it is in these schools. I was a beloved teacher, my classes were waitlisted. I was fit and stylish and until around forty-five I was occasionally mistaken for a student. My last name was different from John's. Outside of the department, not many people knew we were married.

However, when the wave of accusations and the petition came, I found that suddenly everyone knew that I was the wife of the disgraced chair. Toward the end of the spring semester, I was sitting in my office when a group of five young women from my Adaptations class entered, giggling with what was clearly their own sense of self-importance and buoyed-up enthusiasm they had roused in whatever cabal they'd had before. I invited them in, and they exchanged daring glances until Kacee, clad in a flowered baby doll and lace stockings with a Japanime hairstyle—two buns, one on each side of her head—a girl who would attach a pen cap to the fat bottom part of her lip during class and "accidentally" pull her shirt down so that one nipple was exposed, a girl who always laughed too loudly at anything the one very handsome boy said in class, stepped forward.

"We wanted to talk to you, um," she said.

"Okay," I said. They were already annoying me. They were an annoying bunch. Individually I'm able to drum up, most of the time, a sense of patience and tolerance for each student. Even the extremely grating ones. I don't know what happens in one's youth to make one student so tolerable, so pleasant, so secure in themselves, so eager to learn, and what makes other students so irritating. But I pride myself on not discriminating against them because of it. With most of my students, I'm able to understand their need to be seen, and I'm able to focus on that need and let their ticks and blips, their entitlements, their insecurities or overconfidences, simply wash past. I'm able to see them in progress, and to know them in progress. To know that they don't yet fully grasp what they are presenting to the world as they present it.

But if even irritating students can be withstood individually, and pleasant students can be excellent company, students in groups are always awful. They get too much bravery from each other, they forget to behave well. The interaction with this group led by Manic Pixie Kacee was bound to be painful.

"Well, um, we just wanted to say, um."

Becca, a tall girl who took her emotions as seriously as cancer, wearing a baggy turtleneck over a baggy dress over baggy pants (Joke: How do you get into a hippie's pants? Take off her skirt, first), stepped up.

"Well, we just wanted to say, like, you don't, you don't have to, like, do the whole supportive silent wife thing."

I breathed in, white-hot anger rushing up my forearms into my elbows.

Then Tabitha, in her mechanic's jumpsuit, worn unbuttoned to the waist so that her bra was visible, stepped forward.

"Like, you're this hot, brilliant lady. We think you're really hot." I could tell they prized their own opinion of my hotness, their ability to appreciate hotness in an older woman. "And like, it is totally unfair what he's done to us."

"You?" I asked

"Us women," she said.

"Ah," I said. "Not you personally."

Kacee stepped forward again.

"We just want to know when you're gonna dump his ass."

"Cause you should," someone in the chorus piped up.

Careful, Careful, Careful, I thought to myself. Careful. We professors talked about it all the time. Nowadays you must be so careful. It's good, it's good, we would say to each other. It's good, that there's safety. Though we all wondered what we were preparing these students for with all our carefulness, as if the world was going to continue being as careful. But then again maybe it was, we would say. Maybe if these were the people who were in the world, who were comprising the professional culture, then the world would have no choice except to be more careful. And that would be a good thing. People said this crop of youth was weak, but we knew differently. We knew they were so strong—so much stronger than us, and equipped with better weapons, more effective tactics. They brought us to our knees with their softness, their consistent demand for the consideration of their feelings—the way they could change all we thought would stay the same for the rest of our lives, be it stripping naked for male directors in undergraduate productions of *The Bacchae*, ignoring racist statements in supposedly great works of literature, or working for less when others were paid more. They had changed all that when we hadn't been able to, and our only defense was to call them soft. They had God and their friends and the internet on their side. And perhaps they would make a better world for themselves. Their aim was not to break taboos, the way people born ten to twenty years before me, and, in a small way, my generation, had done. No, they worked in a subtler and stricter way. And perhaps it had to be so. And so Careful, I told myself. No anger, no personal attacks, just Grace, Grace, Grace.

The girls stood nervously in front of me, waiting for my response. I cultivated warmth in my chest and brought it up to my face. I pushed the warmth through my smile, letting it settle around my eyes.

"I want to thank you for coming to see me. I'm flattered on two accounts: for calling me a 'hot lady' and for the care that you're extending toward me. It makes me feel hopeful for the future to be surrounded by young women who are as passionate and empathetic as you are.

"Sit down"—I urged them, and they crammed onto the couch and its arms, facing me.

"We all live and work within structures and institutions," I told them. "We can't help it. I work, I live, inside of institutional sexism, racism, and homo- and transphobia, for example. And the difficult thing to understand about these institutions is that we all, however aware of it we are or not, practice sexism, racism, and homo- or transphobia, even if we are female, a person of color, or homosexual or a trans person. And so I'm fully willing to admit that my remaining with my husband—not standing by his actions, necessarily, but simply remaining in relationship to him—may be a product of my own internalized sexism. Certainly how could it not be."

"Right," said Kacee, a band of saliva visible in her open mouth.

"That said, and I say this again, with such deep gratitude for the care you've extended toward me, that my husband and I have had a life together longer than any of you have been alive. And we've had agreements, and arrangements, and compromises throughout that time. And challenges. We're now faced with another challenge. Both a public challenge and a private challenge. I know that you will understand if I beg for *your* understanding, and respect of my privacy, as I decide for myself, as a hot, brilliant lady, how I will handle my marriage of thirty years. Extending me that courtesy is an act of feminism in and of itself."

Ten minutes later I closed the door to my office waving and blowing kisses as they beamed at me.

Assholes, I thought.

But their intrusion shook me. I am clandestine in general, most especially when it comes to my students, and they made me feel exposed. And so while I believed the case against John was both maddening and absurd, I regret to admit that my self-consciousness trumped my conviction. I didn't like to be seen too frequently on campus in his company. And I had never liked him being physically affectionate in the office.

"Please get off my desk," I told him, and he backed away, straightened up and addressed me as though I had been the unprofessional one.

"Did you see Florence's email about the language of the department goals?"

"No," I said.

"Did you see Tamilla's response?"

"No," I said.

"Did you see Andre's response?"

"No," I said.

"Have you checked your email today?"

"No," I said. "I was prepping, and then I was teaching, and then I was researching." He and I had long arguments about how available academics should be. He loved to answer all inquiries immediately, I couldn't stand it.

"Well can you straighten it out? They need some diplomacy."

"Sure," I said.

"Unless you want to come to the gym with me?" He dangled his gym bag in front of me.

In years past, we had gone to the campus gym together from one to two thirty most lunchtimes—cardio on the elliptical, then a weight program given to us by a physical trainer we went to for a few sessions because we had won them in an auction. In Japan, there is the word *nakama*, which is most often translated as "friend" but, as a Japanese colleague once explained to me, is more accurately defined as "close people who do things together." We used to value that idea and talk about it—companionship in marriage: doing things together—not necessarily having to connect, but giving our company. Our regular stints at the campus gym were that, as were our disciplined traveling and our attempts at cultural responsibility.

"No thank you," I said. I now belonged to the YMCA in town. John knew I no longer felt comfortable parading in front of my students in stretch pants, hefting and sweating and bending in full view of their appraising eyes.

He nodded, determined to be amused by my firmness. Just before leaving he paused at the door.

"Listen, I know we aren't really doing the entertaining thing these days."

"We're not, no."

"Right, but I wanted to ask Vladimir and his wife and their daughter over to swim in the pool before the weather gets too cold. They don't know anybody—they're living over on Route 29 in some shitty condo, and I was curious if you wanted to be a part of it, or if I should ask them when you're planning on being out of the house."

I couldn't tell what game he was playing at, if he was playing at a game. I had mentioned that Vladimir had come by in passing because of the book, but I didn't know if John perceived the jolt that he had given me those nights before. Still, imagining the afternoon filled me with elation. The thought of seeing Vladimir Vladinski in my backyard, even with his wife and daughter, of seeing him shy and embarrassed taking his shirt off to reveal his slightly flabby stomach, to see him clad in some hastily bought swim trunks, to pass him a sweating beer or, even better, to serve him a beer as he lay in a cabana chair, to see him bouncing on the diving board, not yet ready to jump in the pool, to see him lifting his daughter into the sky, to observe him in moments of banality—rubbing zinc sunscreen in on his face or hesitating at the door because of wet feet—filled me with yearning. A succession of images, each more tender and intimate, flashed through my mind.

"It would be nice of us to entertain them," I said, hoping that John wouldn't notice anything off about the way I spoke. "Better do it soon though. This weekend, or else it will be too cold. Saturday is supposed to be warm."

"Fine with me," he said, maybe with suspicion, or maybe simply pleased that I had given in so easily.

"There are a few things I'd want you to do in the yard first," I said.

"Jesus," he said. "Fine. Make a list."

"That compost bin has got to go."

"Make a list," he repeated. "I'll do them if I can—"

"Then I'll just hire someone to do them."

"I'll do them. I should have known this would result in my doing labor for you." But he was pleased with me, I could tell.

"When you ask them, give Cynthia my number and we'll coordinate on food."

He nodded. He said my name and I looked up at him. "I miss you," he said, and then turned to leave.

In the doorway he passed Aaron—our lanky, earnest, English Department assistant—bringing me some copies I had requested. At the sight of my husband, Aaron bowed his head and placed the stack of manuscripts on my desk with an unintelligible murmur. I thanked him and asked him how he was. I liked Aaron, he was a sweet senior boy who wrote lengthy, baroque poems about the cosmologies of invented fantasy realms. He didn't answer, and exited wordlessly, his chin pressed to his chest, breathing heavily through his nose, as though he had caught John and me half-dressed, amid some illicit act of concupiscent commingling.

III.

*V*ladimir agreed that they would come on Saturday and then texted
to ask me what they could bring. I felt ashamed. Clearly John had
mentioned for Cynthia to text me about food, and Vladimir had responded because he and his wife didn't occupy the same outdated gender roles that John and I did. I asked if they had dietary restrictions. He
said none, which was a relief, I had gone through a nervous set of hours
when I wondered if he would say something like vegetarian, and I would
have to find the time to test out recipes. I told him they could bring
something sweet if they liked—that we would have everything else—
that we would grill if that was all right with him, and would it be okay
if we had lemonade on hand for his daughter, and did she need floaties,
we could borrow them, and what did Cynthia like to drink? He said yes
to the lemonade, no to the floaties, and said that Cynthia didn't drink
but didn't mind everyone else drinking. Then he sent a follow-up text:

Cynthia wants to know if we should bring our own towels?

I thought about the domestic politics that must have gone into
that text exchange. I could see them sitting, wherever they were, their
daughter banging a spoon on the table. I could hear Vladimir saying, "I
don't think we need to," and Cynthia, sober Cynthia, taking the spoon
out of their daughter's hand and saying, "Just ask her, please," and him
saying something like, "Why don't you text her," and her responding,
"Because you're the one texting now," and him saying something like,
"You were the one who was supposed to text," and her picking up their
daughter and raising her eyebrows at him and saying, "Just ask her,
please. For me," and his threat—"All right, but I'm going to say you're
the one who asked."

Or maybe it wasn't like that at all. Maybe they were in complete synchronization. Maybe she had said, "Do you think we need to bring towels?" and he had said, "I'll ask her," and in deference to the fact that she had been the one to come up with the question in the first place he had given her the credit.

I'd responded, *Nope, we've got plenty! Looking forward to seeing you.* I spent a few seconds rearranging the punctuation, moving the exclamation point from the *you* to the *plenty* and back again.

By Friday I had finished Vladimir's book and read every review (including the painful and abusive ones from Amazon and Goodreads) that I could locate online. Like most books that are full with tone, the last third was not as compelling as the beginning, but the final chapter, and final paragraph especially, was masterful, and shifted me, so that I sat in the library, tears in my eyes, wishing I could put my head down on the table and sob. There was a part of our campus that connected to a network of hiking trails and I stumbled toward them and walked, looking intently at the changing root structures below my feet, letting the spell of the book gradually wear off, like the buzz of an afternoon drink fades into the responsibilities of early evening.

The whole day prior to their arrival I was pulsing with anticipation. I found, but didn't read, pieces of Cynthia Tong's memoir, published in *Prairie Schooner* and *The Kenyon Review*. After my last class on Friday, possessed, but feeling all the while like a fool, I went to a local spa and visited a masseuse for an anti-cellulite massage and a leg spray tan. It was a long, stupid, awkward process, and I despised myself the whole time. The woman who massaged my legs wanted to impress very firmly that nothing could be done about my cellulite. I waited for thirty minutes in a dark room before I emerged and checked in with the receptionist and found I was in the wrong place for the application of the spray tan. I waited another thirty minutes, because the technician had moved on to another client before I saw her, and then was scolded for shaving rather than waxing.

I didn't understand why I booked those appointments. I couldn't really afford them (when the bill came to 217 dollars without tip I felt nauseated), and it was not as though I was in the habit of getting them. It wasn't as though I thought I could become more alluring; it was more that I wanted to erect a fortress around my body—a fortress of care and grooming. A fortress of corporeal dignity. I utterly failed, however. The tan came out dark and orange, there was no discernable difference in my cellulite, and, deeply regretting the idiotic amount of money I'd spent, I resolved to wear pants and refrain from going in the water.

After my appointment I took nearly two hours shopping at several different markets in town before I had gathered all the ingredients and drinks I needed for the following day. I was in the kitchen concocting a pickling brine for the stalks of daikon and carrot when John arrived home.

"What's all this?" He picked up the lemongrass and smelled it.

"It's for tomorrow. I'm making bun bo xao," I said, taking the lemongrass away from him. "It's a kind of Vietnamese noodle salad."

"I thought we were grilling."

"We are—you have to grill the steak for the recipe."

"That's not grilling—grilling is burgers and dogs or brats."

"It's September, we're all tired of that food by now. This is going to be nice and refreshing, the flavors are beautiful, you can make it kid friendly for the little one, and she can have the noodles—WILL YOU PUT DOWN MY JALEPEÑO, PLEASE?"

"Jesus," he said, and tossed the pepper so it hit me in the chest. "It's fussy, that's all."

"It seems fussy now when I've got everything out—it won't be fussy."

"Are you trying to intimidate them? Or impress them?"

"I'm not trying anything—THAT'S FOR THE BABY," I yelled as he pulled out the lemonade and started pouring. "Can you get out of here? Thank you."

"I got rid of the compost."

38

"Thank you."

"They're just coming over to swim, we're not hosting their wedding."

"I'm enjoying myself. I'm enjoying cooking. Please."

"Can I have this beer?" He held up the beers I had bought that were from a local brewery, which had been recommended to me by an affable bearded store clerk with rainbow nail polish and a twinkling smile.

"Of course," I said. He moved in to peck my cheek and I flinched. "Sorry," he said. "Felt like old times."

He lingered in the kitchen for a moment, looking at me. I could tell he was feeling theatrical and I wasn't in a mood to countenance it. He ran his finger around a frame with a picture of him and Sidney and me on top of a snowy mountain.

"Did I tell you that I talked to our daughter today?" he asked.

"You didn't."

"She seemed upset."

"She's upset with us."

"No, not about us. It's something else."

"Oh," I said, and fixed my eyes on the glass hummingbird she had "made" with a kit by melting glass beads inside a metal frame. She had given it to me for Mother's Day when she was ten and there was still a glob of melted and hardened glass in the back corner of the oven that no oven cleaner could remove.

Sidney had chosen me as the beneficiary of her outrage about the allegations against John. She hadn't known about the affairs when they were happening, certainly, one of our rules was that Sidney would never know. We thought it would be confusing, though now I wonder if knowing about our arrangement would have lessened some romantic attachment she held on to in her ideas of who we were. She might have felt more flexible, more pliable, more clear-eyed, more sympathetic. As it was, the last time we spoke she called me an enabler, an accessory, and compared me to Germans who said nothing during the rise and reign of the Nazis.

I couldn't think about Sidney at that moment, however, I didn't want to. I stayed up late, prepping plates of chopped vegetables and cleaning the house (though I doubted they would do much more than walk from the pool to the bathroom). I drank glass after glass of water, as though the liquid would do something to adjust my molecular structure, would melt the frown marks from around my mouth, the puffiness underneath my eyes—all of which I tried not to look at as I passed the mirror. I tried on several outfits in our guest room, away from the prying eyes of John. Eventually I chose a turtleneck rash guard and flowy Tibetan wrap pants. I wouldn't swim, but would wear something that made it look like I might swim at any moment or had been swimming previously. Then, enraged at my vapidity, I forced myself to sit down and read several articles in the latest issue of the *New York Review of Books* before I fixed my nighttime drink. I slept fitfully, furious with myself when I thought about what I would look like the next day with no sleep, my self-directed anger making it all the more difficult to drift off.

Vladimir and his daughter arrived forty minutes later than our agreed-upon time, without Cynthia. With tired eyes, he told me that she had a migraine and was so sorry to miss us. After we said our hellos I left him and Phee to settle at the pool while I pulled out the plates and snack platters and cutlery, using the opportunity to readjust to the change in the dynamic.

Clearly, Vladimir and Cynthia had argued and she had refused to come. Although I was somewhat thrilled by the thought of them fighting, and glad because I hadn't yet read the excerpts of her memoir, I was disappointed she was absent. For one, I had wanted to see him and her together in a social setting so I could satisfy my curiosity about the nature of their relationship—to see if it was affectionate and playful, serious and loving, bickering and distant, collegial, respectful, sexual or sexless, full of admiration or rife with disdain. Secondly, there was the problem of the child and the fact that now he would be spending the entire time caring for her, rather than talking to us. Lastly, and most important, I had truly wanted to love her—to love her so much and so fully that all the reoccurring flashes of Vladimir and his face reflected in the black of my windowpane would dissolve, and I would see in front of me a real-life woman, not an idea, but a full person who I could admire. A neighbor, whose husband I should not and would not covet. For lest you think that I was enjoying my cringing and crushing obsession with Vladimir (which I came to see was lust but at the time didn't fully understand), I want to assure you I was not. I felt tingling and pained and embarrassed. Some fundamental peace within me, already disrupted since spring and the allegations and the petition and Kacee and Dump His Ass, had been entirely capsized. I was swimming in an ocean of electrical impulses. I was a body made of walking nerves. And truly, I had prayed and hoped that seeing his wife and being with his family would give me release.

Phee was very pretty, with chubby cheeks and bright eyes and brownish-reddish curling messy hair. Three is a wonderful age for communication, if you have a verbal child. I remember it, mostly, from some home videos in which I interviewed Sidney. Philomena, like Sidney had at her age, answered every question with a straightforward eagerness. *I am going to preschool and my teachers will be Miss Maureen and Miss Nadia. I am three and one quarter years old. Animals who stay up in the night are called nocturnal and animals who stay up in the day are called diurnal.* I could see Vladimir's lips curling with pride as he coached her through her sentences. Our precocious children. Even though Sidney was by all accounts an unqualified success, I still wish I had paid less attention to her smartness, had cherished her verbosity and alacrity with school much less. She suffered under the weight of her own exceptionalism, I know she did. Over and over she had to show up to the promise of her own potential.

I encouraged the two to get swimming before the heat of the day was gone—by September in this area there is about a three-hour window in which you could even call it warm. Vladimir put Philomena in a little floaty chest guard that looked like modern armor and plopped her inside an inflated donut in the shallow end, where we dipped our feet. He then took off his shirt with an athletic lack of self-consciousness, leaped onto the diving board, and cannonballed into the water, splashing us all, including Phee, who began to cry. He rushed to her and soothed her and spun her around and around in the pool until her tears gave way to laughter.

Vladimir's body was far more toned than I had imagined. His arms were muscular, his chest was firm and hirsute, his stomach was flat and muscled. He was such a specimen that even John commented, in his funny way, "You're so sexy, Vladimir," to which Vladimir, displaying an unexpected sense of humor, said, "I know," and winked. He said that his only hobby other than writing was working out. We spoke about writers who *did* things, like Hemingway or Mailer, who pursued hobbies to fuel their writing. Vladimir said he wished he could be more like them, but he didn't possess the instinct to take up fishing or motorcycling—he wasn't a gearhead, he was a Russian nerd who started weight lifting in high school PE and never stopped. John mentioned Cheever, Fitzgerald, Updike, Roth, a whole list of writers who pursued nothing other than writing.

"Well, sex," I said, "they all pursued or were in some way obsessed with sex."

John shrugged. "It takes up time," he said, and Vlad rolled his eyes with an indulgent generosity, so casual it surprised me.

"Vlad and I went out last Tuesday," John said, as if to answer my unasked question.

"Oh." Tuesday was the weekly gathering at the music hall. I always came back late. John and I didn't always check in on what we did, but I was surprised he hadn't told me—he usually kept me apprised of his goings-on and whereabouts whether I wanted to know about them or not.

"We talked," John said.

He lay in a lounge chair, his belly visibly resisting the elastic of his swim trunks and pulling at the buttons of his guayabera shirt. He stared into the sun, but I could tell from a certain tension around his mouth that he was pleased with himself. My husband is an incredible talker when he wishes to be. Clearly he had taken his new colleague out for drinks and had charmed and convinced him, if not onto his side, then away from personal condemnation. I could see John sitting at his favorite bar in town, buying beers and shots and disarming Vlad with jokes, anecdotes, self-flagellation, and occasional flashes of unexpected insight.

"I see," I said. John smirked, and Vlad dove down to the bottom of the pool and did a handstand, putting his feet in his daughter's face, who laughed and grabbed at them.

As the afternoon went on, I noticed that Vladimir liked to spread his arms wide in gestures that displayed his form to great advantage. When he came out of the water for lunch, he rubbed his stomach slowly and flagrantly, a completely unnecessary use of the towel, meant to draw our eyes to his abdominals. Either he was flirting with us or he flirted with everyone. He hung his towel around his neck and kept his shirt off to eat. He was obviously vain, he ran his hands over his hair many times in order to hide the thin spot on top. When I served the bun bo xao (which really is a simple dish—rice noodles, lettuce, cucumbers, crushed peanuts, quick-pickled daikon radish and carrot, lots of fresh chopped mint and cilantro, tossed with light dressing and topped with marinated steak), I watched as he piled mostly rice noodles on the plate for Phee (who proceeded, in trying to eat them, to fling them so far from her plate that I was finding hardened curls of vermicelli on my porch and yard for weeks) and took an extremely small serving for himself.

I made coffee after lunch, and we sat around the pool, shifting our chairs every now and then to remain in the warmth of the sun. As long as Phee was in the water, circling around in her donut, impervious to her own shivers, she was happy, so we were able to speak more than I thought. "She has the inner resources of a second child," he said. "She's happy by herself, she doesn't seem like a firstborn." I remembered I felt the greatest compliment people would give my parenting was to say that Sidney didn't act like an only child, even though it is in fact proven that only children do better in life and are usually more generous and community-oriented in their adulthood.

"Firstborn," I said. "Does that mean you'll be having more?"

"I'd like to. I was one of four, the youngest. Cynthia is an only child, she doesn't know if she wants another."

I watched Phee trailing her fingers in the water, singing to them as if they were little fairies skipping on the surface.

"Why do you think she's that way?"

"Cynthia?"

"No, Phee."

"Oh, I know exactly why," he said. "It's because my wife left when she was one. Cynthia was hospitalized after her suicide attempt. For six months it was a nanny during the day, and me on nights and weekends."

He brought this up aggressively—the fact like a battering ram he carried around with him, ready to smash in any door of politeness that was other than the truth.

We all knew Cynthia Tong had tried to kill herself. He had told the hiring committee in his interview. It was one of the reasons Vladimir Vladinski got the job.

❦

He stayed until the sun went down. I was glad to have cleaned the house, because after it was too cold to swim we went inside and John played the piano for us and we sang some folk and pop songs for Phee, who danced around the living room, clutching and kissing a ragged piece of red fabric Vlad said that was the only thing she played with. Then he put her in front of the television and we had gin and tonics on the porch, watching the last of the light in the sky. He kept asking if it was all right that they were staying, and we kept insisting how much we were enjoying their presence. He didn't want to leave. It felt like young love, I thought—responsibilities looming, the mounting anxiety of your life building while you clung, lolling pointlessly in bed, to a new someone who gave you a sad and fearful pleasure.

I did worry that something about the afternoon had made us appear parental to him. John wasn't exactly slapping me on the ass, or throwing his arm around me and kissing me, but we were pretending, and enjoying to pretend, a communication and solidarity we hadn't felt in a long while. Had Vlad's wife been there, we would have been two couples, peers, fellow academics and coworkers. But because she was gone, we seemed to take on the role of an august mentor couple. And why shouldn't we, I kept telling myself. John was sixty-three, I was fifty-eight, and although I wasn't *really* old enough to be his mother, I was old enough to be his mother. He continued to flirt with both of us throughout the evening, laughing loudly and repeatedly touching me on the arm and shoulder, so much so that he even commented on and apologized for it and I shrugged it off, pretending I hadn't noticed.

I drove the conversation toward intellectual concerns and politics, forcing discussion like I would do with my students. We talked about the rise of autofiction, and how most of the creative-writing students at the college did not even want to write fiction, but creative nonfiction instead, and primarily autofiction and memoir. I said it was because they were so obsessed with themselves they couldn't imagine existing outside of their viewpoint. John said it came from an anxiety about representing identities and experiences other than their own. Vlad posited it was because they had grown up online, representing themselves via avatars, building brands and presences and constructions of selves before they even knew that's what they were doing. We talked about the rise of populist ideology, both on the left and the right. Cautiously sidestepping any Title IX discussion, we talked about how different the college used to be—rigorous but freewheeling (drugs, drinking, sex)—and how neutered the kids were now, calling their moms every day, prizing friendship over romance. Philomena drank so much lemonade that she threw up on Vlad's shirt. John lent him a linen button-down—the kind of shirt for touring amphitheaters during Grecian summers, and, with it hanging off his tanned body, Vlad looked like Jay Gatsby, or the owner of a yacht. When, finally, Philomena fell asleep on the couch, Vlad picked her up in his arms to leave. Truthfully, he said, he was just so relieved that he didn't have to do bedtime. He had been hoping she would fall asleep in the car ride on the way home, but this was even better.

We watched him go from the front doorway. As his car pulled out of the driveway John leaned down and whispered, "Are you in love?" and I walked away from him so quickly it was as if I jumped. He followed me into the kitchen and began to help me clean in silence, but after a few minutes in which his bustling presence became more and more unbearable, I snapped at him to leave me alone.

"What's wrong with you?" he asked.

"Nothing," I said. I had drunk more alcohol than usual that afternoon, and though I knew I was angry with him, I also knew I wouldn't be able to find the correct phrasing to tell him why. He pressed and pressed, becoming more and more aggressive, until finally I told him to fuck off, and that as far as I was concerned he was a sadist. It wasn't the right word, but I couldn't express how he had taken a beautiful, almost spiritual afternoon, the kind of afternoon one remembers long after it has passed, and ruined it, for no reason, with his cruel and leering comment. In response, he, drunker than me, volatile and irascible, emptied the full recycling bag he was holding on to the floor, so that beer bottles and plastic clamshells tumbled out onto the tile. He told me I was a miserable woman and accused me of taking a shit on every nice thing, all because of what other people thought, not even what I thought. I told him what people thought had nothing to do with anything, and besides, he was the one who took a shit on things, he was the one, he did that, and then I lowered my voice and told him I couldn't go on like this anymore. He told me fine then, please, file for divorce, please, miming begging gestures and histrionically picking up the scattered recycling he had spilled and throwing it back into the bag. I watched his display with what I knew was a look of ugly disdain, then laughed and told him not to worry, that I was seriously considering it. He paused, then threw the empty tin can he was holding at the wall to my right and let loose on me a torrent of blame and expletives so foul and hideous that I can't repeat them other than to say that by the end I felt like there was a sandbag in my stomach, and my head hurt from crying, and my limbs felt limp, and I couldn't finish cleaning, I could barely even walk to my bed before succumbing to a sleep that felt like the heaviness of death.

The next morning we resumed our distant cohabitation, contrite but bruised from our inebriated altercation. I wrote to Vladimir about his book. I told him that I deeply admired it and that I would like to take him out to lunch once the semester "got rolling" to discuss it. I hadn't brought it up the day before because John hadn't read it, and I didn't want to hurt Vladimir or embarrass John. As the day wore on and I didn't hear back from him, I began to feel more and more sick about what had transpired at our home the day before. I went over it in my mind—was I too eager, somehow tense or hovering? Was he mad about the lemonade, or did I talk too much in the conversation? Did I interrupt him—I was known to interrupt, I hated this about myself. Did he think I was merely unworthy of his time and respect? But no, no, I didn't want to work myself up like that, it was Sunday, he wasn't on his email, nobody writes back right away on a Sunday.

At around two in the afternoon I took a drive (with my phone on Do Not Disturb and locked in the glove box) to my cabin near the lake, an hour north and west of where we were, where the reception was nonexistent unless you hooked up to the Wi-Fi. The last renter of the season had gone the week before and I needed to bring in the outdoor furniture and lock up the boats before it was too cold. I had received an inheritance when one of my childless uncles on my father's side died, a moderate sum of money with which I bought a modest amount of property with a little entryway to a medium-sized lake that didn't allow motors. After clearing and replanting the trees and leveling the ground I bought a prefabricated, non-winterized log cabin and had it installed along with a dock. I had purchased it as a retreat for myself, a summer writing cabin, though since it was built I had rented it out, first to help pay for Sidney's college, then law school, and now to help her with her student loan debt.

When I pulled into the gravel drive I was surprised to see that the cleaning service I used had clearly not come. There was a tipped-over garbage can from which trash was traveling across the driveway (the service usually took the garbage to the local dump). I chased crumpled fast food wrappers and drink containers, balled-up napkins, and rotten fruit skins across the lawn. The cabin, when I entered, was picked up, but there was the tacky film of use over all the surfaces, the mildewy smell of damp towels and used sheets piled up by the washing machine, toothpaste marks, and a ring of foundation left on the bathroom counter. The last tenants had been a couple with a young child and a grandmother—like how we used to travel with John's mother before Sidney turned eight (old enough to go to the Frick) and became good enough company that we did not require a babysitter. The small bedroom, where I imagined the grandmother had stayed, smelled of powder; the big one, where the couple and their daughter must have slept, smelled of sweat.

I was sure that there were many years before my daughter would have a child, if ever. When she was very little and I would ask her what she wanted to be when she grew up, she would say, "a mom." And if I asked her what else, she would say, "a babysitter." Now she was a lawyer for a not-for-profit similar to the ACLU and would perform the sign of the hex if children were mentioned. Still, I considered the small bedroom and my eventual relegation to it. If I stayed with John we would get the big bedroom, out of deference to our matriarchy and patriarchy.

But if we split up, it would be cots and sofa beds and small bedrooms for me. My worth would be equal to how helpful, useful, and uncomplaining I could be. I would be tolerated as long as it was clear I appreciated the cots, the sofa beds, the small bedrooms. I would have to demonstrate gratitude for the scraps and crumbs of time, attention, money, and luxury that came my way. I would work for it, with early mornings watching the baby, or nights doing dishes after everyone fell asleep. I couldn't be particular. Particular old women are not invited on vacations. Unless they are very rich, which I was not.

The cabin was wooden inside and out, the logs of the exterior making up the walls of the interior. The main part was one large room, the kitchen taking up one corner, a dining table in another, and the remainder a sitting room framed by two large glass doors that opened out to a small deck and a view of the lake. There was a hallway that led to the two bedrooms, two hall closets, a washer/dryer nook, and a small bathroom. I unlocked the closet where the cleaning supplies were kept. Despite feeling slightly disturbed when I saw the garbage swirling all over the lawn, and irritated that I was going to have to track down the cleaning service to ask what happened, I was looking forward to scrubbing the house. Something to get my back into. I began by drawing the microfiber feather duster over all the high surfaces to knock down the dust, then cleaning the windows, then the mid-level surfaces, and then the floors. High to low, like my mother taught me, so that the last thing to go was all the dirt you knocked down. In the bathroom I wiped down the counters and sink, scrubbed the shower, then the toilet, then got on my hands and knees to wipe the bathroom floor.

The side caddies of the refrigerator were filled with the hot sauce and dressing whims of all the combined summer renters, which I packed into a large cooler to take home. I wiped some stuck maple syrup out of a drawer and brushed some green flakes that looked like spilled frozen spinach out of the freezer. There was a lone ice cream sandwich, "S'more Flavour" printed on its label, in the back corner. I took a bite and spit it out—it was chewy with freezer burn. When the blankets, sheets, and towels were out of the dryer I folded them, wrapped them in clear plastic bags, and packed them in a large Rubbermaid garbage can that kept them safe from mold and mice and moths.

I was about to go pull the kayaks into the storage shed when I was struck with an urge I hadn't felt, not truly, in years. The urge, the want, felt almost orgasmic, like being inches away from someone's mouth, knowing you are about to kiss them for the first time. It was the real and true urge to write—not the "sit down and make yourself write" feeling, in which you perform a number of tricks to start the words flowing, if they ever do, but the desperate desire to actually grip a pen and watch as ink travels over the page. The actual urge to say something.

Of course, there was barely anything to write on in the cabin. Unwilling to destroy any of the books by writing in their back pages or margins, I rummaged through the house until I remembered a pack of Post-its I'd left in the drawer with the long lighter for the grill. I scratched the lone pen against the paper for several seconds before the ink began to flow.

I wrote until the sun went down. Post-it after Post-it, all the while my body vibrating with that near-sexual energy. It was the beginning of a story. A story about improbability, about coincidence meeting circumstance. It was a fairy tale—or the start of one—about what one hopes to happen, against all odds, happening. The voice I wrote with felt new to me—unrestrained. For years I had been trying to cool down the temperature of my writing, to pull it back, pull it back, pull it back—neutralize it, contain it, make it crisp, clear, and sharp, every word carved out of crystal. This writing was nothing like that—it was drippy, messy, breezy. I was working through a mind frame, not a conceit. I was creating a world, not words on a page.

I found the writing so intoxicating that I even considered stopping to masturbate—engorged with the creative juice, to use a hackneyed phrase, that was rushing through my veins. But the sheer ease with which I wrote was too precious. I couldn't stop it. I wanted to preserve this tingling energetic tension that pulsed within me.

Oh, it was him, it was all because of him, I knew. Him and his book and his body, and the way he spread his legs and looked at me in the black glass of the window. It was him and his tragic wife and his sad yet triumphant story. I was writing to him. He who wasn't the least bit interested in me—I was writing to explain myself to him. If I couldn't have him—perhaps I didn't even want him—I at least wanted him to know me. Who I was and how I felt.

I wrote till the sun waned and the Post-its were all used up, then wrenched myself away. I had to prep for tomorrow's classes and review the language of the department goals before a Monday-morning meeting. I didn't listen to anything on the drive back. I thought through the next five plot points in the story. When I arrived home John was sitting outside. I sat down with him. I put my hand on his knee. He shifted toward me and I put my head on his shoulder. That night we fucked for the first time in a year, with a clawing, otherworldly intensity. I woke up in the Big Bed, as we used to call it, in the early morning, and moved to the guest room. I felt exhausted and disturbed, as though a multitude of ghosts had passed through my body the night before.

IV.

*V*ladimir wrote to me at five the next morning. I assumed that he got up early to prep and write and answer emails while nobody could bother him. He told me he was honored I had read his book so quickly and that he would love to get lunch sometime soon. He proposed October 20—more than a month away. It was the last day of classes before study week, a four-day span in the middle of the fall semester when no classes were held in order to give students time to prep for midterms.

He expressed chagrin at suggesting such a far-out date but said that given how much he and Cynthia were still dealing with orientations and registrations and child-care adjustments, he wanted to offer a time he knew he could keep. I was happy for the delay. After reading his book, his visit on Saturday, and then Sunday's burst of writing followed by the unplanned and strange sex with John, I felt as though the past week had been three rather than one. I had forgotten who I was, and I needed the time to remember—to remember myself as a teacher and a colleague and a person whose two feet stood on the ground. I have always taken comfort in putting my mind to my work, and I resolved to engage with some department initiatives and campus activities more thoroughly than I had been in the weeks before.

I was in my home office, looking for my notes for my class "The Gothic Novel, from *Wuthering Heights* to *Beloved*" when John approached, put his arms around my waist, and nuzzled my neck. I stiffened and shifted away from him.

"Where are we?" he asked me. He was sunken and puffy, his jowls hanging, his double chin prominent from my vantage point. The light coming in through the window made his teeth look yellow and coated.

I told him I didn't know. "Are we friends?" he asked. We had gotten that phrase from a novel we had once read. "Are we friends?" "Are you my friend?" Maybe a children's novel. We used it with Sidney too: "Are we friends?"

"I don't know," I said. There was a strong impulse in me to throw away all the resistance I felt toward him. Not out of wanting, but because I knew the little soft parts of his heart. He had grown up in Iowa, been brought up by a mother who adored him and by a father who dismissed him as a pansy for his aptitude in school and his love of reading. He had been pushed around in high school by the masculine forces of the Midwest, by men who loved fighting and hunting and loud shows of ignorance. He had not played football or any sport and had been ignored by the bouncy, cheerful women around whom he developed all his sexual predilections. When he finally got to college, it took him three years to gather enough confidence to kiss a girl.

All that time he wasn't kissing, however, he was watching. He was watching how irresistible the combination of blunt masculinity, physical prowess, and intellectual fortitude were to the kind of women he wanted to attract. This was a different kind of maleness than he had encountered in the Midwest—these men were not the football-playing dullards who ran and smashed into each other because they were unable to express themselves in any other way—this was the maleness of the Rhodes Scholar lacrosse star, the law school Rugby players, the poets who met several times a week for a pickup basketball game. He didn't necessarily like the company of men—he preferred women even as friends—but he forced himself to learn about football, basketball, and baseball so that he could befriend men, so he could talk to them about something. He saw how men who liked men were more attractive to women, perhaps for the assurance that they had a secret life, or deeper, some primate-safety thing. He did hundreds of pull-ups and push-ups and sit-ups and squats in his room until his body shifted from a potbellied flabbiness to a lean solidity (he never had a body like Vladimir's, but when I met him he was tall and trim). All the while he studied—outpacing his classmates, yet driving himself further and further, as if maintaining a vast lead in relation to his peers was the only position that would give him breathing room. He went to the University of Barcelona in his senior year and fell in love with the long gold light and the philosophical bent and the country's literary journey from Cervantes to Lorca to Marìas.

He also fell in love with one of his TAs there—a tiny Spanish woman with long hair who smoked cigarettes with a holder. She was in her mid-forties compared with his early twenties, and she had a son who also attended the college. Emboldened by Spain, by his status as a foreigner, by Moorish architecture and the music that played in the town square until 3 a.m., he began to lurk around her after class. They went for coffee once, and the next day after the lecture, when the college would usually shut down for the siesta, she invited him back to her apartment. She taught him how to address her hard nipples and how to hold back orgasming while still moving inside her. This practice became a ritual that they kept religiously once a week after class. When he said goodbye, at the end of the year, she kissed him, pinched his cheeks like a boy, and said thank you. On the airplane he cried for most of the flight home at the thought of not seeing her again.

The love affair marked some final stage of his development. On his return, he fucked his way through the entire comparative literature department, with a devotion and avidity that might be called (in fact, it is) a sex addiction, in modern parlance. Supporting himself with a combination of odd jobs, he tried writing short stories and poems for several years. When I met him, he told me how he spent years following one woman or another, becoming infatuated, obsessive, then tiring of her for some reason and finding his eye caught by a new one. Then one night he had a dream in which all the women he had ever engaged with gathered on a grand opera stage. They beckoned him up from the audience, then they became the audience, and pelted him with roses that turned to blood, and when he looked down he saw himself waist-deep in shit.

Textbook, I told him at the time. After the dream, he stopped writing creatively and applied for a joint masters-PhD program in comp lit, with a focus on Cervantes. I met him after he had finished his dissertation and was teaching the intro essay-writing course to freshmen, TA-ing some grad courses, and applying for tenure-track positions around the country. I was pursuing my PhD in English and American literature with a focus on women's lit (not as "basic" as it sounds now, I say to my students).

The truth is, we did fall in love. Our hearts would bleat when the other was near. The realness of that early love is something I have returned to again and again as reassurance. We talked for hours, we watched each other walk across the quad, thrilling at the sight of our bodies in distance. We thought there was no one person better in the world. We allowed each other to relax, but we also challenged each other. We helped each other and we moved well together. I was an ideal weight when he met me and had clothes that suited me very well, with long hair that I wore in a high, silky ponytail.

Caught in the throes of love, alcohol, and excess, as well as the late nights and stress of my dissertation (I wanted to finish as soon as possible so that John and I could apply for jobs together), over the next few years I gained a massive amount of weight and smoked like a chimney, so that when we finally married I looked like a little squat toad, wearing a face with no contrast, a bad haircut, graying skin, and dry patches. John seemed to accept my decline with no comment, but my self-hatred swirled and cemented.

Vanity has always been my poorest quality. I hate it in myself, and yet am as plagued with it as I am with needing to sleep or eat or breathe. Despite my ability to read long texts quickly, to analyze them adroitly, to practice exegesis with precision, to publish articles and books on literary form, to write two novels, to raise a child, to be a mentor and friend to my students, still all the while I feel trapped in the prison of vanity. If I can't be a woman who is effortlessly beautiful, I wish I could be one of those women who, gracefully or ungracefully, move through the world unconsciously, with a kind of peace about their physical form. I have never had that peace, I have always felt tortured about my looks. I think my mother used to comment on my beauty (though when I look back at old photographs, I was at best adorable, but never beautiful). By the time I reached a certain age, she was upset with my appetite and tried to control my consumption, leading me to hide food in my closet and eat all I could when she was not around. She pushed the agenda of my beauty even as I disappointed her, remaining short rather than bloom-ing into height, with greasy hair, puffy and lank. When I was young I read without censure, including consuming endless women's magazines and picking up "tips" that haunt me still. To this day I tense my ass at a red light and do calf raises while waiting in line at the grocery store, take the top piece of bread off my sandwiches, and destroy pictures that catch me in an unflattering light. My daily thrum of happiness depends on my number on a scale, as inane as I know that to be.

Which is all to say that in my toady-ness following our marriage, after the photographs came back and I was forced to reckon with the blandness of my face, obscured by flesh and bloat, and the squatness of my body, I suggested to John that he seek out other women. At first I did it like a teenager runs a lighter over their arm hair—to see how it might feel. I felt as though I had hoodwinked this handsome rising star in the academic world, that I had shackled him to me—a woman to whom no one could truly be attracted. When I suggested the availabil-ity of freedom he didn't need much encouragement—he is still a cad, I like cads, and he is one. And after we moved and I had settled into my position at the college and learned to control my excess and reached peak attractiveness, lithe and disciplined, I kept encouraging him so that I could do what I wanted sexually, exploring the vigorous men of the country (I have always held that the most handsome men live in the country, while the most beautiful women live in the city, which is why in both places the pairs are unequal). Then after that halcyon period, and after David broke my heart and I chose asceticism, I ignored his behavior because it gave me room to breathe.

For John has always been a needy man, needing my affection and approval as much as he needed the admiration of the women he engaged with. When he was home he was always following me around the house, slipping his hands into the waistband of my pants or up my skirt. He always wanted to know if I loved him, if I was upset with him, if I was pleased with him. He would dog Sidney with questions about whether he was a good father, about whether he handled the play date well, or whether she had fun, or liked her treat, or if he made her happy or made her laugh. He could go from a faculty meeting in which he was praised to a class in which he was admired to the arms of a young woman who was thrilled by his attention to the dinner table of his adoring wife and daughter telling him that he looked nice, that he smelled nice, that he was a funny daddy, and he would still seem to be unsatisfied—some aspect of himself had not been acknowledged. Though perhaps, in those years that I had to fight to burrow little holes of solitude into the tightly packed days of school and writing and food and lessons and friends and social obligations, perhaps that was merely my impression of him.

By sleeping with him last night I had given him an opening to get some of that approval he was sorely missing—now that he wasn't allowed to teach, that he was politely ignored by most of his colleagues, now that he wasn't, as far as I knew, sleeping with a girl who could blink slowly and wet-lashed in the afternoon light. (After the college banned student-teacher relationships I believe he courted locals and recent graduates, but the allegations had, as of late, curtailed his interest in that pursuit.) He was pawing his way toward me on his tender puppy feet, and if I scooped him up and told him that whatever kind of dog he was, good or bad, he was my dog, and I loved his puppy-dog face, then I would be rewarded with an almost innocent sweetness and delight.

But I couldn't find my notes on *Rebecca*, I was teaching in half an hour, and I needed to get to my office where they probably were filed, then walk the ten minutes over to the other side of campus where my class was being held. I wanted to write out the next scene in my story. I hoped to exercise or schedule a hair appointment, something that would begin to prepare me for my future lunch date with Vladimir. I had to think about how to win my daughter's affection back.

"I'm not interested in being friends right now," I said. "I can't think it through, I'm too busy."

Still hanging on to the lingering feelings from the fight, I saw a meanness creep onto John's face. "So I'm supposed to come when you call? And shove off when you don't want me?"

"No," I said. "You don't have to do anything you don't want to do. You have always done exactly as you've liked. You will not get me into a fight right now, you will not. I won't allow it. I have to teach."

"I think you just don't want to bother with me anymore," he said. "I don't even think you care about any of this."

"Stop hounding me, John," I said. "I know you're getting restless, but I'm begging you, don't hound me. I need time."

After swallowing several times in quick, mad succession, he stepped to the side. As I passed out of the room he let me know that I'd neglected to pluck the reoccurring hair that had, in the last few years, begun to sprout perpetually from my chin.

V

*Y*our office is glorious."

Cynthia Tong was waiting for me by my door when I came back from teaching—a distracted class in which I felt like I was both overly acquiescent to my students' poorly read opinions and overly combative. They could critique only based on representation, they missed the formal elements of a story. Of course *Rebecca* is, in many ways, a story that is erected in misogyny, demonizing women, demonizing the other, but I was not interested in that for them. I wanted them to see how suspense was created, how symbols were utilized, how repetition made the ghost of Rebecca rise from the page. Again and again I told them, you need to see these things, these forms. Oh, they drove me crazy, being so completely obsessed with whether or not people were represented well, wanting every piece of literature to be some utopian screed of fairness.

I had to slide past her awkwardly, so it could seem like I was welcoming her, rather than her welcoming me. I made a gesture toward my couch, but she stood and looked around appreciatively, wanting to impress upon me how much nicer my situation was than hers.

"Are you in the windowless room? I was put there when I first came. Sit down," I said, but she didn't sit, she looked out the window, not in direct defiance—more as though she didn't hear me. The light made a line across her face. She was truly outstandingly lovely, with thick, curling black hair, firm cheeks, a dress shaped like a box that was modest, chic, and sexy all at the same time. She had dancer's or runner's legs, muscles at the top of the calves, indentations above a strong-looking knee, a clear line running up the thigh separating the front muscles from the back. I always noticed that line because I remember a boy I knew in high school telling me how alluring he found it. I didn't have it, and as he was telling me, I found myself understanding a new sort of truth: that there were all kinds and types of bodies, different aspects of physical form, that could spark arousal. That women's bodies were to be noticed and scrutinized and found attractive in all sorts of ways that I had not heretofore conceived. Chins, hands, throats, bellies, asses, legs, feet, all were to be considered and fetishized or dismissed.

"I don't have an office," she said, after staring for a long while at the view of the campus's rolling hills, then eventually sitting opposite me on the couch facing my desk. "They don't give them to adjuncts anymore."

I told her I would look into it, that if nothing else, she should be set up in a shared office. I wanted to make sure she knew from the beginning of our conversation that I was on her side. I complimented her dress and asked her where she got it, I told her I could never pull it off. I told her how much we missed her on Saturday, that I had been so looking forward to getting to know her, that I had read an excerpt of her memoir in *Prairie Schooner* (I had not, yet), and that it was inimitably impressive.

"I wanted to come and talk to you about Saturday," she said, and as she said it a wave of tension seemed to leave her body and I could see in her face the look of a swimmer before they enter cold water for the first time, the mental recklessness needed to trick oneself to jump in before you could stop and think about it too hard.

"I know all about migraines," I said. "I had them until I was around forty-five. The whole world would be insufferable." This was not true—I had bad headaches, but I never had migraines, never had the refracting of light that people describe, the spots, the auras—but I wanted to insist on our similarities.

"I didn't have a migraine," she said. "The truth is that Vlad and I had an awful fight and I couldn't get down from the ceiling after. He had to drug me and put me to bed."

"I'm sorry," I said. "I know all about fights, too."

"I sometimes have migraines," she said. "I think. Anyway, I wanted to tell you that."

"What was the fight about, if you don't mind me asking—you don't have to tell me if you don't want to." There was a fantasy that flashed into my mind quickly—as quickly and intrusively as those horrid images that used to haunt me as a young woman, of shit being thrown in my face or a rapist stuffing my used maxi pad into my mouth to gag me—of her telling me that the fight was about me, about Vladimir's lust for me. No, fool. I pushed the thought from my mind as immediately as I would push back those other images.

"I don't mind telling you," she said. "That's why I came here. To tell you. Do you know I've read both your novels? I loved them. I wasn't going to tell you I read them. But I want to know you, and I want you to know me. Do you think that's strange? But we're working together and now my daughter has swum in your pool and I didn't come and it was so rude and I want you to know why. Listen. I'm going to be frank." She paused and leaned in conspiratorially. "I'm kind of a fuckup."

"Me too." I said to her. I had not expected, when I saw Cynthia sitting quietly in the faculty meetings, that she would be like this. I had been prejudiced—not against her being Chinese American, although who knows what assumptions were lingering unconsciously in my mind. I had been prejudiced because she was a wife. A hanger-on. I was a wife too, but my husband and I were hired for tenure-track positions at the same time. We made equal salaries until he became chair. I sold my first book for an advance that allowed us to make a down payment on our home. This woman, teaching one class, had moved with her husband, parasitic and helpless.

But here in my office, she impressed me. Not because she had liked my novels, but because there was an intense desperation to her, as though after all that she had gone through, the last stop on the train for her was truth, and the pursuit of truth.

She told me what I expected, that when Vladimir had suggested she text to coordinate lunch, she had bristled and told him she wouldn't let the first text she wrote to me concern food. She told him to check with me about towels, because they only had slightly stained white bath towels, and she would have to go to the store and get new ones. She told me that she had gone to a spa to get her legs and underarms waxed to prepare and had bought new bathing suits for herself and Phee. She told me she was so nervous that morning that she was snappy and irritable. When Vlad, after one snap too many, snapped back, she broke down in tears and told him that all she wanted was to show us, me a writer, and my husband—an academic mind she admired—that they were a normal family. (She took a detour to say that she had fucked a couple teachers during her undergraduate and graduate experience, and while in general, looking at the drawn and papery skin that pulled toward their penises, or their crinkled eyes in morning light, she found them sad, she felt herself to be free and aware enough of the dynamic between them and was disappointed in women these days whose first thought after a consensual love affair was of their trauma—me, she said, I know trauma.)

"Vlad is so sick of my moods, he's so fed up with my 'mental health'," she continued. "I don't blame him," she said. "I'm sick of it too. I'm fucking sick of it." Her voice rose with a soft press of emotion that she swallowed. "So then he told me that you already knew we weren't a normal family—that everyone knew—and then he told me—I didn't know this—I didn't know this until Saturday—I sat in faculty meetings and fucking potlucks and I didn't know this—he told me that he told the hiring committee about my suicide attempt." She stopped herself. "Were you there?"

"I was not," I said, "but—" I lowered my head, hesitating.

"You heard."

"I heard."

She turned and looked out at the view again. "He said that's probably why he got the job, because when they asked him why he wanted to move all the way up here, something set him off and he started crying, and it all came out in a burst, and he told them how I had tried to kill myself when our child wasn't yet one year old, and how his responsibility was now to keep me alive, and they could hire me, that I was brilliant, that we were still living in the same apartment where he had found me foaming at the mouth, having shit myself in the bedroom, with a note to keep my daughter away."

At this I might have made a slight noise, because she glanced over to me as though daring me to say something. I held her gaze and nodded slightly, and she turned back to the window.

"I was surprised when they hired me for the memoir-writing class. It's not like a college to just—offer a job. Maybe I should have guessed. He said that when he left he felt ashamed of himself—so unprofessional—but after so many rejections, the offer came within the week." She paused and shook her head. "I mean, students are on that committee, right?"

"They sit in on the interviews, yes."

She pursed her lips and closed her eyes. I felt deeply sorry for her. Before I met Vladimir, when I heard that he divulged Cynthia's suicide attempt in his interview, I had felt a rush of distaste, like I feel when any great writers, or people, really, who have committed suicide are mentioned in the context of that act before their work. I had pitied her position at the college, coming into our small, gossipy department predefined as "damaged."

After he told her this, the morning before they were due to come swim at our house, she had retreated into what she called "the howl," which she described as feeling like one has been caught up in a wave—all sound a roar, all vision static, an ache in every part of her body, a wild pain everywhere. He actually had an injection for her, that's how sick she was, she told me, laughing, "That's how sick I am. He keeps a shot like Nurse Fucking Ratched," she said. "Like Nurse Ratched, like *Girl,*

Interrupted, like *The Bell* Fucking *Jar*, like every seventies and eighties mental-hospital TV movie of the week. Like *Frances*," she said. "Like fucking *Frances*, have you seen *Frances*?" she asked me. I said I hadn't and she said, "Oh, never mind, like every crazy person I've got a morbid fascination with crazy people." She held up a hand to an imaginary objector. "I'm allowed to say 'crazy' when I'm talking about myself. Anyway, I slept for eighteen hours. So I'm sorry I didn't show up."

She took a breath after all of it was finished and laughed, not the laugh of a disturbed person, but the deeply ironic laugh of someone who has never lived without the company of pain. She had fallen inside of and then climbed out of her pain so frequently and for so long that she could not cherish it or give herself any sympathy. I couldn't know the depth of what she had felt—she had gone so much further than I ever had—but I felt I knew about the kind of life that involved a begrudging and humorous acceptance of sadness as the invariable state of experience.

Could it be because we simply weren't sentimental, or we were too intelligent or too sensitive or too watchful? Was that mere self-flattery? What made us sad, and guilty of our sadness, what pit us in this battle against ourselves? And why couldn't we release the way some did, and say, yes, well, depression is a medical condition, I'm just wired a little poorly, I've got an illness I need to take care of, as all my students said. (Which is not to say that Cynthia Tong didn't take antidepressants—I'm sure she did.) Perhaps it was this idea of self-expression and this thought that if we were fully to release this sadness, or if we were to alter it too much—if we were to give up all the obsessions and anxieties that caused us pain—then we would become a kind of person we disdained, someone content with an abstract idea of the littleness of their lives. For our lives were, as writers, essentially little by nature. Writers have to lead little lives, otherwise you can't find time for writing. Was depression simply a hanging on to grandeur?

"I like you," I said. And it was true. She even looked less unapproachably beautiful after she was finished. I wanted to sit with her and talk about all sorts of things. I was thrilled that she loved my books (or said she did). I wanted to ask her what other writers she liked, what other experiences she'd had.

"I like you," she replied. When I told her she didn't know me she said, "I've read your books. I like you. I can tell you have sharp elbows and rough edges. You're prickly, like me. I like prickly people—I trust them. I hate nice people. I like Vlad because he's Russian, at heart, he's Russian. He's brutal and he can't hide anything. I'm a mess," she said, and rose. "Don't let anyone make you feel bad about your husband," she said to me. "I wish Vlad would fuck other people but he doesn't want to. He barely wants to fuck me."

I told her to give it time, that maybe he would.

"Fuck other people or me?" she asked.

I told her maybe both.

"Here's hoping," she said. "What time is it? I have to pick up Phee from the day care at three."

It was five till. "Quick, go," I said. "They charge by the quarter hour after pickup time."

"Shit," she said.

And she was gone, leaving only the light indent of her tiny ass on the cushion of my office couch.

❧

There is a straight two-mile path that cuts through a grove of tall fir trees in the state park at the edge of our town. After I had finished up my administrative duties for the day and forced myself to sit at my desk until my posted office hours ended, I drove over to walk it. If my body is doing something that my brain doesn't have to process, then I am free to think and to work through things. Often, when I am working on a book or an article, I come to this path.

As I would do when I was working on a book or an article, I tried to force myself not to think about Cynthia Tong and Vladimir Vladinski until I had walked the first two miles—one way to the end of the path. Once I turned around, I would allow my thoughts free rein. The first stretch though, I would attempt to discipline my mind. Every time they popped into my consciousness, Vlad, talented, flirtatious, eager, Cynthia, dark, honest, with what seemed like two lifetimes of trouble behind her eyes, I would catch myself and refocus on what was happening in that moment—the sights, the sounds, the smells, my body—an exercise I learned in a mindfulness course the college had offered to the faculty a few years ago.

I hadn't expected to find her so interesting. I hadn't expected that she would be truthful and real. I realized I hadn't ever heard her speak, and I had imagined her voice to be high and bashful. Instead her voice was low and clean, and her words were precise and well-chosen. She wasn't below Vladimir at all, she wasn't even his equal. She was his superior, lowering herself to be with him. Her suicide attempt hadn't been at all about him, there was no Medea to it, no grabbing for love, no attempt to get attention, as most female suicide attempts are interpreted, as I had maybe interpreted hers. No, she had an honorable depression, the likes of well-known writers, a true despair. "Honorable depression"— what does that even mean? Look at the trees, I told myself. Focus on the spaces between the branches, the light fading and filtering through—

He was incredibly talented, of course. She might not have his talent, his assurance, his hunger, or his drive. He might, from the external perspective, lead the relationship, with his accolades, with his career. You have to be willfully ignorant of certain truths to be successful, you just have to, and she seemed to me like the kind of woman who could not be ignorant of anything. The kind of mind that could paralyze itself. Listen, I reminded myself, what's the farthest sound you can hear? The cars along the freeway, the shouts from a soccer game in a distant field—

The sun was coming down and there was a chill in the air. Every so often the trees would rustle from a reckless chipmunk careening up its trunk. There was the outline of the moon, there was the North Star, there was the cashier from the nice grocery store walking her dog. We nodded at each other, acquaintances for more than ten years, two people who had exchanged pleasantries about our kids, her parents back in Bangalore, my daughter the lawyer, but who had never known the other's name.

One thing Cynthia's visit had certainly confirmed for me was that Vladimir was as sexually attractive as I had perceived, not only for me, an older woman who, I would be the first to admit, might have low standards, but for all women. One of the reasons she was with him was that she found him sexy. He wasn't a mentor, he was a prize. This was a disappointment. I had hoped that my attraction to him was something private, born out of a subsurface communication, an invisible thumping current specific to him and me.

A bird cawing so loudly it sounded like a cat in a fight. A woodpecker. My daughter at ten years old, saying, "I don't like nature because everyone is always screaming at you to look at things. 'Look at this deer! Look at that bird!'" My daughter. My good and serious daughter. Twenty-nine and interested in the material of the world. She had no use for abstractions, for fiction, for subtleties and nuances. "Subtlety achieves nothing," she would say. "There's no room for subtlety right now. There has to be right and wrong, and one has to decide and do it fast and not worry about anyone's feelings."

I cycled through memories of my daughter, some real, some photographic, until I reached the end of the two-mile marker and turned around.

It was then I saw a figure walking toward me—a man, with broad shoulders and a confident gait. I had been walking east, so when I turned around to face him he was backlit by the last intense glare of the setting sun. Was it Vladimir? It couldn't be. And yet the way he walked was recognizable—swinging arms and a rapidity that seemed to suit someone who had recently come from an urban area. As he came closer and closer I thought for sure it was him, and I felt like I was submerged in snowmelt water: my skin was prickling, my old, bad tits hard as rocks at the nipples.

It wasn't him. It was just some man in his mid-fifties taking a stroll. His shoulders were broad but his face was squashed, it looked as though he was taking the walk in order to lower his blood pressure. Still, all afire, I thought of this man pressing me against one of the fir trees, rubbing a flat palm over my aching breasts. I greeted him, and he responded in an overly loud voice about the last of the nice weather. I thought ruefully about John and about how only recently now, in his early sixties, did he seem too old for his twenty-year-old students, whereas I, in my late fifties, felt too old for a man in his forties. Older women with lust are always the butt of the joke in comedy, horny saggy birds with dripping skin. But then again, what was I saying, I didn't want to consummate anything with Vladimir. I liked his wife, I liked his daughter, I liked his writing, I liked his personality. What did I even think I wanted to do about it? In truth, when I got to the real imagining of the act, I found myself repulsed by the idea of actual physical contact. I only wanted to think about him, framed by my darkened window.

I quickened to a run, even though my shoes weren't supportive and my hip would ache and lurch for days after. I ran the last stretch of the road to my car, stripping off my coat and letting the cold air rush against my skin. When I sat in the driver's seat, I felt it again, that pressing and orgasmic need to write something down. I pulled out my laptop. Unlike other times in my life, when I needed morning or quiet or the right kind of pen—when I was forcing myself—this writing did not need to be coaxed, it erupted.

I stayed at the parking lot until it turned dark. The jocular man who I had passed rapped on the passenger-side window of my car—Is Everything All Right?—and I nodded and gave him a thumbs-up. He kept speaking at me, but I ignored him, my radio playing Tallis, bending my face closer to the laptop screen. Then he came around to the driver's side and knocked on the window, louder and more urgently, until I turned off the music, opened the window slightly, and asked him, What? Looking hurt, he pointed toward the entrance of the trail. There, a black bear stood on its hind legs, leaning up against a spruce tree, its front paw stretched to hold on to a branch, rubbing its back up and down against the trunk. I smiled and unrolled my window fully to apologize and thank him for showing me. He nodded, walked away, said Stuck-Up Bitch over his shoulder, and gave me the finger.

VI.

I stopped for cigarettes and a bottle of rye on the way home. Checking my email in the driveway, I received a reminder from the Brown summer program and realized I hadn't written Edwina's recommendation letters. I marched myself to the desk and stayed until ten finishing them. It was pleasurable, letting my mind rest on her—an exceptional student, proactive, hungry, curious, charismatic. Her mother was from Saint Lucia, her father Italian American, from Staten Island. She had been raised religiously, but spaciously, always with the room for her mind to grow—in her teenage years she had fallen in with the right Catholics, the liberal ones whose thought verged on the esoteric, who were interested in mysticism and symbolism. She came here on a full scholarship and was constantly worried that she had made the wrong choice not going to the Ivy League school she had been accepted to, extortion-level student debt be damned.

In general, I am very distant from the admission process of our school, but I know from the stress on the faces of the students that year after year becomes more visible, like transparencies of strain that lie on top of each other until they solidify into a mask of perpetual anxiety, that it is not the same as when I went to college. I was a good student, I put in effort, I studied and was neat and tried hard on my tests, but I didn't tear myself apart like the students and parents of today.

I knew college was the way out of my home, which I mainly remember as rooms my father strayed in and out of, with the occasional quiet woman sitting at the breakfast table uncomfortably, waiting for the coffee to brew, made sheepish by my sweeping presence as I imperiously picked up and put things down around her. I had been sent to live with my father because, unlike my two older sisters, it was thought that I showed academic promise, and he was the health-and-safety coordinator for a boarding school where I could go for free. At the time I was indifferent to this leg up. At first I was upset that I couldn't stay back in Texas with my sisters and their boyfriends and the desultory life of cars and dates and marijuana and minimum-wage jobs. Later I resented that I couldn't board with the other girls at the school, and thus was never able to permeate the boundaries of their exclusive world.

Yes, I had academic aptitude, but I never knew my efforts as stress (that didn't come until graduate school). I was excited to do well, and to be petted like a pretty cat who moves with assurance, and I was passionate—so passionate about the books I read and the way they made me feel. I loved that the complexities of my emotions were understood by authors writing hundreds of years ago, I loved looking at their texts and trying to understand what they were aiming to do, to pull my own meaning from them, to point out what others didn't see or notice—the repetition of blue imagery, the recapitulation of motifs of separation. I was good at that. I love and have always loved typing—my fingers traveling and pressing like a musician's, first against the big, resistant keys of the typewriter, then the light, bulky plastic of the word processor, and eventually the smooth, soft clicks of a laptop.

In college I met real mentors who taught me to write and pushed me into academia. I wanted to go there—I didn't want to be in the world, around all those people who didn't read books, who didn't think they were important. I worked hard, I think. I remember falling asleep in the library, waking up once to a teacher (who was probably fifty but at the time seemed ancient, eighty years old at least) stroking my hair with psychotic restraint. But I also felt that I was, as they say, on a track—I was a figurine in an animatronic Christmas display, being whipped around from one end of the window to another. I can see my half-blind pursuit of an academic career only as a blessing. It was merely due to my lack of imagination that I scurried on to my master's and PhD.

Five minutes after I submitted my letters, Edwina sent an email thanking me and asking if she could take me out for coffee the next day. And there it was, that rightness, that ability to not only make the correct and courteous gesture but to do it quickly. This was one of the many qualities that set Edwina apart and would ensure her success. I saw how speed wore on my students—sending some into a brittle and constant state of worry, some into torpor, others into paralysis. If something was not dealt with in a few days, it felt to them like a completely forsaken cause. They viewed lives, roles, opinions, stations as things that got taken from them if they didn't act fast enough. Where was the time for thinking? For consideration? For not thinking? For failure? When I was in college the way to waste time was movies and friends and alcohol and drugs and sex and music. Activities that for the most part we agree now are essentially enriching. They waste time on their little boxes. And they don't want to, they hate themselves for it. But the boxes are there and they are their schoolwork and their social life and their entertainment and their sin and their virtue all in one. God help them.

My gut was thudding with excitement when I made my way down to the backyard—a tumbler of rye in one hand and the pack of cigarettes in the other. I had not smoked in twenty years, after I quit for a bad hacking cough. They had been my master for so long—my friends, my saviors, my trusty companions, my escapes, my rebellion, my illicit yet effective method of weight control—that when I was finally able to excise them from my life, I was too scared to ever go back.

The man's comment in the park upset me. It was always that—a man could always make me feel worse than anything any woman could ever say to me. He could always make me despise myself, make me feel fundamentally self-conscious about my idiotic femininity and my pathetic peevishness, make me understand I was no match for the real power he possessed. In Texas, in Connecticut, in France, in New York, in Missouri, in Mexico City, in my kitchen, bathroom, living room, basement, bedroom, I could click mentally from slide to slide each time a man, with a well-aimed put-down, has made me feel essentially worthless. That bottomed-out feeling, combined with the intense longing stirred awake by Vladimir, the taxing encounters with John, the meeting with Cynthia that had both excited and depressed me, had weakened my defenses. Cigarettes are best when they are accompanied by intense moods—happiness, anger, defeat. No cigarette is better than the one that follows a torrential cry. I had a friend who used to call them "emotion suppressors" but it's more like they complement emotions, like a good wine complements a meal.

I lit one using a lighter (lighting by a match, unless it's an easy-strike match, ruins the first drag). While I wanted to enjoy it more than I did—the smoke felt abrasive and thick in my throat—the transgression against my better judgment was beautiful. My head lightened immediately and sensation was sparkling through my body when I heard footsteps on the driveway coming toward me. Thinking it was John, I kept my gaze fixed forward, as though I hadn't noticed.

"So now you come to his house?"

My daughter's voice rang out of the darkness—I turned to see her at the back gate, illuminated by the motion sensor light that hung over the garage.

"Sid?" I called to her but she didn't hear me. She was fumbling with the gate, pushing at the latch, which had to be turned and then lifted to be released. I rose to walk over and open it for her, when, in her rage, she kicked the door down entirely.

"Don't you walk toward me, skank," she yelled at me. "You come to his house? He lives here with his fucking wife who is my fucking mother, you little skank."

It is always—*funny* is not the right word, but maybe *interesting*—how the exceedingly drunk are truly the most repetitive people in the world.

73

I remember John getting blotto one night in the city (he vomited in the cab and I paid the cabdriver the last fifty dollars we had in apology) saying, while he was in this compromised state, "I Goddamn love you. Do you know that? I Goddamn love you" on repeat. It was uncharacteristic, and I remember feeling pleased for a bit, then tired, then disgusted.

It took me a moment, however, to realize that because I was in near-complete darkness, and Sidney was so very drunk, she didn't recognize who I was. She dropped her attaché and shrugged off her European hiker's backpack like a townie barfly readying himself for a brawl. I said her name again, but before I could tell her that I was her mother, and not her father's paramour, she stumbled toward me and grabbed me by the shoulders with her strong grip. She smelled like a distillery, and her eyes were steely and distant and red-rimmed—waking consciousness buried deep within her. "I'm going to fuck you up, skank." She lost her balance slightly and hugged me into a kind of boxer's clinch. She was taller than me, and far sturdier, and she staggered against me, pushing me so that I stumbled backward.

"Sid, it's your mother, it's Mommy."

I felt her soften for a moment and take in my face. "Oh Mommy," she said, but instead of releasing me she pulled me into a tighter embrace.

Our nighttime sprinklers went off, spritzing her, and she recoiled out of instinct. Still gripping me, she tripped on the hose that was attached to the sprinkler, and, in trying to regain her footing she veered us to the right. I told her to watch out, but she and I collided with the outdoor trunk in which we kept the cushions and the pool toys. Then, like a physical comedian from an old movie, she dragged us away from the trunk and, in doing so, put her foot inside the inner tube Phee had used that was still sitting inflated by the side of the pool. In her attempt to shake it off—it seemed she mistook it for an animal—she, now with one strong arm hooked around my waist, hopped and kicked her leg wildly, hysterically. Knowing there was only one thing that could possibly help I struggled against her, dragging her closer and closer to the edge of the deep end of the pool until I used all my strength to jump into the frigid water, bringing her, who held me as tightly as a raccoon holds a piece of foil in a trap, with me.

It had been cool the past week, so the water was a terrific and icy shock. Sidney let go of me immediately and waved her arms wildly to get to the surface. Before I rose to help her, I allowed myself one gorgeous contemplative moment underwater. Even though she was drunk, and it was very dark, it was still true that my own daughter had mistaken me for a student.

⤙⤚

I climbed out of the pool immediately, but Sidney stayed in, whipping her head back and forth, shaking off the water.

"Mommy," she wailed.

"Get out of the pool, honey."

"Mommy, I need you."

"Okay, my sweetheart, just get out of the pool. Use the shallow end. That's it."

She climbed out and lay her body down on the concrete next to the pool and stared up into the sky. Cold to the point of pain but unwilling to leave her, I stripped my drenched clothes and underwear and wrapped myself in a leftover towel that hung on one of the pool chairs and hadn't been taken in from the weekend. It might even had been Vladimir's towel, I let myself think, as I wrapped it around my naked, goose-pimpled body.

I shimmied beneath her and rested her head in my lap. She turned to the side, snuggling against me.

Her clothes sagged and weighed on her. She was wearing her out-of-work uniform, her standard apparel of a dark hooded sweatshirt over her white oxford shirt, under which she wore both a white T-shirt and tank to minimize her already small breasts, dark selvage jeans, and boots that looked like they belonged to a naturalist in the early twentieth century. She would regret getting the boots wet in the morning—she was as persnickety about the neatness of her clothes as any man (it is my experience that while women love clothes and fashion, there is no one as interested in the preservation of the like-new state of their vestments as a preening man). She made a decent salary, she lived with her partner, and I paid her student loans, and so though she dressed simply, she had a weakness for expensive boutiques that specialized in hand-crafted apparel with clean lines and high-quality materials.

"Mommy, Alexis kicked me out."

Sidney's voice had the forlorn neediness that she had as a child, when she would wake up in the middle of the night with a bad dream, or itching from bug bites, or in pain from a mysterious fever. It was so easy for me to comfort her in those moments, to pull her to my chest and soothe her and let her sleep on me all night. She was never a clinging child, independent and sensitive and usually interested in shrugging me off, and so I cherished those moments, when hurt made her needy, and she clung to me as though I was the only one who could help.

I stroked her wet hair. Like many gay young women, she had the undersides of her head shaved up past the ears, and her light reddish bob flopped a little past her chin when dry. I ran my fingers along the shaved part, the bristles smooth on the way down and textured the way up. It was barely 60 degrees, we would both be shivering in a moment, but I felt a poetic charge in the tableau of us, soaked, our hearts as open and seeping as popped blisters—a sordid and suburban pietà. It reminded me of twenty years ago, when my colleague David didn't show up at our meeting place, and I realized that he'd decided he wouldn't run away with me to Berlin after all, and I lay down on the bare, cold earth of the graveyard (our ridiculous choice for our rendezvous) and let a stray cat sniff, and then walk over, my body.

"She left me, Mommy," she repeated.

"My sweet girl, I'm so sorry."

"I thought you were one of Dad's—" She didn't finish the sentence.

"It's okay, sweetness. But you shouldn't get so drunk, at least not when you're by yourself."

"I took a bottle of rum on the train with me."

"That'll do it."

"Then we were delayed in Albany for an extra hour so I got some beer."

"How'd you get here?"

"I walked."

"Oh my sweetheart. You're safe at home now."

"I think I fucked a man in the train bathroom."

"You think?"

"No, I did."

"Willingly?"

"Basically."

"Basically?"

"Yes. Willingly."

"God, Sid, how do you feel about that?"

"Oh, fine. I wanted to. It was fine."

She was fully shivering now, and I took my towel off and wrapped her in it and helped her to stand.

"Let's get you warm and talk about it inside, okay? I want to hear."

"I don't want to talk. Can you make me some food?"

"Yes."

"Can I stay here tonight?"

"It's your home."

"You're not mad at me?"

"I was never mad at you. You were mad at me."

"Look at those stars."

It was clear out, and they were so dense they seemed connected at the tips.

"I was just thinking about how when you were a little girl you told us that nature was so boring, because all anyone did in nature was tell other people to look at things."

"Were you smoking?"

I didn't answer. She and I took a hot shower together in the big shower, like when she was little. I dressed her in John's sweats and sat her on the couch with a large glass of water, then put on a robe and started in the kitchen. I decided to make her stovetop spaghetti carbonara pie, an old specialty of mine she loved—a sauce made of bacon, tomato, olive, and anchovy (I add olives and anchovies to all tomato sauce because tomato sauce is always better with olives and anchovies) simmered on the stove, to which one adds al dente spaghetti, then cracks eggs into little craters in the mixture, cooking them until they are just set, after which an obscene amount of parmesan is grated over the entire thing and the skillet (oven safe) is put under the broiler for three minutes to crisp the top. The dish is an ambush of calories; it would be good for all that alcohol sloshing around her insides.

I was about to strain the pasta and add it to the sauce that was simmering on the stove when I heard Sidney staggering toward the downstairs bathroom. I turned off the burners, ran into the bathroom, held her hair from her face and rubbed her back as she vomited torrents. After several rounds, in which she alternated vomiting with lying on the cold tile floor, she seemed to have nothing left in her. She brushed her teeth and I tucked her into the guest bedroom, pulling the covers up to her chin and kissing her hair. Next I cleaned up the vomit that had escaped her before she had reached the toilet, a line from the couch to the bathroom, and put the sauce in a storage container. I threw out the pasta, which had been sitting unstrained in the hot water and now looked like a pot of floating dandelion wisps. I washed my face, brushed my teeth, performed my skin regimen of toner, retinol serum, massage, under-eye cream, and moisturizer. I would sleep with Sidney to keep watch over her during the night.

She had kicked all the covers away and pulled her sweatshirt off. I

78

covered her back up with the sheet and lay down beside her, staring up at the ceiling. I must not have slept very soundly, because at 3 a.m. I heard noises below and then John's recognizable footsteps climbing the stairs. He stood at the doorway and looked at me, and I gave him a slight wave before turning my head. I had failed to notice that he hadn't come home.

VII.

The next day, after I had finished my class, I ran into Vladimir. He walked me up to my office and stayed for almost a half an hour, leaning against my door frame. The National Book Award finalists had been announced and we discussed which books we had read and whether we considered the awardees worthy. I sat on the edge of my desk, a position I never sit in, and even pulled one knee up, leaning my chin on it as we spoke. He held the door frame around where the lock was with his right hand, and lifted his left hand over his head, grabbing the frame and stretching his body, like a nymph at a fountain. He was wearing a T-shirt (the heat had been accidentally turned on in our office and it was abominably hot) and I could see both the damp of his armpit and a tuft of his underarm hair peeking through his short, crumpled sleeve. I was overcaffeinated and felt as though I was talking too fast, losing the thread of the conversation. He, however, seemed just as interested in speaking, and we chirped at each other like two frantic birds until the department admin walked over to the doorway, smiled, and walked away, a clear gesture to let us know we were being too loud.

I was elated by our run-in, our conversation. His body, when he was standing in my door frame in his figure skater's pose, seemed to beg for me to come and grab it around the middle. Did he do this with everyone—this sensual display of his corporeal beauty? "Your body was very flirtatious," my college friend said to me when I called her crying after she left a bar without me and I was pushed in an alley and groped by an angry local. At the time, I remember thinking she was right. My body had been offering an invitation, if not a promise. Did Vladimir know that he was communicating with me? Did he think me to be younger than I was? Or did he find me attractive no matter? Was I actually, as my daughter's drunken episode the previous night had suggested, so well-preserved that I was still mistakable for a student? But it couldn't be. He was humoring me, this maternal woman, probably so outdated in her views and opinions, with lines in places I had yet to realize.

After work I picked up Sidney and she and I went to our favorite diner. It was one of the only boxcar diners left in our area, and the family who had taken it over in the nineties had mercifully left its menu alone, except for the occasional portobello-mushroom wrap sandwich posted on the specials. The parents had emigrated from Armenia and borne four daughters and a son, all of whom they homeschooled for religious purposes, all of whom were extremely attractive and reserved, all of whom worked at the restaurant. The daughter who sat us at our booth was chipper but blank, she called us "honey" incessantly but without any force or affection behind it, like she was a telemarketer reading a call script.

Sidney looked awful. Her eyes were bloodshot and her skin was a greenish-gray and there was a pimple on each side of her mouth. She ordered like she wanted to eat the world—everything fried and dripping with cheese and a milkshake. I ordered a Greek omelet, with a salad instead of potatoes and no toast.

"Don't go too crazy, Mom." Sidney rubbed her eyes hard, as though she was weary that I existed.

"What?"

"Would the potatoes kill you?"

"If you had the digestive system I have, you might argue yes."

She dropped the subject with a wave of her hand, dismissing me. I didn't mind. I was too happy that we were speaking again to let her annoyance feel like anything other than the feeble blows that daughters lob against their mothers to make sure they'll still be loved, even at their most peevish.

I watched as Sid took the crayons that they kept on each table in a juice cup and flipped the paper place mat over to the kid's menu side and began to color. It had been the same picture for nearly twenty years, a crowded jungle scene with tigers and snakes and baboons, and she always colored it the same way—blue tigers, green snakes, red baboons, yellow foliage.

I gradually dredged out the information that she had slept until noon, and then sat with John and watched *The Deer Hunter*. She and John shared a love for long seventies-era films with big character journeys that left them feeling cozily wrung out at the end. When she was in high school I would feel slightly left out to find them on a Sunday afternoon in the dark of the den watching *Apocalypse Now*, *M*A*S*H*, *The Godfather Part I* or *II*, drinking chocolate milk and eating bag after bag of butter-soaked microwave popcorn. I loved all those movies once, but they were so long, and I was so busy that even when I tried to sit and sink inside of them I kept popping up, remembering to water a plant or fold a load of laundry, until I was told by my husband and child that my fussing presence was not welcome.

The waitress served us big brown plastic cups of water. I pushed a cup toward Sidney, telling her she needed to hydrate, and she scowled and continued coloring. Gently, my breath calibrated to avoid annoying her, I put my finger on the place mat she was coloring, so that her crayon ran over my finger. She began coloring in a new spot and I put my finger there. I did it a few more times until her guarded grimness cracked a bit, and she grabbed my hand and colored my fingernail in mock fury.

I took her hand in both of mine and asked, "How long are you staying?"

"I don't know," she said, and started to cry.

"Can I sit next to you?" I asked her. In an effort to teach her about the independence of her own body, I had, from the time she was a small child, asked her whenever I wanted to kiss her or lift her up or give her a hug. My mother and sisters had put their hands all over me, I was their little pet to poke and prod at. I didn't ever want Sidney to feel that way—to feel as though her body belonged to me, or to anyone.

She nodded and I slid next to her, holding her in my arms as she sobbed into my chest.

"Tell me what happened." I smoothed the falling strands of hair away from her face. A different waitress daughter came and put Sidney's milkshake down. I mouthed the word *breakup* and winked at her and her face drooped into a little puffy-lipped frown of sympathy.

Sidney told me about how Alexis, whom she had been in a relationship with for three years and living with for one, had, in the spring, broached the topic of having a baby. Alexis was thirty-five and had recently learned the term *geriatric pregnancy*, which made her want to start discussions about a plan, if not the plan itself. Sidney, in the meantime, was reeling from the news about her father, and from the shattering of her perception of her parents' perfect love. She had always clung fast to images and beliefs and traditions. At ten she had been inordinately devastated by the news that Santa Claus didn't exist. She felt as though she couldn't possibly discuss the making of a new family while hers was crumbling to the ground.

Alexis, a self-described Urban Black Woman who was raised in Queens by a single mother, with a father who had long ago moved to Florida and become the head of a family that she had no place within, had little sympathy for her. "You were given everything," she said to her. "They love you. They're grown-up people. Let them live their lives."

They were both lawyers. Alexis worked for a large firm at an average of sixty-five hours a week. It was drudgery, but very well remunerated. Every time I visited their lovely, high-ceilinged apartment I saw the evidence of reckless online-shopping benders piled in cardboard columns in the doorway. The money to buy the stuff without the time to even unwrap it. Sidney's job was more rewarding but paid half as much with nearly as many hours. The last thing they wanted to do during their precious Saturday-night dinners or Sunday brunches was to talk about their problems. So, like the two only children they were, they retreated from the discussions, with the silent understanding between them that when things "calmed down," they might see a therapist.

Two burly men came into the diner. One of them leered at Sidney and me, sitting on the same side of the booth. Did he think we were a couple? I met his eyes and held them until he turned and sat on a counter stool, his pants pulling down and his shirt pulling up to reveal a hairy plumber's crack.

"What is it?" Sidney asked, sensing that my attention was elsewhere. I shook my head, and she continued:

"So at work there was a big case that came up for us, a lawsuit about wrongful termination, and I was given some support staff to help me. It was summer so I had this law student from NYU, and, well, she was very, um—"

She paused and drank her milkshake.

"Beautiful, very tall and, um, fun to be around and passionate and smart, and we were working very long hours—"

She trailed off.

"And somehow Alexis found out," I finished for her.

"She had a summer Friday and was bringing dinner by for me as a surprise. There was nobody else in the office and we were—" She hesitated, and I held up my hand to let her know that she didn't need to elaborate on any further details. She rubbed her eyes roughly, as if to wipe off the memory. "So we talked through it, and I said I would end it, and then our team won the case and went out for drinks and it happened again, and I was trying to be good so I told her, and she said, three strikes, you know, and then one night—this woman, you see, I couldn't, it was like a spell, she was so beautiful and so tall and so—"

"Young?"

"No. No, she was my age. Before she went to law school she was an actress. A real one, commercials and Broadway. I don't know. Being with her was like shooting something into my veins. I tried to resist, and then one night it was two in the morning and she texted me that she was at a bar outside our apartment and I just—left. Just hoped Alexis wouldn't notice I was gone. But of course she did notice I was gone, she's—I don't know what I was thinking—I don't think Alexis has slept through the night since middle school. So I ruined it. She'll never take me back now."

She rested her head in her palms again and sobbed. Our plates arrived and I moved back to my seat. I felt cold. Sid shoveled food into her face, hardly chewing, choking down her milkshake between bites.

"Now you're judging me."

"I like Alexis."

"You of all people should not be judging me."

"I might argue I am exactly the person who *should* be judging you. I'm your mother."

"Look at what you and Dad did."

"We had an understanding."

"You had an understanding about him power raping women?"

She was loud, with an ugly, stretched look on her face. The man with the butt crack and his buddy looked over toward us with amused expressions. I was reminded of Dante's *Inferno*, when Virgil rebukes Dante for watching two souls argue with each other, telling him it is wrong to ogle two beings who are embroiled in their own suffering. I told her to quiet down. She looked at me like she wished me dead, though when she next spoke, her voice was lowered.

"How could you not be sympathetic to me?"

"Of course I'm sympathetic to you."

"I messed up. She should give me another chance."

"She might."

"We were going to go all the way."

"What's that mean?"

"You know, all the way. A kid, a house. A life."

"But it seems like you didn't want that."

"I just wanted time."

"It seems to me like you wanted to act in some way—to sabotage it. Because you weren't ready."

"Never mind."

She slammed her cup onto the table and got up as if to leave. I asked her where she expected to go. She sat back down and asked me not to psychoanalyze her, that she needed a listener. I apologized, blamed my upbringing, and sat quietly until I saw her posture soften.

"Are you taking the week off work?" I asked her tentatively.

"No, that's another thing." After all her adolescent histrionics, her face took on the fatigue of a grown-up person, and I finally could imagine her sitting at a desk and being trusted with a task.

"You got fired?"

"No, I didn't get fired," she snapped. "But Charlie—"

"The other woman?" I clarified.

"She got a job there. I mean, of course she did, she's brilliant. I asked to take leave. I think I have to find something else. It's going to be too complicated, and Alexis will never take me back if she's working there."

"You love your job."

"I can get another job I love. I think. If I don't expect to get paid well for it."

"This woman ruined your life."

"It's not her fault. Or it is, I don't know. But it's not like I can prevent her from getting hired. My ass would get sued every way but straight." *Every way but straight*—one of John's phrases. Sid laughed. She loved the old Texan/Midwestern expressions John and I traded. She used them to contrast with the rest of her overeducated liberalese. In high school she was fascinated when she learned that Bob Dylan lyrics were cited by judges to elaborate on obscure laws in court filings. The folksiness blended with the officiousness delighted her. More than doing good, and to my great pride, she was a do-gooder, far more than her father or I were or would ever be, she loved the language and jargon of the law. She loved the way phrases could become solid, and then could have their solidity stripped from them, all by interpretation, all by language, language, and more language. Fighting with words, she would call it when she participated in Lincoln-Douglas debates in high school. She was so awkward then, so homely and horse-ish, with bad makeup, poorly fitting clothes, and a sawing, toneless laugh. But when she stepped onto the debate stage her tongue was loose and her mind was quick and precise. She could find and dissect holes in the arguments of her competitors nearly instantaneously. It was when I saw her there at that podium that I knew, despite everything, despite all my weakness and guilt, that she had something in her she could use to take care of herself.

I, of course, was thrilled when she told me she was dating a woman. What a relief, I thought, to free oneself from the heterosexual prison. Straightness: the predictable container in which all possible outcomes seemed already etched into stone—happiness, unhappiness, complacency, strife—a life in which we were all operating inside of a story already told, even as we sought to live an authentic existence. Even as we tried to say to ourselves that it wasn't who we mated with but the quality of the thoughts in our brain that made us radical, we knew that the patterns of our life were the patterns of our parents, were the patterns of all the dim, sorrel-chomping sheep living unexamined existences in all the homes all over this thoughtless, anti-intellectual country. We knew that the stuff of our lives was the stuff of normalcy, and how normalcy and its trappings and expectations were always there. There would always be couple friends who were a bit more square than you, who you would have to play some hetero game with. There would always be family who would ask the women to do the dishes while the men played chess. How fortunate for her, I thought, to be able to evade all that. She told us she was queer, attracted to men still, and that she would appreciate if we didn't label her one way or another. She was Sid. Fine, fine, fine. As long as whatever she chose, she wouldn't have to take on the identity of the anxious woman who got dinner on the table while the men sat on the porch. As long as she didn't have to act the part of the schoolmarm to a good-natured rascal of a partner who did whatever he liked and was loved more because of it. And if she did choose to cook or clean or worry, at least she could maybe do all those things for a woman who understood, not a man who, by virtue of being born with a thing between his legs, had absorbed from an early age that it was all right to sit back and enjoy being served.

"How are *you*, Mom?"

She swung her attention to me abruptly. It was clear from the question that she had something to say about how *I* was, or how she thought I should be. Immediately I felt my face lengthen, my eyebrows lift and a frown form at the sides of my mouth.

"Fine," I told her. I caught the eye of one of the Armenian daughters—she made a questioning gesture about the check and I nodded. "Let's go on a walk. You should get some outside time today—you'll feel better tomorrow." Sid acquiesced. It was a joke in the family that I thought everything could be solved by exercise and fresh air, but over the years I had gotten Sid to share my view—she ran cross-country in high school after I told her she needed a sport for college and ran the marathon a couple of years ago. I could tell she was doing well when she spoke of running. She was compulsive, she needed replacements. When she wasn't running she was probably drinking too much, or screwing too many interns, apparently.

I was leaving the tip when her eyes caught the remnants left on my plate.

"You didn't eat your omelet."

"I ate half of it."

"You look thin."

"Thank you."

"I don't mean it as a compliment."

"I'm not hungry." Panic bumped up against the edge of my voice.

"You need to take care of—"

"Sidney, let's go. I'm old. My metabolism is so slow. You eat less when you're old, it's just a fact. You need less. You want to talk? Let's GO."

And once again, the bumpkin at the counter, shirt riding up and pants riding down, his face greasy from his burger, with little white shreds of napkin stuck in the stubble of his mustache, looked over at us. He smirked or smiled, I couldn't tell which. I gestured for Sid to go ahead of me and she walked out of the diner. He watched her pass, looking ostentatiously at her rear as she exited. A power move, performed to assert himself and to warn me. The look was to let me know that no matter how androgynous she may come across, he could still find a hole to stick his dick in if he so chose. As I mentioned, it was an old boxcar diner, and so the exit was extremely narrow. I spent some time pretending to count change in the plastic check tray, then after Sid had fully exited I took an unused straw from our table and, as I squeezed past the man, took the opportunity to plant it directly in the exposed darkened crevice between his left and right buttocks, so it stuck out from his flesh like an erect tail.

VIII.

*D*eep purple-blue sat on top of an orange horizon, and the trees turned inky black against the sky as Sid and I walked a loop that began at the base of an apple orchard, climbed up to meet the Appalachian Trail, then circled back around, dipping into a marsh, over an old railway track, and back to the little gravel pull-off where we'd parked. It was threatening to storm, the clouds moved quickly, a cluster of loosed metallic balloons crossed the sky at such a pace it was as though they were being chased.

All I wanted, the entire walk, was to talk to Sid about Vladimir. When she noticed my half-eaten omelet, I admitted all the thoughts that I had heretofore pushed away. I realized I was completely and utterly lovesick. It was love. I had restricted my caloric intake nearly all my life, eating half portions, carving little lines around globs to delineate what must be left behind, even throwing food into the trash; but there was only one other period in my life when I left food on my plate without even thinking about it, which was when I fell in love with David. There was a burning in my body, an extra level of excitement keeping part of me fed and running that required no sustenance. It was longing for the love of Vladimir Vladinski, junior professor and experimental novelist. Longing was energizing my muscles and organs and brain. Longing was replacing my blood with fizzy, expansive liquid. I loved him.

I have always been amazed at the mind's ability to do several things at once. I remember reading to Sidney when she was a little girl—for hours I would read to her—and often during those times I would be in a completely different thought space and would have no consciousness of any of the words that were coming out of my mouth. As Sid and I walked the trail she told me about trends on social media (I didn't have accounts, mostly because they made me feel undignified, and I relied on Sid to keep me updated), television shows that she watched, articles that she read. She gave me a long report on *The Deer Hunter* and how it was much campier than she remembered. All the while I was thinking about Vladimir. I imagined us in a flat in a European city, it didn't matter which one, so long as the language outside was not English, the murmur of an incomprehensible tongue surrounding us like a curtain of privacy. It would be my flat, with open shelves and a big slop sink and cut-up fruit lying on a wooden slab on the counter. There would be one small bedroom with windows on two sides, big old windows that either stuck or flew up wildly, and a mattress on a floor with crumpled and cool white linens. We wouldn't live together, that wouldn't be what anyone wanted, that wouldn't be compatible with a *life*, but he would come to me, some evenings, a few afternoons a week. We would drink wine, or not, we wouldn't need the wine, we would spend hours in a tangle on the mattress or walking around half-clad with books in our hands. (I had to pause the reverie to consider that lately I was having more and more hip problems, so I would need to probably raise the bed, and inserted an antique iron frame beneath the mattress.) I might feel desperate and half-crazed by where he went when he was away, but I would restrain myself, cherishing the time we did have. I would write stories in reserved and pulled-back tones, like Mavis Gallant, about the life of the expatriate. I might teach, yes, I might teach, maybe a few wealthy students, one-on-one, a class here or there at a university. Not a university life, not that anymore—maybe the equivalent of a community college, something very incognito and undemanding. There would be something sad about our love, mainly when I started to become too old, to become Léa in Colette's *Chéri*, and his eyes would pool with tears on the day that I told him he could—he *must*—go. Of course, I didn't really picture my own self in all of this. I pictured some amalgam of film stars, with doctored teeth and antiaging programs, and money spent with fun, mean trainers who put their bodies through all sorts of tortures. I didn't picture my already withered top lip with the bulging scar at the tip from the ingrown hair I had attempted to dig out with a razor blade five years ago. I didn't picture my upper arm aloft, flesh hanging like a ziplock bag half-filled with pudding. I certainly didn't picture my own breasts, which had always been more conical than globular, and which now, on a bad day, looked nearly phallic.

We had reached the pinnacle of the hike and were on our way down when Sidney impulsively grabbed and held me close to her. She smelled like grease, metabolizing alcohol, and piney men's deodorant.

"What are you gonna do, Mom?"

"About what?"

"About your life."

I was confused. Had she heard me thinking? No, I had been nodding at something she was saying about a man who claimed to espouse personal responsibility but, in fact, espoused fascism.

"What do you mean?"

"Are you going to leave Dad?"

Oh, that. Leave Dad. Dump his ass. At least she had some skin in the game. At least it had something to do with her.

"Do you think I should?"

"I feel like if you stay with him you're giving some signal that you condone his actions, and I don't think that makes you look very good."

"To whom?"

"To the college, to all these women that you mentor. I think the optics are bad."

"That's a cliché."

"For a reason."

"Another cliché."

"Fine, but I'm saying it doesn't look good."

"You want me to destroy our family?"

"I'm a grown adult. You and Dad have been on separate tracks since

I've been conscious. We're just three people, how much do we really identify as a family?"

Her comment hurt, she saw it did, and apologized.

John and I had one child on purpose, but one of the great questions of my life was about whether that had been the right thing to do. He had a vasectomy when she was a toddler, which meant the issue was decided. We had agreed on it, but when it was finalized I was filled with grief. When David and I had talked about running away with each other, part of my excitement had been the thought of another baby, with another man, more things to love in our house that would be so filled with love. Once Sid got over the shock, I thought, once I was allowed back into the fold and we all came to an understanding, as painful as it would be, she would have a complex and interesting relationship with her half-brother or -sister. We might even have two, I had fantasized, and by the time we were old at Thanksgiving there would be his daughter and my daughter and our two children and their partners at the dinner table and scads of children running underfoot, a big, raucous family gathering in which someone was a professional chef and bossily did the cooking while the men did all the dishes.

As it was, our holiday dinners were usually only the three of us and often took place at restaurants. Some years we invited old friends, but the relationships between our children weren't ever as easy as it was when they were small and we could foist them together, no matter their preferences.

She cautiously stroked my cheek and brushed a hair away from my eyes.

"I want you to have the life you want, Mom, not some compromise."

Always, the touch of my daughter thrilled me. I still marveled at how cellular the love between a mother and child was—how little I had to think of it, how much I simply felt it.

We reached the car. In silence we strapped in and I started up. The road from the trail back to town was long, with fat, winding curves, swooshing and swooping past woods and farmland.

"I want to be honest with you honey. You have always done exactly what you wanted to do. Every time you leaned in one way or another, your father and I were there to support you."

She drew a breath in, to defend herself.

"That's not a criticism, or a judgment, it's a fact. And it's as it should be. You're a force for good in this world, I think, because of it. Also, I think more importantly, you have ideas about what you want and ideas about what will make you happy. I'm so glad for that. I'm so glad you know what you want. I've never had a clue. I've wanted people, I've wanted acclaim, but it's all turned out so lukewarm. Other than being your mother, which has been the most unmixed and positive part of my life, it's all been a series of ups and downs, and I don't expect any more."

"That's a horrible way to live."

"Your father does all the business stuff. The taxes, the bills."

"That stuff isn't hard."

"He does the chores around the yard, he fixes things that are broken, he does upkeep on the cabin. What would happen to me if I got divorced? I'd move into some terrible condo—"

"Dad wouldn't get the house!"

"I couldn't afford the house on my own."

"He could pay alimony."

"Sid, I always knew. And he knew that I knew."

"That's so gross."

"Why?"

"Because, oh God, you were enabling him, with these underage women."

"None of them were underage."

"Under-mature, then."

"How was I enabling anything? It's not like I built him some secret chamber for his trysts, or groomed or cultivated women to go engage with him. I knew them by sight, if at all."

"But didn't you understand there was a power dynamic?"

"Of course, but aren't we attracted to power? When I was a young woman it was said—and maybe it was a powerful man who said this, I'm not sure—but it was said that men were attracted to looks and women were attracted to power. Yes, he had more power, but I imagined that made it fun. He could bless them with his approval and what's more arousing than that? You've got to understand, and I'm not saying this is right, but we were all still thinking about sexual liberation—about freeing women from feeling that if they were sexual they weren't serious, or good, or that they would be judged. We didn't think of sex as trauma. He didn't drug them or coerce them, he didn't even have anything to give them."

"He wrote recommendation letters and gave grades. He was responsible for their future."

"None of those women suffered professionally or academically because of your father."

"They're saying they did now."

"They're reacting to a moment now."

"What about the ones who wouldn't sleep with him?"

"They came to him. He didn't pursue."

"Are you sure?"

"No, Sidney, I'm not sure. I haven't ever wanted to know as much about this as I know now."

"But didn't it hurt you? Or make you angry?"

"The only time I ever got angry was when it affected our schedule. Once he forgot to pick you up from soccer, and that made me angry. Once he missed a dinner with the dean. That made me angry. But in general it made him happy. And when he was happy my life was easier. I am not, and was not, some woman staring into the distance and waiting sadly for her husband to come home. I won't be seen that way."

"I feel like you've endured your whole marriage being tough for the sake of being tough."

"What do you want me to say? That I'll divorce him? Maybe I will. But I'll do it because I want to, not because other people think I should, or the 'optics' are bad, because there are things you simply don't understand."

"Like what?"

I drove past the turnoff for our house, making my way toward a country road that would lead me into a neighboring town and then eventually back onto the highway and around again.

Sid didn't know about the doe-eyed student. She didn't know about Boris the artist, Robert from the business department, Thomas the contractor. She certainly didn't know about David, whom she was familiar with from departmental gatherings, and whose daughter was only a year younger than she. She thought I was a faithful, saintly ostrich of a mother, head in the sand, while my dirty-dog husband romped wherever he pleased. I remembered, when she was eight years old or so and found a lighter in my purse. "Why do you have that?" she had asked. When I feigned like I was puzzled and told her I didn't know, she said, "It must have been someone's birthday," and warned me to be careful in case it lit itself by accident and set my purse on fire.

It wasn't that I didn't want Sid to know. Part of me longed to tell her war stories, tell her of Boris's barn, the half-finished art more erotic than his dry, anticlimactic kisses, or Robert, always in his suit and tie when he met me at the motel room we rented each week, or the time I got a rash from the sawdust on Thomas's hands. I wanted to tell her about my obsession with David and how our romance was so intoxicating that I was ready to leave my whole life, including her.

I also wanted to keep my own secrets. It was a pact I held with myself, a game. If I didn't tell anybody about certain things in my life (notably the things that I would most like to divulge) then, like the men who hold themselves back from orgasm to preserve their life force, I would accumulate some inexplicable strength.

In the corner of my eye I saw Sid bite her thumbnail and tear off a sheaf, layered like mica.

"Let's cut your nails when you get home."

"Let's?"

"Cut your nails when you get home."

"What about Lena?" I felt her eyes scrutinizing my face.

"Who?"

"Lena the babysitter, the one I had growing up."

"Your father never did anything with Lena."

"Yes he did. I saw them, I remember, it's an early memory. I came into the kitchen and I saw his head in her neck and his hands wrapped around her, and she was giggling. She saw me and pushed his hands off her. I remember I asked if he was trying to get something from her pocket, and they both laughed."

"That was me."

"No it wasn't."

"Yes it was."

"I remember what I saw."

"No, sweetheart, you don't remember it right." And I told her how when she was little, John had been groping me in the kitchen as he was wont to do, and she came in and asked that exact question. And he had said, "Yes, I'm trying to get something from your mom's pocket," and she had said, "Give it to him, Mom," and he had leered and said, "Yeah, Mom. Give it to me."

"You know how unreliable memories are, my love," I told her, but Sid just shook her head.

When we arrived home, John was gone again. I hardly minded, though this was the second night he had left the house without telling me where he was going. Sid had a bottomless hangover stomach, the kind that can be fed and fed and never gets full, so when we returned I warmed the carbonara sauce waiting in the fridge with fresh pasta and eggs and we shared a bottle of Malbec. She went to bed and I brought my laptop and cigarettes outside. There was an email from Edwina, apologizing for failing to confirm our appointment, telling me it was a busy time, telling me how much she valued my mentorship, asking if we could reschedule when things calmed down. Though I had completely forgotten we were supposed to meet, I was slightly offended. It seemed unlike her not to fix a new date. But then again, I expected my students to have dips and peaks in maturity and accountability, and I wrote her telling her not to worry and of course, and signed it with *x*'s and *o*'s. An email from John appeared, with the subject "D-Day." Where was he that he was forwarding emails? In the dark in his office? His face illuminated by the blue light of his computer? Alone in some bar with his phone? It was the date for the first day of the dismissal hearing that would decide if he could stay on with the college: October 20.

I lit a cigarette and drew hard into my chest, letting the smoke permeate all the little crooks and spaces of my lungs. Students were innocent to tobacco nowadays, they called smoking a death wish, considered it a suicidal tendency. Many of them had no idea what it felt like, they thought tobacco affected your mental state, like marijuana. October 20—why was that date so familiar? Sid, mercifully, hadn't brought up that she saw me smoking. She said she remembered going into the pool, but besides that the whole encounter was blurred in her brain. To my knowledge, she never found out that I had smoked. I had kept it secret from her, because I didn't want her, when she was fifteen or eighteen, to have some image of me, in the past, smoking mysteriously. Nothing is more alluring than a mother-before-she-was-a-mother, an unknowable and irresistible figure. My own mother smoked until I was ten. After she quit, she struggled with an excess forty pounds until she died. I started smoking at fourteen when her Australian colleague offered my best friend Alice and me a cigarette in the parking lot of a company picnic. I was crazy for his height and his sunburn and his accent and his white-blond hair. He taught us how to suck in, hold the smoke in our lungs, and release. I prided myself on not coughing. After a few drags, Alice stood up and passed out briefly from the head rush, and the man and I, I forget his name, carried her into the shade and pepped her back up with Hi-C and ice cubes. Once she revived, we chased and teased each other, dropping ice cubes down each other's shirts. As the summer went on he hung around the two of us more and more, and we smoked and mixed the rum and vodka he brought us with pineapple juice and ice. One night when my mother was out with her boyfriend and my sisters were off on a beach trip with friends, he and Alice came over and we sat on the couch to watch the 1976 Summer Olympics in Montreal. He had both of his hands on our legs during the long jumps, and up our shorts during the sprints. By the time we were watching now–Caitlyn Jenner set the world record for the decathlon, we were squirming horizontal on the itchy woolen couch. I remember I had one breast exposed and another still in my white lace bra, and I didn't know whether I should undo the whole thing—if I looked ridiculous or asymmetrically appealing. At a certain point, he guided my hand to his penis. Not knowing exactly what to do with it, I jerked it wildly until he took my hand off and pushed me away. I fell off the narrow couch onto the floor. I had the feeling of failing a test, and watched as he kissed and groped Alice, who, always more knowledgeable than I, held him expertly. Disgusted with myself, I retreated to my bedroom, leaving them entwined, and cried myself to sleep with self-pity. That was my last summer in Texas.

The moon reflected on the pool. I made a mental note to call the guy to come and cover it this week. Oh God, still so much self-hatred could ripple out from those adolescent memories. Always the shame, not of being too fast or engaging with a perverted Australian man who was at least thirty, but of being laughable—of being a slightly chubby girl of fourteen with one fat-nippled breast hanging out of a bad brassiere and not knowing how to give a hand job. Some of my students, when they read Victorian or Edwardian novels, would become so angry at all these heroes and heroines whose lives are ruined because they are afraid of embarrassment, but I did not know of any emotion more powerful, more permeating, more upending than that. You could die seemingly pointlessly or loveless to avoid shame, but shame could also make you feel as though you wanted to die, as I still felt, forty-four years later, when I pictured myself on the floor, looking at the beige strands of our wall-to-wall carpet as Alice and the Australian writhed above me. Then I remembered why October 20 was so familiar: it was, of course, the day of my lunch date with Vladimir.

IX.

*W*ithout any formal discussion or request, Sid stayed on with us the following week, mostly shut up in the guest room, emerging every once in a while to jog or to make food. She was considerate, overly so, her consideration a way to keep us at an arm's length. She didn't have a car but ordered groceries and beer to be delivered to the house and washed her dishes immediately after each use and did small chores like taking out the garbage and rotating the laundry. I say "us," but I only knew for a fact that she kept her distance from me. She and John might have been having heart-to-heart discussions whenever they were alone, I didn't know. Whether it was being back in her childhood bedroom, or because I had somehow failed to be the confidante she'd wished for, after that day at the diner she became as aloof as a teenager. In the unlikely occurrence that we were all home together, we moved around the house hushed and with care, like silent monks on balance beams. I had a futon in my office that I made up as a bed for myself. When Sid learned I wasn't sleeping in the Big Bedroom she offered to switch with me, but I insisted that I preferred having unlimited access to the office, and as long as I had enough pillows the futon caused only minimal damage to my back.

I wasn't being sacrificial. In fact, I was aflame with ardor and inspiration, and the only place that felt like real life was the seat at my desk, looking through the slats of the wooden blinds to the street outside, writing my story. I still refused to call it a book, because to call it a book might snuff its flame. It was like when I first met John. If I had met him a year or two earlier, it would have been impossible for me to believe that this tall and handsome lothario could seriously return my affections, and I would have somehow ruined it. If it had been a year or two earlier, our coupling would have been doomed. But as it happened, when we came together I was at the height of an upswing of good fortune. I was the most well-regarded student of my year, beloved by my teachers; I was passionate and interested in my subject matter. A beautiful future stretched out before me. My confidence calibration was such that the night after John and I first kissed, I acted with utmost restraint. Unlike every other romance I'd had, which I had either entered begrudgingly or ruined with anxiety and clinging, I could sense exactly the correct level of communication, the perfect blend of distance and attention needed to manage him. For the first and only time in my life, it was possible to act like those women who prided themselves on their success with men, the ones who preached ideas of manipulation, about letting a man think he was right while secretly getting what you wanted. Which is not to say I didn't fall in love. I did. But somehow I intuitively understood exactly how to manage it—how to neither clamp down nor let go, but keep gently pulling the thread until I found myself unpacking boxes in his apartment.

It was like that now, whenever I sat down to write this story. The writing felt like what I imagined skiing the slalom felt like to an accomplished skier, just the right amount of exertion and planning and foresight, the rest of it easy grace. I instinctively knew to never speak of it, or even think on it too much when I was away from the desk, except for the walk here or there when I allowed my mind to rest on it. The act in front of my computer was an act of evocation, of conjuring. It gave me shivers of pleasure, like the vibrations I used to feel the third or fourth time a new, infectious pop song played on the radio. The familiar and the new. The sensation would surge as long as my fingers moved over the keys.

I took pains to distance the story from Vladimir. It was written in the third person, it took place in the 1960s, it concerned a certain subculture. I based one character physically on him, a minor figure. But I infused it with the energy of my desire. And even as I held off the idea of a finished work from my mind, I kept thinking about him and me on some panelists stage, at some book festival in some smaller city like Calgary or Austin or San Diego. Award winners, both of us, we would be put up at the same hotel and would meet for a martini in the dark of the bar. However ridiculous it was for an older woman like me to lust after him, the force of my talent, the brilliance of my work, would blur my lines and firm my skin. It would be one night, maybe two, and then over, but there would be a crystal of connection formed between us. We would be linked for the rest of our lives. This fantasy floated alongside my expatriate fantasy, fantasies of meetings in bathrooms, and the re-occurring image of him reflected in my window. They gave me a float-ing feeling as I moved through my circumscribed world, teaching my classes, answering my emails, exercising, driving my car, grading papers, meeting students, attending faculty meetings.

Like every year, the cold came more quickly than expected. The day after the pool guy came there was a sudden frost, and the dirt froze into a spongelike formation that crunched when stepped on. That morn-ing I pulled out my white woolen cardigan sweater that I bought from the Salvation Army in my twenties and layered it over a long flannel nightgown with bulky fisherman's socks and my indoor sandals. Even I could admit I was getting bonier, the cold seeping more easily into my marrow. Sid, in a neck gaiter and a hat, was out for a run when John approached me in the kitchen. He was wearing an old sweatshirt that clung to him in unfortunate places and shorts he knew I hated.

"Are you coming to the first day of my hearing?"

"Good morning to you."

"You haven't said anything to me in the last three days. I just want to know if you're coming."

"I don't think so."

"Got it. Fuck you." He moved violently through the kitchen, bang-ing doors and slamming the carafe of the coffee maker down with such force I was afraid it would shatter. I could tell that he wanted to stalk off but couldn't bring himself to do it. I felt a pang of pity for him. Where was he going at night? He seemed so lonely, so alone.

"John." I moved forward and put my hand on his forearm. He pulled his arm away and looked at me with thick red rings surrounding his nearly lashless eyes.

"Do you even love me anymore?" Something soft rose up in his voice.

And what was I to say? Most days, these days, I didn't feel as though I loved him. Most days I thought of him as a problem I would have to solve eventually, when I felt like making the effort. Despite what Sid said about perception, I felt as though it would be more humiliating to divorce at the height of the scandal. It would make it seem like I hadn't known about the affairs, that I was another victim, that I stepped into the light of knowledge on the day the petition was delivered to the dean. If we were to divorce, then I preferred to do it after everyone had forgotten. Five years from now, perhaps, when the freshman class was gone, and some old faculty had retired, and nobody remembered John on campus. But as he stood in front of me, vulnerable and wanting, I couldn't tell him no, I didn't love him. I felt wildly protective of that soft part of him that reached out for me like a child. John was usually pulled back and cynical. Dignified. In a departmental gathering or a faculty meeting I would sit back and admire how he could dominate all the whining, sputtering academics with his removed dignity.

A loud succession of thumps sounded from the back room that led to the porch. "It's Sid," I said, and ran to let her in, but when I got there I saw that the noise was coming from a cardinal charging the glass doors, intent on murdering its own reflection. Last year a developer had cleared the forest down the road to build condos, and since then I'd found two dead birds lying outside these doors. I kept meaning to research what I needed to do to stop them. I grimaced, feeling sick, and pleaded with the bird to stop. I put my hands on my knees, my stomach churning.

"Take the other end of this." John picked up a throw blanket from an armchair. "We'll hold it against the glass."

We stood there, each raising a corner against either side of the door frame. Too late. The bird rammed harder and harder, shaking the panes, until there was a soft thump on the ground, and the corpse lay still on the concrete.

"The symbolism is a bit heavy-handed, don't you think?" said John.

It was a joke we'd said to each other for thirty years. Whenever we passed a deer slain by the side of the road, or a violent storm crashed down on us. Disarmed, I addressed him with a note of affectionate anger in my voice.

"Why do you wear those shorts and then ask me for something you want? You know I can't stand those shorts."

But I hadn't read the moment correctly. I had thought he'd melt and sweep me up jokingly, and I'd tell him that of course I loved him, that I'd consider coming to the hearing. Instead he looked at me sadly, shook his head as though I were responsible for all the tiredness in the world, and left.

I sank into an armchair like a felled tree. I was angry at myself for creating my own trap. Now I felt as though I had done something wrong. Now I felt as though I had to run after him. "I love you, baby, I love you." What did I truly want from him? Did I want a day, a month, a year of domination? In which I could scream at him and mock him all I wanted with impunity? Did I want him to grovel at my feet? It wasn't that, exactly. I wanted him to accept the role of the penitent. But you can't ask someone who feels like a victim, as John most certainly did, to live apologetically. And there it was, that twisted logic. Even as we railed against victim mentality, against trauma as a weapon, we took the strength of our arguments from the internal sense of our own victimhood. John was acting just like the women who accused him. He had been wronged, goddamnit. While there was a part of him, I knew, that understood I was suffering too, he still cherished the sense that he was the most drastically injured party. He grasped his being wronged like a precious gem in a velvet pouch. Yes, he was like all the rest of them, desperately holding on to his own pain.

By the time I arrived on campus, I was shaking with anger. I was late, having stood stock-still in my bedroom staring out the window, a cavalcade of thoughts crashing down on me. I remember reading that Edna St. Vincent Millay gave instructions to her housekeeper not to interrupt her if they saw her standing still—that was the way she would compose poems, on two feet, staring into the middle distance, writing and rewriting lines in her head. I never had that organization of thought: my rapt pauses were all about conflicting feelings, images and memories running and bumping into each other—more like a chaotic battle scene than the unfurling of insight.

At any rate, I was hurrying to my Women in American Literature survey class when I saw Edwina, my treasured star pupil, walking with Cynthia Tong along the green. I waved, and they waved back with overdone fangirl adoration. But it was the gesture of two people who were clearly together in thought, while I stood on the outside. When I began teaching, when I was young and fresh and within a decade of my students, there were certain women with whom I related deeply, women who became my friends. Even briefly watching Edwina and Cynthia crossing the quad, I saw this was happening with them. So quickly, only three weeks into the semester. Jealousy burned at me, anger fired from my womb. Edwina hadn't put her off, she hadn't said she would make a date with her and hadn't followed through. I had written an email to her with x's and o's and they were giggling with each other like new roommates.

In class we were comparing selections from Kate Chopin, Charlotte Perkins Gilman, and the diaries of Alice James. "Why are all these white women so obsessed with being female?" asked a blond, female student who never did the reading. "Don't they recognize their privilege?" When I ventured to say that Chopin, for instance, began writing after being left widowed with six children as a means of support, she shrugged. "But she still walked through the world as a white woman." When I asked her if that meant she shouldn't write, she said, "No, she shouldn't complain." When I asked what writing that was not-complaining looked like, she said, "I don't know, like James Joyce." Another student, thankfully, interrupted and said the women were of different times and different literary movements than James Joyce. "And different countries," said another. "Also he was very privileged," another burst in. "I just don't know why we have to read these whining women," the student countered, and another, defending my honor, said, "The course is Women in American Literature." "Women couldn't vote or get legally divorced at the time Chopin was writing these works," I said. "They may seem outdated to you now, but—" Then I stopped myself. I hated this class more and more every year. The wide scope of the subject matter made it impossible to take the time to fully examine any work we studied, and the brief timeline of a semester made every choice of every class objectionable, as though every week I was saying, "This is the American Woman." I wanted to take it off the course catalog, but it was a cross-listed requirement-fulfilling class in both the Gender Studies and English departments, and therefore hard to shift. "I want us to talk about what they are doing in their work. What is the symbolism they are using, what is the metaphor? They are writing at the time of Freud, Darwin, and the tail end of transcendentalism. How do we feel those movements affected . . ."

I felt so tired when class ended. The student who had challenged me hurried out of the room, all her bravery gone when she was not performing for her classmates. Starving, I stumbled to the school café and bought soup that came in a waxy paper tub, a seasonal apple pastry that they stocked from a local farm, and some ashy, lukewarm coffee. I found a booth in which I could sit in a patch of sun, and collapsed into it. It would be poor form for me to fall asleep, surrounded as I was by students, but that was all I wanted to do—to close my eyes and let the heaviness overtake me. I must have closed them momentarily, because it was behind the dark of my lids that I heard a strident "Yoo-hoo!"

When I opened my eyes, there was a halo of light surrounding a mass of hair that could be compared to a lion's mane were it not so shiny and well-coiffed. Florence. Florence once said at a faculty retreat that the only thing she would bring on a desert island was a round brush. "And that's all you need to know," I said to anyone who would listen. She taught postmodernism, apparently quite well, but it was nearly impossible to imagine her reading a book. She was around forty, and her uniform was aggressively "hot": short dresses, high-heeled boots, big earrings, ripped tights. She had enviable long legs, which she would furl and unfurl excessively, like an anthropomorphized spider. Her use of uptalk was deliberate and defensive, and she spoke primarily about recipes and restaurants and her children's extracurricular activities. In most faculty meetings she complained about labor and how she didn't want to do it. She purposefully misunderstood the pact that tenured faculty had: the exchange of volunteered service for the security and freedom of her position. After she got tenure she never published, and she was late to everything. She was contradictory as a way of life—challenging any statement or assumption made in our meetings. She could be fun— there was one night about six or so years back that she and I embarked on a caper after a dean's cocktail hour that ended up with her getting a summons for public urination—but as a colleague she was a dud.

She had been especially irritating about John. Like many beautiful-ish women, she was obsessed with the idea of men sexually trespassing. To hear her speak, she had never had an encounter with any man that had not resulted in some form of the man expressing his longing for her or taking advantage of her. I secretly thought she was offended that John hadn't invited her to join him in a tryst, although she was the kind of woman John would stay away from out of instinct. She had led the charge to say that he could not teach this year, even before his hearing, and she resigned from the budgetary committee, saying she could not sit in the room with "that man," though we all knew she had joined the budgetary committee only after a performance review that threatened penalization if she didn't sign up for at least one working group (I, for example, was on four).

I straightened myself up to greet her and saw she was with David. David, my old lover, currently the interim chair while John was suspended. In the past, God, almost twenty years, David had declined. When we came together he was a lean, compact man with a shaved bald head that I loved to rub my hands over, to feel between my breasts. He had a strong forehead and a prominent nose, which could physically arouse me by sight. At the height of our coupling, I would catch a glimpse of his nose during a meeting and could manipulate myself, using the ridge of the chair and my muscles, into a small, secret orgasm.

David was now fifty pounds overweight and dissipated. He no longer shaved his head, but wore a little tonsure of short hair surrounding his shiny pate, a style that made him look like the character-actor version of a tax accountant. His nose had lengthened into a beak, with an extra bit of hanging cartilage at the tip. He dressed as an afterthought—I am sure his wife bought shirts and slacks for him in bulk and he accepted them like a prisoner accepts their uniform. Ah, but I shouldn't be so mean to David. For years I had focused on his flaws. It was the only way I could survive his great betrayal. Was I pleased when I compared him with my husband, whose light hair and eyes allowed him to fade so gracefully into age? Who was still vain, who used the gym more than the library, who dog-eared pages in fashionable men's catalogues? Certainly I was. But I would wager that David, with his meaty, masculine fingers, could still be a thrilling lover: focused, playful, receptive. He had marked the end of my experimentation, the commencement of my unimpeachable existence. Our affair lived in my thoughts like a once-loved but mostly forgotten piece of music, popping into my head occasionally, bringing all sorts of feelings.

He lost a son, many years after we ended things, in a freak accident at a lake. At the funeral he had embraced me tightly and whispered in my ear, "See?" I didn't see. I knew what he meant, but I didn't see. During our affair, he had not had any understanding, unspoken or otherwise, with his wife. Guilt about leaving his family had prevented what I had believed at the time was my greatest chance at happiness. His son was born a year after we ended things. I assumed he was putting all his sexual energy back into his marriage, doubling down on the life he chose. His "See" seemed to suggest that he believed the punishment would have been much worse if we had gone overseas, that the death of his son was already a result of his transgression. Understandable in the moment, at the peak of shock and sadness, but ultimately ridiculous. Grief makes people wild in their thought. As if we are ever punished or rewarded in that kind of way—a random tragic death in exchange for a secret indiscretion. Since his son died David moved through the world heavily, as though his entire body was draped in the lead apron one wears for X-rays. I never liked that "See." It was like a line written by an aspirational Ibsen or Strindberg or Bergman, some Scandinavian obsessed with being haunted by their actions—a line that sounded like a profound truth, but meant nothing.

"Tired?" Florence looked at me with irritating sympathy. I shook my head. "No, I just closed my eyes for a moment."

"I'm exhausted," she said. "This fall weather makes me tired. Hot in the sun, cold in the shade, I close the door of my office and take a twenty-minute nap, then wake up and eat some chocolate-covered raisins and it's like I'm a new woman. Do you nap, David?"

He nodded. "Yeah, I'll take a nap. I like a nap."

"I love a nap. How about you, do you nap?" She sat herself down at the table and beckoned for David to grab another chair.

"No," I said to her. "I hate naps."

What I truly hated were conversations about sleep. It felt like all anyone talked about—work and sleep. When Sid was young the world seemed obsessed with sleeping—her sleeping, my sleeping, my husband's sleeping—the schedule, the tiredness, the endless tiredness.

"Wow, you're amazing." Florence winked, to herself it seemed.

"Are you joining me to eat," I asked them, "or is this an ambush?"

David smiled. "More the latter, unfortunately."

Florence batted him on the shoulder. "This is not an ambush, don't say that." She kept looking nervously at him; it was clear they'd banded together to come and tell me some news that I didn't want to hear.

David looked around the café. "Maybe we should walk," he said.

"Scared I'll make a big scene?" I asked him.

"Not at all!" Florence flipped her hair so that it looked like an ocean wave on the top of her head.

"Yes," he said.

An image cracked in my mind at that very moment. It was of Vladimir and Cynthia, with faces more weathered than now, holding hands on the front steps of the English Department building, posing for a photograph. John and I, when he was promoted to chair, had posed for a shoot such as this. In quick succession I saw flashes of them posing, climbing the stairs to their offices, kissing chastely, and then Cynthia walking into my office, which was now hers. I stood outside, visible from her window, except I was costumed like a leper in a church musical, with distressed and tea-stained Ace bandages dripping from my arms. I reached toward her in supplication. From her mind's eye she zoomed in on my face, and it was toothless, tearstained, covered in dirt.

I finished my soup and coffee, put the pastry in my bag, and threw out my garbage as they waited for me by the door. I was seized by the impulse to run. This felt like the walk that a doomed man takes with a couple of Mafia stooges. The walk Camille Claudel took with her brother before he locked her up in that insane asylum for the rest of her life.

We left together in silence. There was a narrow, poorly designed rocky stairway that led from the café to the grounds. David held tightly on to the railing and limped down the stairs. When I asked about his injury, he told me that he had helped move Mercy, his daughter, in with her fiancé over the past weekend and had injured the lower right part of his back. "Fiancé," I said, and congratulated him. "He's a great guy, we really like him," he said, nodding sadly. "They don't want a big wedding, so that's a relief." And we fell into silence again, trudging over the grass until we reached a footpath that encircled the campus.

Florence began.

"You know that John's trial begins on the twentieth?"

"His hearing," I corrected.

"Were you planning on attending?"

"No," I said. I was in fact ambivalent, but I didn't want to admit that ambivalence to either of them.

"Good," she said.

David started in. "Look, you know the times we are living in."

"Certainly I do."

"Absurd, you have to be so careful, you get no support from the administration—nothing to back you up—the students rule the roost—you know what I mean."

"What are you getting at? Did I do something wrong? Something offensive?"

Florence shook her head vigorously. "No no no no no no no no no no."

"So then what is it?"

As Florence seemed unable to speak, David nodded at her to show he would take over. If there weren't such a discrepancy of attractiveness between the two, I would think they were together.

"Please, David, just say what you're going to say, this is agonizing," I said.

Without deciding, we all stopped walking.

"A number of students have expressed that, given the circumstances of John's case, they find your presence in the classroom to be objectionable, even triggering. They feel as though you were complicit in the alleged indiscretions. They have asked that you stop teaching classes immediately until the hearing is over. Depending on the verdict, they asked that we then reassess the situation."

A heavy ball sank into the base of my stomach, and my arms and chest tightened in anger. "And what does the department say?"

"We don't think that the students should have the say about who comes and goes here," David said quickly.

"Still," Florence cut in, "we want them to feel heard. Some of the students have suffered sexual assault, and to be in the presence of a rapist's wife—"

"My husband is not a rapist."

"Maybe not according to you—"

"According to anyone."

"He used his power and position to find women thirty years his junior to fuck."

"And that's still not anywhere near rape."

David put his hand out to quiet Florence. "Let's not say that word. She's right, it was never used."

He went on, "The department is almost mortally wounded by this whole mess. Enrollment is down—"

"Enrollment is down in all the humanities. You both know how it is. Nobody wants to be an English major anymore. The ones who used to be on the fence and chose it as a default—they all want to go into psych or environmental studies or poli-sci. We're dinosaurs, all of us—"

I smiled at them, but neither returned my smile. Florence was staring at me, tight-lipped and perturbed. David looked at the ground.

"You'd still be paid," he said.

"And then what?" I tried to keep a shriek from rising in my voice. I started walking again, and fast, and was pleased to see Florence's chunky heels sinking into the muddy mulch.

"A student walked by and saw John sitting on your desk the other day. You were laughing together. It would be unprofessional in any circumstance, and with the allegations, students feel as though they're surrounded by a hostile learning environment." Florence was the one yelling now.

"Is this coming from the administration?" It seemed as though the curving hills of the campus were tilting, like paper waves in a puppetry performance, and I was a flat figure held up by a stick, bobbing up and down between the waves, getting tugged out of the frame.

David looked sternly at Florence, and then placed his hand on my arm, which I shook off like it was a diseased crow. "This is coming only from the department. As you might have already gathered, we can't make you do anything. You have a contract. We are asking that you consider this for the good of the students."

"Who would teach my classes?"

"I would teach the Gothic Novel class, and we were thinking Cynthia might take over the Women in American Literature class. She's interested in taking on more classes, she told David. You're only teaching two this semester, right?" Florence said this so quickly, and I thought about how long the department meeting must have been to come to this decision.

"How would that work?" I felt as though an iron band were being wrapped around my chest. I tried to remember the fairy tale in which someone wraps iron hoops around their chest in order to prevent their heart from breaking. Oh, what was that, why couldn't I remember it? When he gets his heart's desire they come pinging off, Ping, Ping, Ping.

Florence busied herself locating and picking off invisible hairs from her sweater. "If you wanted to maintain the syllabus, you'd give us your notes."

I laughed. Give my beautiful notes, written with gorgeous precision for each class—a legal pad per session? Written in my handwriting, the one aspect of myself I felt was aesthetically perfect? My classes were part of my art, they were journeys. I held out a raft for students at the beginning, which they all boarded, and once they got on I skiffed them down the river of experience, pointing out things they should notice, on your left, thematic resonance, on your right, imagery, giving them a chance to reflect, to notice for themselves. At the end, I reminded them of where they had come from, what they saw, what they might take with them on the next journey. Give away my notes. It would be like a singer giving away a song. Come, stand in for Nina Simone, she'll let you sing "Mississippi Goddam." Idiocy.

"Does the entire department feel the way you do?" I quickened my pace, enjoying Florence's stumbling, David's limping.

"There was a meeting of the tenured faculty and the vote was five to two," David said, huffing.

The currently tenured faculty (excluding John and me) were David, Florence, Tamilla, Andre, Ben, Priya, and Julia. Vladimir, of course, was tenure-track; he and the other adjuncts like Cynthia would be excluded from any discussions, thank God.

"Five voted that I should stop teaching? And two wanted me to stay on?"

He nodded. "Five voted that we should ask if you would consider the proposal. Two thought that the measure was too drastic."

I made a quick tally sheet. Priya was my age, she was my friend, she was New Criticism to the core, she wouldn't have voted against me. Neither would Andre, an older Frenchman who shook his head in amusement whenever the debacle was mentioned. That left the rest of them: Tamilla, Ben, Julia, Florence (all under fifty), and David.

"And you both were part of the five?" David and Florence nodded.

Given there was a divide, there was something far more treacherous about the fact that David had chosen against me. If the vote had been unanimous, I might have understood it—though our affair was ancient history, he would still not want to seem preferential to me for any reason. But there had been room for him to side with me and he hadn't. I don't think he believed that I should stop teaching. I think he was simply scared and wanted to protect himself. He wanted to hang on to his hat while the wind was blowing. An old white man, he was both savvy and spineless enough to be afraid of coming out on the wrong side of history. I thought about his stubby little penis peeking out from below his now bulbous stomach. A little white-capped mushroom. I thought about how it might feel to take garden shears to the top of that mushroom, how it might feel to watch the inside of his fat feminine thighs get soaked in blood.

I stopped abruptly and turned on the two of them. David, breathing hard, Florence, half hobbling. I wanted to tell them they could go fuck themselves. My brain was employing a liberal use of fucks. There was no fucking way I would ever stop teaching my class unless they fucking dragged me out of there with campus security. That it was completely fucking illegal to try a wife for the crimes of her husband and they were fools and should know better. That each one of them, and everyone else who had voted for this decision, as if they could even make such a decision, would be on my shit list for the rest of my life, and I would come and find them and exact my revenge upon them. Hostile learning environment? I could sue for a hostile work environment. I could sue endlessly, I could cripple this department.

But as I faced them, I felt the words fall away from me. A rush of confusion clouded and coated my thoughts. My eyes crossed. I felt spikes in my chest, like a large burr had lodged behind my breastbone.

I closed my eyes. When Sid was three or four, at her little hippie preschool, they used to teach breathing techniques to help the children calm down. *Smell the flowers, Blow out the candle.* I still thought about those words whenever I was trying to collect myself. *Smell the flowers, Blow out the candle.*

When I opened them, David was once again looking at the ground and Florence dropped the arm that held her phone.

"Sorry," she said. "Childcare."

I didn't let myself contemplate the slight. I mentally cut her out of the picture, like a figure in a cartoon that runs through the scenic backdrop, leaving a hole in the shape of their body. I looked up at the balcony of one of the covered walkways, where the students were crossing back and forth to class.

"I'll think about it," I said. I turned abruptly and began walking through the middle of the field away from them as quickly as I could. The ground had thawed in the sun and squelched beneath my feet, sucking at my shoes as I stepped. I walked straight toward the English Department and made my way around to the back, where the dumpster was, crouched beside it, like a surreptitious teenager, and lit a cigarette. I slid against the wall and sat down on the pavement, leaning my back against the brick. I envisioned myself as an ancient, mangy addict sitting outside of Penn Station in New York City, a half-hearted sign propped up, hoping to gather as much money with as little effort as possible for fentanyl, bumming cigarettes and McDonald's fries in the meantime.

Which student had complained about me? Oh, but it didn't matter. I could picture the cafeteria, outfitted with gas fireplaces so it looked like an upscale ski lodge, and three Formica tables pushed together to create a long banquet, at which were seated ten or so students, mostly female. I could see the different body types and the different foods, most probably incongruous—the thin ones with cream-sauce pastas, the thicker ones with lean proteins and salads. What started out as a question, "Oh my God, guys, do you think it's weird that his wife still teaches?" grew into more and more of a rallying cry, as together they decided that my presence was offensive, that it made them frightened, that it reminded them of bad people and bad events that had happened to them, or to their cousins.

Picturing them in the cafeteria, I started to view their utensils as little pitchforks that they moved up and down. I understood not only the bonding that comes out of complaining but also the incredible sense of identity that comes with discovering why you think something is wrong. I wanted them to feel that fire, that was what college was for. They were enacting a right of all young people, unearthing what they felt were the systemic wrongs of the world. It was their right to look at us murderously, longing to stand where we stood. It was their right to believe that they could do our jobs better than we could. We, who had experienced enough bitterness in life to expect flaws, faults, and complexities in every situation we encountered. They had grown up with a constant stream of global warming and gun violence burbling on low from their parents' radios as they were driven to and from soccer or clarinet. Their lives, for the most part (at least the majority of students who attended this liberal and very expensive college), were cloaked in the postmillennial blanket of peace and prosperity, while terrible threats loomed in the shadowy corners of the larger world. They were overpraised and overpressured. There were teenage billionaires, twelve-year-old YouTube stars, and no jobs for them once they graduated. Once Trump became president, the illusion, the one imparted to them comfortably from the driver's seat of a minivan, the idea that the world would slowly get better, that "the arc of history is long but it bends toward justice," was upended.

Or something. I shook off my grandiose thoughts. I didn't know them or understand their world at all. I prized myself on liking them. I defended them at dinner parties. The Kids Are Alright! I liked their action, their strict moral code, their stridency—

"Ma'am." From my seat on the pavement I saw the wheels of a golf cart and looked up to see a square woman from campus security wearing wraparound sunglasses and a fisherman's hat.

"You need to put out that cigarette right now, ma'am, this is a no-smoking campus."

"I know. I'm a professor here."

"I'm going to have to issue you a ticket, ma'am."

"I'm a professor here, I *teach* here. I'm not a student."

"You should know better, then, ma'am."

"Stop calling me ma'am, please. This is the first time I've done this—I just had some bad news—"

"In the future you can walk beyond the perimeter of the campus, ma'am. It's right out that way."

"I know where the perimeter of the campus is, thank you."

"Can I get your name, ma'am?"

"Why?"

"For the ticket I'm about to write you."

"May I have *your* name?"

"My name's Estelle. My mother died of lung cancer. I have one job on campus, and that's to issue tickets to illegal smokers. Name."

Estelle drove off into the sunset, her back emanating triumph. She did it! She nabbed another culprit! It was a good day, baby, I heard her saying to some wiry wife in an A-line skirt as they drank stupid home-brewed beer. I even nabbed a professor! Wasn't she a piece of work. I showed her!

I held the ticket in my hand. Fifty dollars. A hundred for repeat offenders.

X.

*W*hen I told Sid what the department had requested, she smirked and shook her head with the reassuring arrogance of a licensed and accredited attorney.

"They can't do that."

"Well, I know they can't, but they didn't say I had to. They asked me to consider it."

I was making martinis for us in mason jars. Before I left the college that day I wrote emails to my classes and all other pertinent people, telling them that I would be taking off the next day due to a cold. As I expected, there was an email from Priya, saying that she was sorry, and she thought I should walk around with the red letters *AW*, for Adulterer's Wife, pinned on my breast as performance art. I wrote her back a quick note of thanks, and wanted to write more, wanted to ask her over for dinner to talk about it all, but my fingers felt leaden against the keyboard.

Seized with an urge to consume, I went to an upscale butcher shop that had recently opened in the area and bought expensive T-bone steaks from a very handsome, well-muscled butcher. I tried to imagine him tracing the tip of his knife over the curves of my body to cheer myself up, but the fantasy failed to displace my doldrums. I stopped at the organic market and purchased dark black kale and designer anchovies and a nineteen-dollar brick of parmesan and olives and seeded crackers and an uncut boule of whole wheat sourdough and goat cheese and salami and raspberries and a flourless chocolate ganache torte.

Usually I went to some undignified liquor warehouse for alcohol—the wines were good enough and the prices were better and the salesclerks left you alone. Today, however, I stopped at the boutique in town—used only by tourists—and let an Englishman talk me into three thirty-dollar bottles of red and a new, artisan vodka. I wanted to take substances into my body like an immoral and immoderate businessman traveling on a company credit card. I wanted everything that passed my lips to be decadent, full of sulfites or iron, with mouth-screwing flavor, to taste rich and deep.

I found Sid in the guest room, glassy-eyed and grumpy, playing a multiplayer video game on her laptop. I demanded she shower, put on a button-down, and meet me downstairs. Sensing my desperation, she complied. I stripped, ripped, and washed the kale and set it out to dry, rinsed and patted the steaks and shook them with salt and pepper. (I am of the opinion that good steak should have no seasoning other than salt and pepper.) I lightly boiled an egg and then broke it into the bottom of a wide, low salad dish with anchovies that had been mottled with garlic and olive oil. To that I added the kale and a massive amount of freshly grated parmesan, and then massaged it until it shone. I set out the cheese, salami, bread, crackers, and olives and decanted the wine. I pulled out my tray of cocktail fixings with the firm intent of getting completely and gloriously wasted.

The air was chilly, but daylight savings was still a few weeks away, so I pulled out extension cords, ran them into the backyard, and plugged in two heat lamps so that Sid and I could sit and watch darkness fall and the evening creatures peek out from the bushes. There were always a disturbing number of deer, covered in flies and ticks and savagely ripping the heads off all the flowers—those you saw every night. Often you would see a fox, sometimes reddish rabbits, and very occasionally a beaver or an opossum. One year there was an ancient-looking tortoise from God knows where who lived nearby the pool for a month as she laid her eggs.

Sid and I set up a folding table and I put the steaks on the grill. By the time they were ready I had drunk half my martini. I ate like a beast, ripping chunks of flesh with my teeth, stabbing enormous fork-fuls of the salad into my mouth and letting the oil smear all over my face, shoveling crackers and cheese, alternating my red wine with my martini to wash everything down. Sid and I tore the sourdough with our hands, soaking the pieces in salted olive oil. I had a memory of my mother, back when I was twelve or so. She was a nurse's aide, and after she and my father divorced she picked up shifts as a waitress at a local Irish pub, the kind that exists in most towns in America, with burgers and onion rings and soggy fish and chips and a perpetual stale-beer-mixed-with-cheap-floor-cleaner-topped-with-cigarette-smoke smell. Friday nights I (and I suppose my sisters if they were home, though I don't remember them ever being there) was permitted to stay up and wait for her to come home. I would read and watch late-night TV and try on her makeup in the bathroom mirror until around 11 p.m., when her shift was done. She would come in bearing two grocery-sized bags full of pub fare, and a couple bottles of Coca-Cola, and she and I would feast on the soggy, greasy food and the sugary desserts until we could eat no more. I remember us silent, content, and chewing. It was the one time my mother and I shared a common appetite together, perhaps the time we were the closest.

I looked over at my daughter. She was staring out into the bushes, her mouth full. There were sickly gray rings below her eyes and the drawn expression on her face made her look like a daguerreotype of a morose Progressive-Era female intellectual.

"Have you spoken to Alexis?" I asked her.

She nodded. "She might come here to visit." She said it gloomily, examining what was left on her plate.

"That's great," I said, forcing cheer into my voice. "Right? Isn't that great?"

"I don't know." Sid shrugged. "Now there are terms."

"Terms like what?"

"Terms like getting married and having a child."

Alexis was funny. People were funny. Besides having a serious job and a decent income (that would be significantly reduced if I stopped renting out the cabin to help pay her student loans) there was very little about Sid that suggested she was ready to live the kind of life Alexis wanted. Maybe Alexis imagined she'd be the reliable one, the caretaker, the one who packed the lunches and went to the school events, while Sid flitted around like Puck, doing fun things like throwing the baby in the air and loading the car for spontaneous beach trips. Alexis had her own career though, she would need help and support, and the lack of responsibility and accountability from my daughter would soon become oppressive.

I chose my words carefully so she wouldn't take it as an indictment.

"Maybe you want different things," I offered.

Her face froze in annoyance for a moment, but for whatever reason, she let it go.

"Could be that's all it is," she said. She used a hunk of bread to sop up the bits of kale and cheese and meat juice left on her plate and then gnawed it like an animal.

I took our dishes inside, refilled our wine, and brought out slices of cake, which gave way under the sides of our forks with pleasing, geometric neatness.

The light grew dim and creepy. I thought about my story. If I were to stop teaching I would have a significantly greater amount of time to work on it. I could finish the first draft in a month, perhaps, if I was diligent. I could have another published book before I turned sixty.

"I'm thinking of doing it," I told Sid.

"Doing what?"

"Stopping teaching."

"Are you kidding me? Why?"

"I don't want to be teaching if people don't want me there. If I'm making people uncomfortable."

"It's not about them being uncomfortable. Trust me. It's about them winning. What will it look like if you stop? You'll basically agree to be seen as an accomplice when you had nothing to do with what Dad did."

"But maybe you're right, maybe I am an accomplice."

"Listen to me. I can call you an accomplice because you're my mother and he's my father and I don't like the idea that you were telling me a lie this whole time. But if you're an accomplice, most everyone is, right? It was common knowledge, right?"

"Right."

"So don't quit, please."

"I don't know. My day may be done. Nobody wants to hear from me anymore. Always I run into some struggle with my students. I used to find it fun, trying to get on their level, trying to understand where they were coming from. Adapting, for them, for the moment, not wanting to be left behind. But now I think that maybe I should be left behind."

"Don't be silly, Mom. You're an extremely youthful person. You look young, you act young, you think young. You're just down on yourself right now."

"How young?" I turned to Sid to make sure she wasn't just puffing me up.

"What do you mean?"

"How—young do I look?" I was drunk, or I wouldn't have asked. When she was growing up, wanting her to find her worth elsewhere, hating myself for my obsession with my appearance, I never once asked Sid how I looked, even as I longed for her praise. When John would call her cute or laud her clothing choices I would tell her that it was only the inside that mattered. Even as I obsessed, I never spoke of my weight, my wrinkles, my grays. Before the awkward adolescent years I would swoon at her long-legged grace, her wide mouth and white teeth and luxurious hair, but would keep my thoughts silent. It had worked, in a way. She was a confident but not a vain young woman. Or whatever obsession with her looks she had absorbed by osmosis she also kept hidden far below.

She looked at me with an indulgent smirk. "You don't look a day over forty-five." Then she patted me on the knee and said, "Really."

My whole face burst into a wide, almost painful smile. I was so pleased, in fact, that tears threatened to roll down my cheeks. I slammed the rest of my martini and retreated to the kitchen with the excuse that we needed more wine.

Sid brought out a portable speaker and turned on some music, so we didn't hear the car pull into the driveway. We were faux-modern dancing in the backyard, making funny shapes with our bodies, pretending to pass electrical impulses back and forth that would shake us from top to bottom. After our martinis and two bottles of red wine I unearthed some maple bourbon, which we were bopping over to and shooting straight. I had a brief moment of clarity in which I noted that the pool was covered and we wouldn't fall in. This time, I wasn't sure one of us wouldn't drown. With each undulation and move of my body I imagined I was shaking all the frustrations and negativities up and away from my inner self and flinging them away from me, back out into the atmosphere, to be absorbed by the universe. You don't get through a PhD with a concentration in women's literature without encountering some New Age–ery, and drinking could bring out my mystical tendencies.

Sid was the one who grabbed my arm and pointed her out. Standing at the back gate, held up with duct tape as it wasn't yet fixed from Sid kicking it in, was a woman, watching us. As soon as my eyes fixed on her I realized how drunk I was and how nearly impossible it would be to keep a steady course as I walked to greet her. "Come with me," I said to Sid, and grasped her arm. We approached cautiously, like Dorothy and the Scarecrow entering the dark forest, arms linked.

As we drew closer to the gate I saw that it was Cynthia, wearing a slightly forced smile, like she had just opened the door on me going to the bathroom.

"Hi there," I said, hoping I wasn't slurring my words. "This is my daughter, Sid." I felt very aware of Cynthia's sobriety in the face of my drunkenness, and how judgmental she might be if she knew the full extent of the evening's bacchanalia.

They exchanged hellos. Sid, perhaps because she was an only child, was always good about participating in conversations with neighbors or my colleagues. Unlike other children who would twist themselves away and stare at the floor when questions were asked of them, Sid would always stand placidly beside me and look adults in the eye when they spoke to her. It would mostly make me proud, though sometimes I would feel badly for her, the mini adult by my hip, so pressured to appear mature beyond her years.

After a long moment of silence, Cynthia gazed past me toward the pool and spoke. "I didn't want to bother you," she started. "I was on my way to campus and realized I was passing right by your house—" Later I considered that she had never been to my house before, so she couldn't have been "passing by," she must have deliberately looked up my address, but at the time I didn't think of that. I murmured that it was no bother, I asked her to come in and beckoned for Sid to help me lift and drag open the broken gate.

She protested that she couldn't stay, then said, "I heard that they asked you to stop teaching."

"They did."

"I wanted to let you know I think that's totally fucked-up. Honestly, it makes me livid."

"Thank you," I said to her, reaching my hand over the gate and awkwardly placing it on her shoulder. "It's nice of you to come and voice your support." I was so wobbly, I didn't want to take my hand away from her for fear I might stagger. I felt like I was underwater, unable to poke my head through the surface.

"What are you going to do?" she asked me, looking at my hand.

"I don't know yet," I told her. I could think only of Vladimir, so much so that as I looked at her she almost transformed into him, and it was him standing in front of me at the gate, him enduring the weight of my outstretched hand instead of her. I supposed I could keep my office even if I wasn't teaching. I could still see Vladimir in the hallways and travel with him to the coffee stand, run into him in the parking lot. In my mind I saw the weather getting cold and the two of us in parkas and woolens, leaning against the cars, freezing but unable to break from our conversation with each other.

"Well, let me know if you need anything, letters—whatever—" she said. She looked once again at my hand that was still resting on her. Rooting firmly into one side so that I didn't tip over, I slid my palm down her upper arm (rather sensually, I am mortified to admit) and allowed myself to squeeze her firm tricep before I took the hand back, scraping my forearm against one of the fence posts as I withdrew it.

Was it just my drunken imagination, or did I see her shudder and ever so slightly pull the shoulder I had touched away? In a flash I remembered that Cynthia would be taking over one of my classes if I chose to stop teaching. Did she really come here to offer support? Or did she come here to spy? Was she already counting her money like a little fox counts on the flesh of a lame hen? Was she actually on her way to campus? Or was she driving over here to kiss my ass and then getting back in the car and driving to David's, who was due to become chair, to kiss his? Where was Phee? What was she doing out at this hour?

I stood there for too long, staring. Sid, more sober than I was, asked her if she was sure she wouldn't like to come in, have some cake or a drink, but she once again refused, saying she had to work tonight. She murmured that I should let her know if "there's anything I can do." Then she seemed to examine my face for several seconds, as if searching for clues to a puzzle. Not finding what she wanted, she smiled weakly, turned, and walked toward her car.

"Just don't stab me in the back," I said softly. She stopped and pivoted to face me. I instinctively stepped away from her. Even drunk, I didn't want a confrontation.

"What?"

"Nothing."

"Okay," she said, and proceeded to get into her car. The moment before she ducked her head into the driver's side, I saw an expression settle on her exquisite features. It wasn't anger or scorn or any of the emotions I would expect her to feel had she overheard my comment. Instead, even with my consciousness just brimming at the surface, I saw that I had made her nervous, and as I watched her leave it seemed she took the K-turn in the driveway too quickly, like a jittery thief escaping the scene of a crime.

XI.

The following day I woke in my old marital bed. John was not there. My head felt as though someone had taken a vegetable peeler to my brain and roughly scraped away the topmost membrane. As I hoisted myself up, an explosion of white floaters appeared in my visual field. I was wearing the same clothes from last night. I went to the bathroom and tried to will myself to vomit, but nothing came out. I looked in on Sid, asleep in the guest room, in her pajamas, under the covers. I looked in the office and saw John sleeping on the futon. Again, I didn't remember him coming home, but I barely remembered anything from last night, and I prayed I had not thrown my hungry, booze-soaked body upon him, begging him to make love to me.

With relief I recalled I'd canceled my classes—planning in advance for this day of mental squalor. Well, yes, and so I deserved it. I started the coffee, and while I was waiting downstairs I pressed a bag of cut-up frozen mangoes to my face. Water, I needed to drink water. All the water in the world. Later I might ask Sid to go buy me a green juice from the little health food store off Main Street. And a kombucha, I liked those. I began a mental list of what I would eat and drink that day. (Most people think it's best to compensate for a hangover by eating, and while that works for young people like Sid, I have found in my dotage that starving and dousing a hangover with excessive hydration is a much more effective tool for recovery.) I would let nothing pass my lips other than water, coffee, and the green juice until one in the afternoon. After that I would allow myself to eat high-water-content fruits and vegetables (watermelon, cucumbers, cantaloupe, celery, lettuce, tomatoes) until 5 p.m., at which time I would make a chicken soup (no noodles or rice) with a healthy amount of spice to burn and scour my insides. I would do an old aerobics DVD that forced me to sweat.

I gathered a collection of half-perused periodicals from the coffee table and ran a bath in our clawfoot tub. A few years ago I purchased a walnut bath caddy that lay midway across the mouth of the bath and an ipe bath chair that sat below the water and supported my neck and bottom so that my tailbone didn't ache while I soaked. The bath setup always made me feel like Julie Christie in *McCabe & Mrs. Miller*, though my legs would never bend in such straight and appealing lines as hers did. I poured my coffee and a glass of water. I brought my drinks, along with the *Paris Review*, *New York Review of Books*, *Harper's*, and the *New Yorker* to the bath caddy. I swapped the bag of frozen mangoes for a fresh bag of frozen peas. I urinated, and noted that John and I couldn't have had sex last night, as there was no sting or ache. Then I slipped into the water, took a long drink of coffee, rested the peas against my face, and closed my eyes.

I slid into a doze, the feeling of blanket after blanket gently placed on top of me. When I opened my eyes the peas were mushy, the bath was cool, and there was a clatter at the sink. John stood there, teeth bared like a wolf, flossing.

"Hi," I said.

"Oh, hi," he said, smiling. "You were in quite the state last night."

"I don't remember."

"Well, it was almost fun, though when I wouldn't have sex with you, you threw a bit of a fit."

"I'm sorry."

"Don't be. I enjoyed feeling valiant and refusing you in your compromised state."

"Thank you." I turned away. He was acting a little phony, a little arch, and I wasn't in the mood. I remember, back when I lived in New York City, eavesdropping on a woman asking her boyfriend if he wanted to get a drink. Clearly, she wanted one. He replied in a reserved and pious tone that he wouldn't be drinking tonight. His refusal embarrassed her, and her voice rose to a high pitch: "We Never Want the Same Things at the Same Time!"

For so long, this was how it felt with John. If he came to me light-heartedly, I would want seriousness. If he came to me gravely, I would feel irritated. If he came to me lovingly, I would react icily. If I came to him in supplication, he would mock me. If I came to him in strength, he would ignore me. We were so pitted against each other. Perhaps because we were so desperate to hang on to our own identities, our own separate I's. We insisted on living our own lives in our own minds and could never truly merge. Perhaps we were undisciplined, or perhaps it was because we didn't go to church, didn't live by a moral code, didn't believe anyone was watching. We had come into adolescence in the 1970s, of age in the 1980s—we were brought up swaddled by the most selfish and individualistic decades in the history of the United States.

Then I remembered his fat thumbs texting students. Meeting them in hotels. Acting agog at the sight of their bodies, their breasts like small, round flotation devices. Even if I didn't care, even if I liked the space, had I been doing what Sidney had said? Had I been talking myself into a compromised existence for the sake of being tough? Why did I feel as though I was still trying to figure out how I could be a better partner for John?

"Do you think you brainwashed me?" I hoped I looked a little bit alluring from the bathtub.

"What are you talking about?"

"All the women. Was it brainwashing? The fact that I allowed it?"

"You suggested it in the first place."

"A very long time ago."

"We didn't want a conventional marriage. That's what we said. That's what you said."

Yes, that was what I had said. And yes, that was what I had wanted. Strangely, I hadn't thought about the idea of a conventional or an unconventional marriage in months—since the petition. I suppose because I had been foisted into the clichéd role of the wronged wife. We had wanted to live unconventionally, in a new way, invented unto ourselves, and now I was playing the most timeworn part.

Our conviction wasn't truly behind it, because then we would have shared our life choices with Sid. If we believed in an unconventional marriage, I wouldn't have been the one to make all the dinners and arrange all the play dates and schedule all the lessons. We lit a couple of fires in unexpected places, but we weren't willing to burn it all down.

"Hey." He was feeling moved, I could tell, he swelled slightly with import. "I heard what the department asked. I'm sorry that this all has affected you. I find it truly boneheaded."

"Where do you go at night?"

He finished flossing, rinsed his mouth, and spit a stream of blood-tinged saliva into the sink.

"Nowhere." Then he pulled his elbows behind him to stretch his chest, farted, and left the room. As a matter of habit he flicked off the light on his way out, stranding me in the dark.

I hadn't planned on being so mentally compromised that I couldn't contemplate my response to the tenured faculty, but my loose brain and sweaty palms lasted well into the day. I was overwhelmed with burning humiliation for whatever had occurred between Cynthia and me, no matter how many times Sid assured me that I was fine. "She's hot," she said. "She is," I said, and then pictured how ridiculous I must have looked while dancing, how sloppy I must have sounded when I spoke, and how strange it was that I would threaten her, when the whole reason she came was kindness.

At 6 p.m. a little clarity broke through my brain, bringing with it a craving for more alcohol. Once more I wrote to pertinent people and told them I wouldn't be able to teach the next day, as my cold had worsened. I had papers due in my Gothic Novel class, and wrote them a strict email requesting the essays in my inbox at the end of class time. As a teacher, I've found that strictness is often an effective way of diverting from one's own laziness. Sid mixed martinis and made us some not-half-bad French dip sandwiches with sautéed onions and the leftover steak (my resolve for a liquid/vegetable diet failed around three, when I became ravenous). I preserved a modicum of sense and limited my drinking to one reasonable martini and a large glass of cheap red. We ate the rest of the cake and watched Billy Wilder's *The Apartment*, which Sid had never seen.

"Disturbing," she said at the end, after the credits rolled on Shirley MacLaine and Jack Lemmon playing cards together. I wondered if *The Apartment* was the first film that ended by depicting love as a kind of jovial camaraderie rather than passion. MacLaine and Lemmon didn't even kiss at the end of the film. It seemed as though all films now, unless they had titles like *Desire* written in red letters against black backgrounds, portrayed true love as the coming together of two fun friends. No wonder that I perceived, mostly from their short stories, that my students found nothing more romantic than lusting after a platonic member of their social group.

Sid, though, wasn't interested in that inquiry. What was disturbing to her was that there was such a delineation of women presented and that the movie had no qualms about that. Shirley MacLaine was deserving of love and a better situation because she was sensible, funny, beautiful, and well-spoken. The other women who had affairs with the executives of the corporation were presented as fools and sluts. They were curvy and spoke with regional accents and were less beautiful and thus deserved our ridicule, while Shirley MacLaine's gamine, refined character deserved our sympathy and support.

Of course, until very recently we had all thought that. We had all thought that there were certain kinds of women who deserved to be taken seriously, women you saw in the office, for example, and certain kinds of women, women you saw in titty bars, for example, who didn't. We believed they were different and we all thought it, men and women alike. You could separate your ideas about them with ease. You could respect some and denigrate others. I understood Sid's and her whole generation's rejection of the excuse that "it was a different time." That kind of excuse leads to cultural stultification, it perpetuates misogyny and racism, it is general and not interesting. I didn't believe Billy Wilder should be held up as a moral paragon, or even as a good man.

But what I was becoming so frustrated with, and the reason I felt more and more like not teaching, was that I believed that art was not a moral enterprise. That morality in art was what happened when the church or the state got involved. That if you insisted on infusing art with morality you would insist on lies and limits. Truth could be found only outside the confines of morality. Art needed to be taken and rejected on its own terms. Art was not the artist. Were these all simply platitudes I had absorbed without question? I felt more and more mixed up about it recently. Should we only portray the world we wanted to see? Should we consider certain stories "damaging," and restrict them from a general audience, not trusting them to take in the story without internalizing the messaging? Hadn't we all agreed that morality in art was bad? But art did cause damage, and I was affected by films I had seen when I was young, and I was ashamed when I watched an old film and saw racist depictions I hadn't seen before, and I was glad to be ashamed. But did we all have to see ourselves in the presentations of types? Did I have to feel like every wife and mother was presenting an overarching narrative of Wife and Mother that reinforced or rejected my own experience?

Sid was indulgent with me that night. She said that I was clearly a good teacher, because I was entertaining the questions and not just roundly dismissing them. For her, she said, the misogyny of *The Apartment* was primarily distracting and kept her from enjoying the film the way it was meant to. It was meant to be agreed with in a certain way, and she couldn't agree with it. When I suggested the movie was interesting as a document, as a way America saw itself at a certain time, as an example of the trajectory of film, of a new kind of comedy emerging, a new kind of hero, and that the crowd scenes were choreographic marvels, she told me that while she understood that I was interested in that way of thinking, she wasn't. She was a lawyer, she wanted something different from her intake of art. When I cited to her that Ruth Bader Ginsburg's favorite teacher was Nabokov, because he taught her how to appreciate literature on a formal level—to look for the tricks of the writer, the art of the novel, to see more than just the story—Sid shrugged and told me she had no doubt that Ruth Bader Ginsburg was smarter than she.

XII.

The next day I felt clearheaded, if not energized, and resolved. After my conversation with Sid I felt a renewed urge to engage with my students, to prove myself as a teacher. I realized I had been approaching my classes, my entire presence on campus, with a bowed and apologetic posture. I had been teaching fearfully, as though I had to be agreed with, as though I weren't a skilled enough instructor to allow for multiple opinions to exist in the room at the same time. I needed to listen, to make myself permeable and receptive. Naturally I made them all feel uncomfortable—I had never officially acknowledged the scandal. I had never, in any public sort of way, mentioned the accusations directly.

I wrote an email to the tenured faculty.

Dear Esteemed Colleagues,

I want to thank you for your dedication to the well-being of our student body. There is no doubt in my mind that your wish for my suspension (I believe that is what you are requesting) comes from a place of deep caring.

In the effort to be direct and upfront, I will say from "the get-go" that I do not accept your recommendation, or urging, or whatever you may call it. I will continue to instruct my classes. If you insist that I halt my normal duties, you give me no choice but to respond with legal recourse.

That said, I understand the great rift that has come about in the depart-ment, for both students and faculty. I believe I have shirked my responsibility when it comes to openly discussing the events that have caused such a rift. I will admit that I have felt personally wounded at the idea that I am at-tached to these events, and have ignored and avoided said idea at all costs.

Pride, obviously. Thanks to your confrontation, I am now aware that my pride must be swallowed, and my silence must end. I will be speaking to the allegations and the hearing in my classes, and sending a department-wide email to all majors, inviting them to a coffee hour in which I will talk a little and listen much.

Attached to this email is my class schedule. If any of you wish to come and observe my address to the students, you are most welcome. Questions and comments are also welcome, although for the sake of everyone cc'd on this email, please do not reply all.

From then on, and for the next two weeks, I felt strong, centered, and focused. In both of my classes I gave the following speech, which I wrote and memorized:

"I want to start by saying how much I admire you. In my (ahem) years of teaching, I have not encountered a generation of students as committed to improving their structures, institutions, and worlds as you are. I am impressed by you, and terrified of you.

"First, an apology: I'm very sorry that on the first day of class I did not speak to the suit brought against my husband. Remaining silent was a gross misjudgment on my part. When my daughter was young, and I noticed that something upsetting had happened to her, in school or on the playground, I would tell her that if she would only speak about it, the bad feelings would evaporate. It's magic, I would say, talking is magic.

"So now, to attempt some magic. Many years ago, before any of you were students at this college, my husband, John, had consensual relationships with several students. These occurred prior to the rule that expressly forbid relationships between students and faculty. I assure you, he was not the only one.

"I knew of these relationships at the time, though I don't

wish to go into private details. I support him staying on at the college. He did not violate any rules, and he has not engaged with a student since then. I'm willing to discuss this with you, and I'm willing for you to prove me wrong. I will certainly accept the results of the hearing—which may reveal more than I yet know.

"As to that, I want to say that I am an 'Independent Woman,' to paraphrase Beyoncé, and John's actions are not my own. I believe, deep down, you understand and respect that.

"That's all. I don't wish to talk; I wish to listen. In an attempt to dismantle any power dynamic, I invite you now to anonymously write any questions or statements you may have and pass them to the front and I will do my best to answer them."

The address proved successful. The students passed up little slips of paper and I read their questions out loud in a tempered tone. They ranged from aggressive, "How can you live with a sexual predator?" which I answered, vaguely, "I'm curious to see if the hearing proves that John was a predator," to intrusive, "Are you polyamorous?" which I answered by winking and asking them whether they thought that was any of their business. I urged them to answer as well, letting them discuss for the entire ninety minutes of class, nodding, only occasionally pinching my thigh to keep from reacting. Having been heard, they released their resistance. I even managed to win over the student who had criticized Kate Chopin—she came to me at the end of the following class and sweetly asked if I would look over one of her short stories. None of the faculty came to observe—I knew they wouldn't; they could barely make it to their own courses. Similarly, only three students came to the coffee hour I had suggested, and they were all my pets, there to offer solidarity and affection. The only thing that felt odd was that Edwina neither attended nor responded to the department-wide invitation I sent out, and I started to wonder if I had said or done something that had caused her some offense. But she was probably simply involved in her own interpersonal situation, I told myself, a heartbreak or a rift with her peers. As a professor one shouldn't overestimate one's importance in the lives of students; they care about their friends and lovers far more than they care about you. It is critical to remember that. Whether they love or despise you, you are usually not much more than a minor figure in their dramatic landscape.

I made a point to lift my head as I walked on campus, meeting eyes and saying hello to everyone I knew. Vladimir and I ran into each other frequently, in hallways, in the cafeteria, and at the coffee stand. Whenever we met we lingered, discussing students, new books that were overpraised, and old books that were underappreciated. Often we spoke of the twentieth, and how we looked forward to a long and uninterrupted conversation. Every time we parted it was as though we had to tear ourselves away.

I felt willing to face all that I had not faced before. Besides working every day on my book (I was nearly halfway through a draft and confident enough to call it a book now), I read Cynthia's memoir excerpts. Well-written, terse, biting, they centered on the day that her mother committed suicide, when Cynthia was ten years old. I didn't think she would make much money from it—it was too good, written without an ounce of sentimentality. I sent her a note with a list of my favorite sentences. I enrolled in a 6:30 a.m. boot camp at the Y. I went to the dentist and had my teeth whitened. I contacted and met with several contractors up at the lake to collect estimates for winterizing the cabin. I opened a separate bank account, a thing that, to the disbelief of some of my friends, I hadn't kept since before my marriage, into which I redirected my salary and put half of our savings. I did a face mask every other day.

That summer, John had enlisted the services of Wilomena Kalinka, a lawyer from town who Sid deemed "fine." "As long as you have a woman, as long as you prepare." He had initially wanted to represent himself at his hearing, but Sid had convinced him to bring on counsel. He argued he was sure to be dismissed, so what was the point of paying someone. She told him that he had to prepare in case civil suits were brought against him after his dismissal. As the hearing loomed, he spent more and more days at Wilomena's office, in the front room of a historic house, with "W. Kalinka, Juris Doctorate, American Bar Association" stenciled in white letters on the leaded-glass entrance. He would come home from her office around dinnertime, change, and leave once more. Sid grew increasingly agitated about his absences and begged him to tell her where he went, at first in a joking way, and then in earnest frustration, but he evaded her questions just as he evaded mine.

My nights were full of feverish and intense meditations on the lustful joinings of Vladimir and me. He would run his fingers, ever so lightly, from my earlobe down my neck. He would press me against a bathroom sink from behind and reach around and grab my breasts. He would slide his hand up my leg while I drove. Those simple flashes were enough to send me into an erotic frenzy. I would masturbate, climax, step outside to smoke, then return to the futon in the office and repeat the process two or three times. At night when I dreamed it was always of him. Often he would stab me with a kitchen knife, and I would see black-cherry pools of blood on my tile before I woke.

Two nights before John's hearing Sid convinced me to follow him so we could discover where he went every evening. She could no longer bear being excluded, like when she was a small child and would get so upset when her father and I would disappear into the bathroom to discuss an issue she was not supposed to hear. I didn't think it was a good idea, but I agreed because I was so pleased that Sid wanted to treat me like a comrade. It felt like a new stage in our relationship. I pictured the two of us in Argentina, visiting the birthplaces of Borges and Cortázar, sitting in outdoor cafés with red wine and seafood buried in rice, or in Norway, waking in the middle of the night to see the aurora borealis, or in New York at a lesbian bar—Henrietta's if it still existed. "This is my mother," she would say. I would be attentive, supportive, and interesting for her friends, who would come to see me not as a parent but as an equal member of their group.

We weren't particularly subtle in our pursuit, but John wasn't particularly careful or attentive as a rule. We jumped into my car the moment he pulled out of the driveway. Once he reached Main Street we let a pick-up come between us. There was a long, uninhabited stretch of road before one of the college entrances, and once I realized he was taking that, I turned with a screech to approach the campus the other way. I acted excited for Sid, who was palpitating with the idea of the chase, but as soon as I realized he was headed for the building that housed the English Department, a hard lump rose in my throat. Poor man, had he been going to his office all this time? Sitting in his very well-appointed room, maybe at his desk, maybe in one of the two leather club chairs, or lying on the tartan chesterfield, considering the life that would no longer be his? For while I had my writing, John had nothing other than the college. He had made the program what it was today, developed its curriculum, brought on most of the current staff. He had helped students go on to achieve master's degrees and PhDs and become well-regarded writers and influential scholars in their field. Our program was ranked second in the nation in colleges of our size. He was proud of the status, he felt responsible for it. We were considered diverse and progressive, due to his insistence on active recruitment. All over the internet, alumni and students would refer to our department as "a special place."

One could observe the staff parking lot for our building from the general parking area, which sat below it on a hill. Sid and I pulled into the lower lot in time to see John walking from his car toward the back entrance. Just as he approached the door, it was flung open toward him, a square of bright white light against the heavy dark of 9 p.m. Standing in the doorway, one hand at her neck, the other pressing against the metal bar latch, stood Cynthia Tong.

✑

I prayed they would say a few words and she would continue out to her car, the whole run-in a coincidence. But then I saw John touch her face, and she pulled him in by the hip, the door closing behind him so that they seemed to be swallowed by the night.

We watched in silence as the light in John's office turned on, and then I started the engine and backed up without looking, nearly hitting a Subaru behind me, and drove out of the parking lot at an irresponsible speed.

"Where are we going?" Sid asked.

"Home," I said. The image of John and Cynthia was thudding in my brain as if lit by a pulsing strobe, and I fixed my eyes on the white line of the road, like one is supposed to do in dense fog, to stabilize my thoughts.

"Don't you think we should go in?" Sid shifted her body so she could look over her shoulder out the rear window, trying to keep her eyes on the building as I drove away.

"For what?"

"To see what they're doing."

"We know what they're doing, honey."

"I didn't think it was so clear."

"Sid, it's nine o'clock."

"So?"

"So it's clear."

Sid turned back to face me, chewing the inside of her lip, an old habit. "That was the woman I met the other night, right?"

"Right." Had Cynthia been on her way to meet John when she came

142

by the house that night? Or worse, had she come looking for him? Had he given her our address, or had they met there before, an afternoon tussle in our marital bed, arranged for a time when his family was sure to be away?

"Why would she do anything with Dad?"

"She's a complicated person." Sid waited for another answer, so I offered, lamely, "Women like your father."

"Yuck," she said, but there was a heaviness to her voice, a drip of sadness clogging up her sinuses.

Then her phone buzzed, and she gasped. Alexis was arriving at the train station in fifteen minutes, hoping to be picked up. She had said she was coming, but she hadn't said when. I was relieved—I didn't normally enjoy spontaneous guests but I didn't want to spend time processing what I had seen with Sidney. I felt remiss that I hadn't parented her out of this shakedown, that I hadn't told her it was inappropriate for us to go tracking Dad together. Warmed by her attention, by the idea of us as partners, I'd broken a long-held pact I had made with myself to never go chasing after John. And what was I doing inserting Sid into all this? She may be a grown woman, but that didn't mean the actions of her parents had no effect on her psyche and well-being. Wasn't it finding out about John and the allegations that had spurred her into the affair with her colleague in the first place, upending her life, forcing her to leave her job, stranding her in her old bedroom turned guest room in her childhood house and town? Without work she was completely adrift, all the running in the world couldn't counteract the amount she was drinking and eating—she looked perpetually puffy, distended, and ill.

Sid spent most of the ten-minute ride hunched over her phone, texting furiously with Alexis. The pace their thumbs could move. I forced myself to note the scenery around us as I drove. The elementary school, the old post office, the sandwich shop. It wasn't until we were parked in the pickup area, watching the train pull into the station, that Sid turned to me and said, out of obligation, "How are you feeling about all this?"

I told her I had feelings about it, but I didn't want her to worry. She was to worry about repairing her own relationship, if that was what she wanted. She took this as offensive.

"What do you mean, *if* that's what I want?"

I said I thought that was what she was communicating to me, that she wasn't sure if she wanted to commit in the way that Alexis was asking. "Not wanting to have a child is not the same thing as not committing," she snapped.

I nodded. The bond that we had cultivated over the past few weeks was already being severed by the intrusion of her "real" life, which came toward us now in the figure of Alexis, toting a hard-shell rolling suitcase and wearing a very well-tailored power dress with soft leather flats, her braids loosely pulled back in an elaborate gold hair clip that looked like the branches of a tree, adorned with jeweled leaves.

She came around to my window first, greeted me, and told me that she had thought Sid would be the one to pick her up. She was mortified; she hadn't realized I would have to come out at this time of night.

I told her not to worry, that it was just a coincidence and no trouble. Sid jumped out of the car to help her put her case in the trunk and I listened to their conversation as she rearranged the grocery bags and snow-clearing equipment to make room.

"You look beautiful, Lexi." I saw Sid perform a half bow of appreciation.

"I was in court today. We got the verdict." She waited a beat. "Now you're supposed to say, how'd it go?"

"Sorry, babe. How'd it go?"

"I won."

"You're incredible."

"Tim told me to take the week off."

"I'm really happy you're here."

"Maybe you are, maybe you're not."

There was a moment of silence, a touch or a kiss.

"You look rough," said Alexis, soft care in her voice.

"I know. I miss you."

Alexis climbed into the backseat and Sid followed her. In the rear-view mirror I watched as Alexis squeezed her leg, scolding. "Babe, your mother is not a chauffeur."

I spoke into the reflection. "Thank you, Alexis, why don't you come into the front seat." We often played the little game parents played with partners, pretending we were more aligned than she and Sid.

"I would love to," she said, and thanked me again for coming to pick her up. I wished Alexis would be a little less polite with me, it enforced a distance between us. Whenever they visited, she and Sid became a conspiratorial unit, having what I imagined were honest conversations behind the closed door of the guest room and then emerging and making removed small talk with John and me. Still, I liked her considerateness better than Sid's childhood friends, the entitled spawn of fellow academics who opened my refrigerator without asking, borrowed my books without telling, and on summer days used to drop by and swim in my pool whether Sid was there or not.

"I love your clip," I said. Awkward around most women, I had trained myself to notice something on their person I could compliment. Compliments made you supplicant, equal, and master all at once. Supplicant because you are below, admiring; equal because you have the same taste; and master because you are bestowing your approval. In my life I've been wounded more by compliments than I have by insults. (Once when I asked an acquaintance what they thought of my second novel they said, "I can tell you worked so hard on it.")

"Thank you," she said. "A friend made it for me."

"Who?" Sid asked from the back. And they proceeded to discuss the friend who Sid thought was someone she met at a picnic but realized was someone else she had met at a party.

Excused from the conversation, I let my imagination return to John and Cynthia. The picture they made at the door grew more and more surreal in my mind; they became like figures in a biblical illumination, emanating golden rays. Had Cynthia been wearing an off-the-shoulder bandage dress? Had she been barefoot and standing on her tiptoes? Was she holding a glass of champagne? Was there a red rose wrapped around her upper arm, its thorns drawing blood? No, Cynthia didn't drink. I didn't see what she was wearing. She was so attractive I couldn't help but feel aroused thinking of John feeling up her firm, voluptuous legs. Were she and Vladimir all but divorced? Was he soon to be free?

"Babe," I heard Alexis caution Sid. "We'll talk tomorrow. Okay? I'm exhausted. Tonight we're just going to celebrate."

My date with Vladimir was two days from now. Did he know? Could I tell him? It struck me that Cynthia had taken Edwina's affection from me, she would have taken my class had I not resisted, she had Vladimir, whom I wanted, and now she had taken John. For what, for spite? She had youth and a body I always dreamed of, a body that would stay muscled and smooth well past her middle age. She had even, unlined skin and straight white teeth. She had attended the most prestigious writing program in the country, and her work would be better reviewed than mine ever was. She was the survivor of great trauma, she had something to *say*. I was jealous of every bone in her body, every moment of her history. She was acting wildly, I was jealous of that—jealous of her extremity, the fact that she was drawn to John, for who was the baddest boy on campus right now, who was the ultimate taboo? She had just arrived and was already so reckless—what would happen when the true, three-year-in boredom of small-town life worked on her? I wanted to push her into the mud and kick up great puddles of splattering filth, defiling her face, her clothing, her stylish shoes. I also wanted to worship at her feet, have her tell me all her secrets and methods for living so completely and exactly as she wanted.

At home Sid and Alexis sat outside, drinking wine next to the heat lamps. They half-heartedly invited me to join but I refused. They didn't truly want me there, and I wasn't in the mood to converse. I was so overwhelmed with thoughts I decided to grade papers. I needed a task that consumed me, nothing imaginative, no room for digressive thinking. I had learned to focus during my PhD, when I had to read complicated texts for hours at a time. People want books to absorb them, but one could force attention upon a book. It would be back and forth for the first half hour, but if you meant it, you could rope your mind into sublime and single-pointed concentration. I printed, stapled, and arranged my students' papers on my desk and with great effort began to read and mark them. My whole body felt as though I wanted to bolt from my chair but I put a stress ball between my legs and pressed hard against it with my thighs. Eventually my mind settled and I worked fluidly—underlining interesting sentences, correcting muddled paragraphs, questioning sloppy word choice, and writing a paragraph of evaluation on a piece of yellow legal paper that I attached to each of their documents. After two and a half hours I rose from my desk, creaky and stiff. It was midnight. The girls had gone to sleep, there was no light coming from beneath the bedroom door. Alexis had brought her white noise machine, which blared the sound of a rolling rainstorm. Something about the aural barrier caught my breath, and I felt a sob collect behind my upper cheeks. I pictured Alexis pulling Sid into the bedroom like Cynthia had pulled John into the building, enclosing them in their own private world, leaving me alone, bereft, in the dark. I checked in the guest bathroom to make sure there were clean towels and saw that Alexis had hung her neat, segmented toiletry bag on the back of the bathroom door. Feeling rude and unloved, I opened it.

I suppose I could have deduced that anxiety-ridden, perfectionist, high-powered Alexis would have some pharmaceutical products. I noted that in one clear zippered segment of her bag she had a variety of prescriptions. When I examined them I saw that among a few medications I couldn't identify, she had a bottle of Xanax and a bottle of Seconal. They were full, and I had no doubt she was measured in her use of them in a way I never could be, meting them out sparingly—taking them only in extreme circumstances, on an airplane or an insomnia-ridden night before a big court day. Pull This Lever in Case of Emergency.

Seeing the pills, I felt an inspiration begin to form. I thought of the white, cracked crumple of John's hands running frantically over Cynthia's hips. How much the lure of her taut beauty must ensnare him, turn him into a child, material she could manipulate, an object she could possess. Even when I had been her age and yes, somewhat beautiful, I had never let myself own a man in the way I assumed she did. The afternoon all those years ago, when David failed to meet and run away with me, I hadn't chased him down and tried to lure him back. I hadn't used the sexual power I knew I had over him to bend fate to my will. No, after lying on the ground for half an hour I had risen, bought a submarine sandwich (not a food I usually allowed myself), ate it in the car, semolina dust and bits of lettuce falling all over my lap, returned home, and unpacked my suitcases. After two failed attempts to meet him for a coffee and discuss what happened, I gave up, telling myself that closure was a myth, a concept fetishized by people under thirty.

Such a missed opportunity, I thought. And as I looked in the bathroom mirror at the webbing around my eyes, my frowning jowls, and the shriveled space between my clavicles, I felt desperation at the idea that I would never captivate anyone ever again. A man might make a concession for me based on mutual agreeability, shared crinkliness, but he wouldn't, he couldn't, be in my thrall. Images of Sid as a two-year-old rose in my mind as well, the way she looked at me then, fixed and obsessed, like I was the sun and the entire world, the origin and limit of consciousness. All that was gone forever. It was true, wasn't it, I would never experience power over another human being again for the rest of my life. I thought of Vladimir and tried to picture him as he might be in this exact moment, in his natural habitat. He was in bed, asleep but sitting up, a scratchy old camp blanket over his knees, wearing a cut-up college T-shirt, one hand clutching a book, the other, himself.

As I conjured him, I found my hands unzipping Alexis's toiletry bags, opening the caps of the Seconal and Xanax, and removing two of each pill. Like a painter might conceive of the outlines of their next piece, a plan began to form itself in my mind, blurred but distinctly edged. Yes, there was something I could *do*, some action I could take. I didn't have to accept what I was allotted and pretend I was grateful for it. I put the pills in a vintage pill case I used for travel and placed it in my underwear drawer. No, I was not required to accept the world's rejection of me without a bit of a struggle. I went outside and smoked, trying to keep both my eyes and my mind on the stars. I changed into my night shirt, performed my skin regimen, and, fearing that my active mind would prevent my rest, took another Seconal from Alexis's bag, swallowed it, drank three large glasses of water, and read until I blacked out.

The next day, one day before our fateful meeting (as I have taken to calling the whole event), I prepared. I packed a large suitcase with both John's and my clothes, and my elegant daytripper with toiletries. I filled a sturdy canvas bag I had gotten from a conference with books and some other administrative supplies. I loaded them into the back of my car, along with a case of wine and a bottle of vodka, sweet and dry vermouth, bourbon, bitters, and a bottle of cachaça. I would visit the grocery store the morning of our meeting for the rest of the provisions. I tidied up my correspondence, finished my grading, drove to campus, and gave my students' papers with my notes to the department admin for them to pick up when and if they wanted. I went to the Y and yanked dementedly at the handlebars of the elliptical trainer for seventy-five minutes until I was drenched in sweat. That evening I smoked the last cigarette in the pack. After I extinguished it I emptied the flower pot that had served as my ashtray into the large trash bin, pulled the bin to the street to be picked up the following morning, and firmly resolved to smoke no more.

XIII.

On the morning of October 20 I showered, then turned on the harshest light to shave and pluck and trim every errant hair I could find. I massaged my cellulite with oil and clipped my nails. I used a blow-dryer, smoothing spray, curling iron, hair powder. I took twice as long as usual applying my makeup—priming, concealing, blending, setting.

Lately John tended to sleep in past eleven or twelve, but today he was up as early as I was and cornered me in the kitchen, where I was taking a few moments to finish my coffee before leaving for the grocery store. He was shaved and wearing a suit and looked quite handsome, really.

"D-Day," he said. "I'm going to meet Wilomena in town before the hearing begins." I could tell he was nervous: his face was pale and fixed, his breath high in his chest.

I looked out the window at our maple tree, its yellow-red leaves fidgeting in the wind. I knew that if I took in too much of his worry I would cave with compassion and decide to accompany him to the hearing after all. "Remind me when it is?"

"It starts at eleven."

"How long will it be?"

"A week, a month, three months, I don't know."

"How are you feeling?" I rubbed my finger against the fraying edge of our laminate countertop that I'd wanted to replace for years.

"I thought you didn't want to know anything about it."

"You can tell me or not, I was just asking." I pinched one of the tattered plastic threads to pull it free.

John brushed my hand away from the counter. "Don't pick at that," he said, and walked loudly out of the kitchen.

He stopped at the bench on the back porch to tie his wing tips. I followed him and put a hand on his shoulder. I wanted to say something about Cynthia and what I saw the other night, but I was too ashamed to admit I had been following him.

"Will you text me when the day is over?" I asked instead. "I don't know when I'll be home."

"Neither do I," he said, annoyed, and then, maybe because he felt some twang about the institution of our marriage, his brow softened and fell over his eyes. He looked old and battered. "I'll let you know when we're out."

He finished tying his laces with a yank, stood and grasped me in an awkward side hug, planted a hard kiss on the top of my head, and walked away.

I moved through the grocery store with swift precision. Seasonal fruit, grapes, bananas, lemons and limes, herbs, carrots, lettuce, tomato, avocado, garlic, onion. Good cheese, good crackers, good bread, bacon, sausage, a roasted chicken, tubs of premade salad and slaw, nuts, chocolate, large bottles of sparkling water, coffee. Eggs, milk, yogurt, popcorn, vinegar, olive oil, butter, flour, sugar. Most of it went into freezer bags, lined with ice packs. It would all need to keep until later in the afternoon.

The Women in American Literature course, my final class before the study break, was inspired and energetic, the conversation lively. We discussed selections from *Mrs. Spring Fragrance*, a work I was sure they wouldn't have encountered in high school (it was always better when they hadn't previously been exposed), a collection of short stories written by Sui Sin Far from 1912 that explored American expectations of assimilation. After class I returned briefly to my office to drop off notes. Edwina stood at my door, waiting for me.

It was petulant and foolish, but I still couldn't help acting like a bit of a spurned lover with her. She had received several emails from me over the past two weeks, either directly or as part of a group, and hadn't responded to any of them. I greeted her distantly and let her follow me into my office rather than invite her in. She sat on the edge of the chair across from my desk, which I stood behind and neatened, with what I knew was obnoxious and demonstrative officiousness.

"I know this is last-minute," she said, "but I wondered if you wanted to grab that coffee."

"Oh no, I can't!" I said, rapping papers against the hard surface. I was acting like a phony, I could tell I was disappointing her.

"Okay," she said, and looked down at her hands like she wanted to cry. "Well, I wanted you to know that I got an interview with the film company, so thank you."

I immediately regretted my coldness and stopped what I was doing, letting my voice drop into a sincere place, low in my chest. "I'm so glad," I said. "I didn't do anything, just told the truth about you."

At that her face twisted into a pained grimace and she started to cry, tears flowing so freely they dropped onto the lap of her jeans.

"What is it?" I asked. I was used to students crying in my office, but Edwina wasn't the type to break down. "Edwina, are you all right?" I closed my office door, pulled a chair, and sat down beside her.

"It's so stupid," she said. "I'm embarrassed."

"But you want to talk about it, otherwise you wouldn't have come—please tell me."

She took a moment to get her breath under control. "I—I got an F on my first memoir-writing assignment from Professor Tong."

"She's not a professor, she's an adjunct."

"Well, she—I got an F. Look at this. I've never gotten an F in my entire life. I've never even gotten a D. The last time I got a C was on a test in high school precalc." She pulled the paper out of her satchel as she spoke and thrust it in my face.

I didn't register the contents of Edwina's paper. All I saw, scrawled diagonally across the front of the double-spaced typed words, was "THIS IS A LIE." I looked at the next page and it was the same. I wanted to laugh but looked at Edwina's face and swallowed it. God, I loved Cynthia.

"Why does she hate me?" Edwina asked, pleading. "We, like, bonded when she came. We went out for lunch and she gave me her number and said to text her anytime and—I don't know, I was really excited." So Cynthia had been trying to woo her after all. Was it purposeful? Or merely shared good taste? As teachers we all want our favorites to favorite us in return.

"Oh, Edwina," I said. "She doesn't hate you at all. I bet she wrote the same thing on every paper. And if she didn't, you should take it as a compliment."

"Why?"

"She's a firebrand, she wants to shake you up. She wants to make you go deeper, write from a more honest place."

Edwina shook her head. "Everything I said was honest."

"Not factually honest, emotionally honest. You're a good judge of character. Think. She's trying to disrupt you is all."

"Should I drop the class? I want to go straight to a master's program. I don't want to fail—"

"No," I said, though if I wanted to maintain primacy in Edwina's affection, I knew I might be arguing against my best interests. "I mean, you could, if you didn't enjoy it. Haven't you ever had this kind of teacher?"

"Never," she said. "Maybe I had teachers who said they were strict graders, but I could always handle that."

"She just wants to get to you, believe me. I think you should stay. She wants you to prove her wrong. Think of it as a fun challenge. Trust me, by the end of the semester she'll be in love with you. I promise."

Edwina sighed, looked down at her paper, and placed it neatly back into her folder. She sat for a while, seeming to deliberate, and then without meeting my eyes she said, "John's trial started today, didn't it."

It was the first time she had ever mentioned it directly and I found myself nervous as I realized she did, in fact, have opinions about it. "It's a dismissal hearing, not a trial, but yes."

She continued to look away. "Well, whatever you want, I hope that's what you get."

"What would you like to have happen?" I asked her. Edwina was so level, not inclined to melodrama or whipped-up outrage. Erudite and inclined to please, she always formally engaged with the literature in my classes. I thought of her as a rarity among her peers, someone who preferred succeeding to nursing wounds.

"It doesn't have anything to do with me," she said. Her face was tense and she was breathing hard out of her nose.

"Why not?" I asked. "You're in this department—you can have an opinion. Everybody else does."

"I don't have an opinion because it would never happen to me."

"Not to get into sordid details, but it has been several years since he's been involved with a student." I felt a prick of annoyance. How many times must this be said?

"Even so. It's not about me. This is a white girl thing. White—woman thing." Her chest heaved, and she turned to face me with daring eyes.

"I see," I said. I nodded at her, and a feeling of dull dread opened in my rib cage, right below my heart. I hadn't considered that she would have this response. If I interpreted her reaction correctly, this scandal brought up a different anger in her—an anger about a world of complicity between white teachers and white students, where they shared secrets with each other and patted each other on the back and sometimes fucked each other, all the while keeping students of different races out of their interior, intimate circles.

I fumbled, feeling the need to defend John, who was a cad, as I have said, but not, I thought, a bigot. "No, Edwina, the reason it wouldn't happen to you is not because you're not white—"

"Please," she interrupted me. "That's not what I mean. I don't even want to talk about it, actually."

"No," I said, "I want to explain. Listen, the reason it wouldn't happen to you is because you're—" I struggled with my words. I wanted to say, "Serious," but I knew the implications that would come with that—was I saying the women he engaged with weren't serious?

"I'm going to go," she said, and thrust herself forward in her chair, threatening to rise.

"No, listen. It's because you know what you want," I said. "He thrives off people who are conflicted, lost, adrift. You're none of those things. He wouldn't know what to do with you if he tried. And you forget—he's a flirtatious man, don't get me wrong, he has a reputation, but—mostly those women pursued him. You would never have done that."

She sat back, crossed her arms and legs, and looked toward the door, shaking her head. "They were girls, they didn't know what they were doing."

"Do you think that about yourself? Do you not know what you're doing? Is that how you want to be treated?"

"I know that I would do a lot of stupid things if I felt like I was allowed, but I don't have that privilege." I could see that despite her best effort, tears were once again pressing against her eyes.

"Would I ever have pursued a teacher? No," I said, "but everyone has the privilege of having experiences and making mistakes and being forgiven."

She sat back and huffed. Hurt dimmed her expression and she took a few deep breaths to calm herself. "No, they definitely don't." Her mouth twisted, dismissing me.

I knew I had made a misstep. The students she was surrounded with, all these white non-scholarship kids, these kids with so much money, they could make mistakes and have them cleaned up in a way that was impossible for her. "I understand what you're saying, but they should, right?"

"I'm confused," she said, though she wasn't; she was using the word *confused* in the way so many of my students did, to mean they disagreed or didn't like what one was saying. "Do you mean John should be forgiven? Or the women?"

I didn't know what I meant, I felt turned around, my words weren't coming out the way I intended. "I think I was talking about the women. But both?"

"You say he preyed on young women who were adrift, then you say they have agency. You say you would have never done it, but everyone involved should be forgiven."

My insides quivering, I managed a smile. "You're good at debate. You remind me of my daughter."

"I actually don't have the time or resources to care about this," she said, and she lifted her hands, palms facing down, closed her eyes, and lowered them with an exhale, as though to press against the earth. "I just want to live in a world where I can pretend that stuff like this doesn't exist. I have more important things to think about."

She rose, holding her backpack by the loop at the top. "Thanks for the rec letters again," she said. "I'm not mad at you, I just—don't care."

And she left the office.

I sat, looking out the window, feeling sickened, worried that I had lost the admiration of Edwina forever. I understood something I hadn't fully admitted before, which was how cleaving the act of choosing could be. John's history was not necessarily disruptive and painful to me, or even to the girls he engaged with. His affairs were painful because they created an atmosphere in which some women were chosen and others weren't. It was mostly through stories and lore—but it nevertheless turned all the female students of the English Department into candidates, to be selected, dismissed, or ignored.

But that had been the case throughout all my education, I thought, and we females had all shrugged and monitored our behavior, believing we were the ones personally responsible for either inviting in or keeping our male intellectual stewards at bay, or being deemed worthy or unworthy of that kind of attention. Moreover, didn't any kind of choice, romantic or not, create a discriminatory environment? We discriminated when we bestowed honors, when we gave prizes and awards at the end of the year, of which Edwina had received several. The act of choosing was embedded in academia, it was meant to be a place in which a student could rise, could distinguish themselves. We had to select some students over the others and those selections caused more pain, at least in my opinion, than the amorous fixations of an over-the-hill professor.

I didn't fully finish my thought, because Vladimir said, "Knock knock," and walked in. He was a delight to regard—a black V-neck T-shirt, black jeans, distressed leather blazer, neck chain, high boots. Again, he was so fashionable it was almost arch, like he was impersonating a member of the Italian intelligentsia in a late Antonioni film.

"Don't you look nice," I said, rising to greet him.

"I dressed up for you," he said. "Plus I just got this blazer and I couldn't wait to wear it."

"It's stunning," I said, and he popped his collar, squinted his eyes, and pursed his lips in a male model pose, then shook it off, embarrassed.

"We match," he said, recovering. I was wearing an ensemble I had considered for weeks, a long-sleeved jumpsuit that was modest but had what I thought were youthful lines. It was black as well, and I wore it with taupe platform slides I prayed I would not twist my ankle in.

"Ready?" I beamed my whitened teeth and threw my work bag over my shoulder, stumbling a bit as its weight hit me on my upper back.

We made our way out of the building to the parking lot. John's car was parked beside mine. I imagined him in his hearing, crumpling a half-drunk plastic bottle of water, the label shredded, silent and red-faced as his colleagues conferred on the end of his career.

Once we were in the car, Vladimir asked where I was taking him. I acted intent on adjusting the settings on the dashboard and spoke in what I hoped was an offhand way so I could gauge his response.

"I was thinking we'd go a little farther afield," I said. "I know a little farm place by a brook, it has a screened-in glass terrace, with a fire, it's lovely." I was jangling with nerves, I heard myself as I spoke, my voice false and tight.

"Amazing," he said. "For once in my life I'm completely free this afternoon. Well, till five."

"We'll see about that," I said, started the car, and pulled out. He laughed, then after a moment cautiously protested that he did in fact need to be back by five. He and Cynthia switched off in the evenings after a five o'clock dinner with Phee.

"What does 'switching off' mean?" Now that I was driving and could keep my eyes on the road my self-consciousness began to fade and I felt more at ease.

"She goes and works at my office. She's trying to power through the end of her book. She's up against it—the publishing company is pressuring to take back the advance if she doesn't get the draft in soon."

So that was what he thought she was doing. "So you're home at five, and then she goes out for the night to work? What if you wanted to see a movie or a friend?"

He shrugged. "It's temporary. She needs to get it done more than I need a social life. We'll get a payment on delivery of the draft. We're drowning in debt. Sorry, I shouldn't mention that."

"Why not?" We were on the road out of town now, and wide vistas of farm scenery spread out all around us.

"Nobody wants to hear about money troubles."

"Who doesn't want to hear about money troubles?" I said. "Money is real life."

"Thank you," he said. "I'm glad I'm not the only one who thinks so." And I was pleased to detect an acrid note to his voice, directed, I imagined, at his wife's financial irresponsibility.

I felt encouraged by his tone. "Marriages are so different now," I said. "John and I had no schedule. He came and went as he pleased. I was content to '*keep his dinner warm*,'" I sang, then said, "I mean, not really, but—"

He interrupted me. "What's that from? I know that."

"Oh God, a musical—*How to Succeed in Business Without Really Trying*."

"That's right. I was in the chorus in high school."

"My father had the cast album. He loved musical theater."

"I love musical theater too," he said. "Cynthia can't stand it. I tell her that I think musicals are like novels, but she doesn't think that's a good excuse."

He expounded on his theory, that while plays were more like poetry—contained, hermetic, and symbolic—musicals, because of their breadth and the function of the melodic and harmonic motifs, their peaks, valleys, and "numbers," were actually useful structural comparisons to the novel.

I nodded and murmured assent enthusiastically, but when he finished we were silent. American academics, like the rest of America, become shy when our conversations get too earnest. It is one of the reasons that I both love and am put off by conversations with Europeans, who never undercut their assertions with the discomfiture of having been emphatic, the way Americans do.

And Vlad, though born to Russian parents, was an American boy. "Didn't you mind it," he said, leading us back to a more comfortable track, the personal track, "that John would do whatever he wanted while you were at home with your daughter?"

"It wasn't like that. His freedom gave me freedom," I said. "And we had more babysitters. Parents today are so crazy about spending so much time with their kids. I love Sid but I never felt guilt about hiring a cheap college student to come and watch her while I lived my life, did my writing, saw friends, went to the gym."

"Yeah," he said with a sigh, indicating that the complications of his situation were beyond any simple solution. Though they weren't, I thought. We make our lives so complicated, when often all that's needed is a bit of time and space. I flicked a glance at his sturdy knees bursting against the dark denim, pressing against the glove box. When I next spoke, I tried to bring a smile to my voice, a sense of irresistible and fun wickedness.

"I think you should text Cynthia and let her know you're not sure when you'll be home."

He scoffed. I could almost hear his eyes rolling. "She'll go ballistic."

I tried to keep my voice in that light, insouciant register. "So give her the privilege of being the injured party for once. Listen, it's almost two—this place is still quite a drive from here. Be expansive. I think it'll be good for you both, Vlad. Trust the old woman."

He was quiet. I could tell he was thinking. I kept my eyes on the road and listened to the clicking of keystrokes on his phone. "Done," he said. He sounded giddy, disbelieving his own actions.

"Good for you," I said, though I hated that phrase and its empty support of what was usually a lazy or at least self-oriented act.

I heard the soft bloop of a response, and Vlad exhaled and texted back.

"What did she say?"

"She said, 'Have fun, stud.'"

And I could feel an air of tension that had been swirling around the both of us dissipate. We were free. Thank you, Cynthia, I thought, graceful, funny Cynthia.

I patted the small strip of seat to the left of his leg. "We're going to text her the number of a student I know who babysits when we get to the restaurant. I'm paying."

"I don't know. I don't like leaving Phee with someone I haven't met."

I patted his seat once again, this time allowing my hand, when raising it, to brush ever so slightly against his outer thigh. "Vlad, you have to let go a little. You can't be a parent and an academic and a writer if you don't let go. I know this girl. She works part-time at the college day care. Phee has probably met her. I can fully vouch for her character."

He nodded. "Okay. Thank you. I think Cyn will like that." And I took a moment to silently marvel that everything was going so perfectly well.

We paused at a four-way stop sign and let a comically slow tractor pass. A group of dirty cows crowded against a fence on our right, their milk bags heaving. Vlad's voice settled. "You know it's hard for me to let go. I have to hold on tight. She's been better in the past few weeks. Ever since she started getting back into her book. I wouldn't even have considered this a couple months ago. Still, she's barely sleeping, which can be a warning sign, and it feels like it could always just—crumble. One wrong move and—" He stopped himself, to keep the emotion from overtaking him.

I squinted in the sun to do something with my face, then proceeded along our route after the tractor finally cleared. As enthralled as I was with Vladimir, he took too much melodramatic ownership over Cynthia's psychological well-being. He acted as though it were *his* burden and his alone. I felt umbrage, as a fellow female, that Vlad insisted on bringing up her troubles nearly whenever she was mentioned. It smelled of condescension and a gooey fetishizing of her suffering.

"I'm glad she's doing better," I said, remembering her and John in the doorway. No doubt she was elated by her little affair. Nothing boosts one's spirits like secret plans and schemes and meetings and new hands and a fresh mouth to fixate on. Good for her creativity too. I'm sure she was writing with a renewed sense of energy, like I was when I thought about Vlad. Though I hadn't consummated anything, and she got to feel the burning memory of someone's touch while she crafted her sentences. How would I feel if Vladimir touched me? Would I lose myself completely? Would I dissolve? Become nothing but particles?

"Vladimir Vladinski," I said, attempting to shift the tone.

"Yes, my dear?" he asked, countering me.

"Today I want *you* to think about *you*. Should we talk about your book now? Or wait until the restaurant?"

"I don't know." He sounded pleased and modest, and though I kept my eyes on the road, I could tell he was smiling. "Let's wait until we sit down?"

"That's fine with me," I said. "I'll tell you now that I think you're a genius, and I think you're going to be very famous."

He laughed. "Literary fame. That and a dollar will get me a dollar."

"You'd be surprised," I said. "Things will happen for you, I know it."

"You're kind to say so."

I allowed myself to glance at him and saw that his cheeks were taut and his eyes were shining with pleasure. "I've embarrassed you. We won't talk about it until we get to the restaurant."

At my request he found the cast album of *How to Succeed in Business* on his phone and played it using the Bluetooth on my car speaker. We sang along to the songs—tentative at first, then with full-throated abandon. I took the female parts, he took the male ones, we messed up the words of the verses and came in strong on the choruses. The more we sang, the more brash and emboldened and confident I felt. He was happy, I could tell. Happy to be free, happy to be a genius, happy to be a beautiful man with his elbow out the open window, squinting at the sun in the October afternoon.

XIV.

*A*fter we had texted babysitter information to Cynthia, were seated by an eager Italian man, and had ordered our food and received and poured our bottle of wine (I filled Vlad's glass twice as full as mine, and being male, he did not notice), we turned to discussing his book. I had reread it over the past few weeks and made careful notes about theme, symbolism, his deft use of irony, his startling word choice, his use of plot as metaphor, his vivid set pieces. When I was a young and insecure teacher I decided that the greatest service I could do for my students was give them my focused attention. Kill them with care, was my motto. If you're unsure of your brilliance, give your time. A student who feels seen by you is yours forever. And even though it cost me hours of sleep, and probably came at the expense of my fiction career, the habit of close reading has become the way I teach and the reason that, until all this hoopla with John, I was one of the most popular professors on campus.

Our table sat against the glassed-in wall of the porch looking over the brook. Vlad couldn't stop exclaiming about how charming it all was. The decor was a little outré—red-checked tablecloths, Chianti bottles coated in wax holding candles, large old fake cheeses hung with straw in the rafters—but the fireplace and the contrast with the rural upstate New York exterior that surrounded us made the decorations feel special rather than silly.

I pulled my notes from my bag. I couldn't meet Vlad's eyes as I was speaking—he was too interested and eager. I alternated looking at my notes and at the brook outside, watching a long-beaked bird pick at the carcass of a frog, digging and pulling at its gelatinous corpse.

"What I find so remarkable about your book, Vlad, is that you've created a work of extreme restraint that never reminds the reader of its leanness. You move so deftly from scene to scene it feels continuous, and only after I finished did I realize how impressively you pushed time forward. Your use of tense is fascinating, as well as the switch-offs between first and third person. I took these shifts as our narrator's shifts in self-knowledge, and the impossibility of knowing the self. We reflect, we identify, we seek distance, we seek intimacy, all tactics fall short when it comes to actual perception—the views of ourselves are always conditioned. The writing is like a trapdoor: it gives the reader a sense of knowledge behind and around what the prose is presenting—a fascinating sleight of hand. The recurring appearance of paintings and photographs forced me to consider the representation of experience as it was being represented, which was dizzying and exhilarating. I thought often of John Berger and not only *Ways of Seeing* but also his photography book—do you know that one? I'll lend it to you. The character of the boy is pitiable, lovable, hilarious, tragic, and the relationship with the father has a warm and lived-in feeling. Do you know those rides that spin so fast that you're pinned against the wall? Yes, like in the Godard film *Breathless*, or sorry, what is it? That's right, the Truffaut film *400 Blows*. I know they are so different but I can't help but mix them up in my mind because I watched them all during one specific time in my life. So anyway, like in those rides, I feel like what is in the center, what everyone is afraid of falling into, what everyone is spinning to avoid, is the body. The material sense of aliveness, animal-ness, humanness. And yet the body is there—it's the pit, it's the center, it lives, molten at the core. I admire that the body is there but that you skirt direct mention of it—ever since Roth and Updike it seems as though men can't write a book in which the physical is present but not didactic . . ."

And so I continued. At one point Vlad interrupted to ask if I minded if he recorded what I was saying. I said of course not and that I was also happy to provide him with what I had written. Our food came—we both ordered salads and soups. As I spoke, I occasionally topped up his wineglass and watched his eyes become glassier with the effect of the alcohol. I went through my pages—three legal-sized sheets—and when I finished I leaned back in my chair, pleased with myself. I was comprehensive, and complimentary without fawning. I told him I thought he might pay more attention to compression as he neared the final third, my only substantial criticism.

"I want to kiss you," Vladimir said. And though I knew it was just an expression my heart rate seemed to double, and I felt queasy. He told me that it had been a very long time since he had gotten feedback like that—in fact he had thought the days of hearing his work reflected or analyzed in that way were over. He would be reviewed in the future, he would hear from advisers about what he could change to help sell a manuscript or from publishers about parts that weren't clear or from a copy editor about usage and grammar, but he hadn't expected to hear someone fully reflect his work back to him—what he was trying for—with such specificity or rigor.

"Cynthia's a good reader," he said. "But her advice is always so holistic. She'll say, 'cut this part' or 'that guy seems fake.'" He waved his hands at me, as if to say I was "too much." "I knew I was excited about our date for a reason."

"Well, I didn't want to read your book. And then I was very jealous of you when I first started it. But then I realized it was very good, and when something's very good, it doesn't make me jealous, it makes me happy that it exists."

"No more—I'll float away on my own inflated ego."

I put my elbow on the table and leaned my head against my fist, in a gesture of total attentiveness. "How's the next book coming?"

Badly, he said, he didn't have enough time to work on it, so he could never find the kind of rhythm he needed for an honest start. It was hard in the condo—he missed his writing space in his apartment. It had been a closet, he had stared at a blank wall—there had been nothing picturesque about it—he had sat in a folding chair that murdered his back. Still, it was where the first book came from. Also, as a first-year tenure-track junior professor, he needed to publish in some journals, so he had to keep working on an essay he was writing comparing Zamyatin's *We*, Huxley's *Brave New World*, and recent trends in apocalyptic television. The essay was taking him forever, because as he was writing it he kept forgetting why the topic had ever been interesting in the first place. Finally, with his next book he felt he needed to "swing for the fences" and write something really big—historical, maybe, or with multiple perspectives, or concerning a social issue. He felt scattered, he kept changing topics, he couldn't settle on something true.

"I think, what do I care about? And for a moment I'll convince myself that I care about veterans from Afghanistan, or drone operators, or Russian political hackers, or sex slavery, or cults, or the friendship between Babel and Gorky. And I'll do all this research—this will be it, this will be my big novel. And then I'll start to write and it will feel so dead and so false that I can't go on. I think, genre twist, I think personal, and then I'll think, why am I trying so desperately to find what to write? Doesn't the world have enough books in it? I should just give up."

The waiter approached and inquired about dessert. Vlad asked for a cappuccino, but at the risk of appearing domineering, I told him to hold off and asked for the check. "Their coffee is terrible," I said after the waiter had left. "Not worth it. And also—" I hesitated. The lunch had gone better than I could have dreamed. My dining companion, I could tell, was in an agreeable emotional state and a high level of intoxication. If I were to enact the next steps in my plan they would most probably succeed. And would I want them to? I pictured the alternative—driving him home, dropping him off at the front door of his condo, watching him walk inside, a bomb of hollow sadness falling upon my breast, knowing we would most probably never engage like this again. He would find appropriate friends, other parents his age, "that sexy playground," as Grace Paley named it. I would get older, we would become familiar with each other, in faculty meetings we would get on each other's nerves, our interactions would be reduced to mostly brief, pained, "so busy" smiles as we passed each other in the hallways, as it was now between David and me.

No, I couldn't bear that. I let myself look at him, fully in the face, nurturing a feeling of warm affection: loving the puffy bags beneath his eyes, the large pores on his chin, his spiky nostril hairs, his self-doubt, his neediness . . .

"I want to show you something," I said, as though confessing an intimate secret. "May I take you somewhere?"

He said I sounded mysterious and that he was intrigued. And that yes, he would go with me anywhere I wanted. He breathed heavy sighs—"I haven't felt this kind of release in a long time," he said. "Do you remember that fairy tale, where the soldier or the prince or the pauper—I forget who—puts the bands around his chest to keep his heart from breaking?"

"You stop that," I said. "I was just thinking of that story recently."

"I feel like that, sometimes. Like I need to keep myself held together with bands of iron. For my daughter, for my wife. I have to use the bathroom."

He stumbled away from the table. I'd had one glass of wine, he'd had the rest, and our harvest salads and minestrone soups—no breadsticks for low-carb Vlad—couldn't effectually sop up the wine, which came in at an astonishing 15.5 percent alcohol level. (Not too many years ago, you were unlikely to encounter a wine greater than 11 percent; somehow in the past decade we had internationally agreed we needed to get drunker faster and for less.) He had mentioned his "wife" again. "My wife." "Mine."

I checked my phone. I had a missed call from John, but no voicemail. He'd texted a photo of attractively arranged wrap sandwiches on a platter with the message *The execution will be catered*. I searched the internet for the story about the iron bands and found that it was a small detail from Grimm's *The Frog Prince*. In the story, when the prince is turned into a frog, his manservant is so grieved that he has three metal hoops soldered around his chest. When the prince is kissed and turned back to human form, and the manservant is driving the couple home to the kingdom, the manservant is so happy that the hoops snap off. Strange, the detail of a servant loving his master so dearly. Homoerotic, perhaps, which is fun to consider, or a teaching tool of oppression, most likely.

I'd paid the check by the time Vlad returned. He protested, but I waved him off, telling him I wasn't the one saving up for a down payment on a house. As we were gathering our bags the owner turned on a Cuban dance song, and Vlad assumed a stiff upper carriage and gracefully cha-cha'd out the door.

"I was a salsa nerd in high school," he said. "Florida in the nineties. I was this skinny, zitty kid but they liked me at this one place. I cleaned the floors and got to dance with all these thirty-year-old women in stretchy flare pants and belly chains. It was"—there was a dreamy, sexualized look on his face—"formative."

My cabin was only a twenty-minute drive from the restaurant. When we arrived and Vlad exclaimed about what a perfect idyll it was, I fought the urge to tell him that he could have it. I wanted to. In the past, early on with friends, and later with boyfriends, I had always been overgenerous—giving away my doll if another child said she liked it, or spending an egregious amount of money on Christmas presents for girls I admired and receiving nothing in return, or giving men free use of my car or place, which often ended in disaster.

I told him to go look out at the lake—and while he walked ahead I opened the trunk and slipped my toiletry bag, the limes, and the cachaça into my work tote, which was voluminous enough to conceal their contents. I yelled that I would be inside when he was done, and hurried into the kitchen. If I was to do what I had planned, I would have to do it now. I wasn't sure how compulsive Vlad was—he was Russian, he probably had a high tolerance, he clearly liked to drink, but he was also ambitious and a father. I couldn't tell if he would have more than one cocktail. I pulled out the pill box from my toiletries and rolled a Seconal between my fingers. Would it be possible to seduce him on my own? He seemed to be flirting with me, speaking about sex in indirect ways and suggesting that he and I had a special connection. But no—that was only my own projection, he behaved that way with everyone, I was sure, and besides, compared with Cynthia I was repulsive, an old woman. Real life did not work out like that, with surprise reciprocity—that was a juvenile fantasy, a foolish ideation. I resolved to stay steadfast to the plot. Pushing deliberate thinking from my mind, as though I were in an exercise class and someone was telling me to complete the motions, or, more, like those moments when I turned off my critical brain and forced myself to "just write," I crushed the pill with the sugar for his drink, muddled the limes, and mixed them with ice and cachaça. I'd started fixing another caipirinha for myself when he tapped at the glass doors that opened into the living area.

"Vat is zis?" he said in an over-the-top accent when I handed him the drink.

"Some renters left cachaça." I showed him the bottle. "And some limes. You were just talking about salsa—I figured, we had to."

And it had been a sort of coincidence that I had brought that cachaça (I had brought more options should the mood have been different). But caipirinhas were the drinks that John and I had fallen in love to. Near the university where we first met there was a tapas bar—we would go after classes and get deliriously drunk. First with groups of other academics, and then as friends, until one night I convinced him to take me home with him. I remember those nights as half-lit, sparkling and sultry, my body elated with the romance of romance. When I was packing up and came upon the bottle in my liquor cabinet, I remembered and longed to re-create that glorious, fizzing confidence I had felt in myself, in my appeal, on those nights. Also, caipirinhas were incredibly sweet; if there was a medicinal taste to the Seconal, the sugar would probably mask it.

Vlad drank fast. He sat in the medieval beer-hall chair with the carved initials—saying it made him feel like a lord. A chilling wind rattled through the uninsulated gaps in the wooden walls, so I pulled out and turned on the space heaters I had brought up when I was conferring with contractors about winterizing the place.

"This is my dream," Vlad said. "Somewhere like this—not my home, somewhere else that was mine—where I could get away and write. Spend forty-eight hours in a fever—stay up all night, banging it out."

That had been the intention, I told him. But when we realized, idiotically, as we were professors, how expensive college was, even for a double-income household, I knew that if we didn't want to cripple Sid's chances with debt, we needed a greater income stream. We got the most money from long-term renters—people who stayed for a month or longer—and there were summers when we didn't even get a week up here. Then Sid had gone to law school at NYU, a perfect fortune even with loans, aid, and a small scholarship, and spent a miserable summer interning in a corporate office before she decided she simply couldn't work in that environment, that she had to do something meaningful. Working for a nonprofit with her debt would have been utter drudgery—we ran the numbers together and we were shocked—and, well, I wanted to see her both happy and making a difference, of course I did. She wasn't being selfish or lazy—and what else was my life for if not helping my one child do good for this world? As for winterizing the house—the expense could not be justified. I was so busy during the school year it would be nearly impossible for me to spend significant enough time up here, it would require so much work—the township didn't even plow the road when it snowed.

I told him things were different now, though. That I was making plans—that I wanted to make it accessible all year-round, that I planned on using it quite a bit more in the future.

"Because of John?" He had drunk most of his cocktail but was still cogent. Having never drugged anyone before, I wasn't sure how long a shift might take. I looked at his glass and saw the sugar, and what I presumed was the crushed pill, settled at the bottom beneath the ice. My heart seemed to beat faster with each sip he took. "Can I mix you another?" I asked.

"You're bad," he said, and then, again in his accent, "Vell vhy not." I forcefully stirred up the sediment, but made it much weaker this time, worried about the interaction between too much alcohol and the medication. My hands were sweating, my stomach was twisted up. Vlad noted I had barely touched my drink, and while I had planned to take tiny sips, keeping myself alert, his encouragement was all I needed to drain most of the glass. A quiet settled on us then, an awareness that we were alone together.

"What town is this?" he asked. I told him a false name—the words coming out of my mouth before I considered them.

"Never heard of it." He checked his phone. "Cynthia said the babysitter arrived." Then he frowned and pawed at the screen. "Is there no reception here?"

"Cell service is bad," I said. "But you could hook up to the Wi-Fi."

He put his phone back in his jacket pocket. "What do I need it for."

I handed him his refreshed drink, we clinked glasses, and he took a long sip. We had the obligatory talk about how rare it was, these days, to not be reachable. He said how when he was in the Peace Corps he would have these transformative moments, camping by a small village, when he would become aware that there was no one in the world who knew where he was, and no way for them to find out. These were the only times he felt the burden of ambition lift from his chest, understanding himself to be an animal among animals, a miraculous, meaningless life-form that had grown from the earth only to be absorbed back into it. I said I had nothing as glamorous to offer, but there were times in the past when Sid was at school and John was away, and I would go for a long drive to another town, or take the train a few stops north and sit in some establishment I would normally never frequent, simply to be somewhere nobody would expect. But I was so safe, I told him, even when I would tell myself to try to get lost, I wouldn't let myself stray too far from what I knew. I wasn't an explorer at heart. I was a woman who had been taught to protect her body above all else, and a writer. I lived the small writer's life—chained to my desk, my couch, my bookcase, my thoughts.

"I need to read your books," Vladimir said. "Cynthia loves them." His speech was not yet slurred, but his head began to move up and down in a slow, rhythmic motion.

I said he absolutely did not. They were failures, I said, I would be mortified. I spoke too quickly, though, and with too much force. I didn't think Vlad had read the books, but for him to admit he hadn't so casually underlined how little he considered me. His wife clearly thought about me a good deal more. Which made sense, as I was, in some ways, her competition. I remember, at the height of my obsession with David, trailing his wife after she left her office building. I followed her as she stopped by the grocery store, then the laundry to pick up dry cleaning, drove through a McDonald's for some illicit treat, picked up her daughter, and then drove home, where from a distance I watched her pull into their attached garage. I remember how enraged and pathetic and excited I felt, to see her shadowy figure moving behind the blinds, thinking about her touching the mug that David drank coffee from, or fluffing the pillow his darling head had crushed.

Vlad tried to rise and then immediately sat down. "Head rush," he said. I told him to stay sitting, ran the tap until the water was clear, and poured him a glass. He drank it all, I refilled it, he drank another, and then shifted in his chair, composing himself. I felt remiss. This had been a mistake. I should confess to him, make him hate me, sever this relationship completely.

"I have them on my bedside table," he said.

"What?"

"Your books. I want to read them but I'm working my way through all these—" He paused and closed his eyes tightly, trying to gather his thoughts, to find the words that were escaping him. He reached for his water glass and I leaped up to refill it. I didn't like what I was seeing, I didn't like watching him battle with a slipping awareness.

I tried to keep my voice playful, masking any concern. "As long as you're looking at my name last thing before you turn out the light."

"That and your foxy author's photo."

My mouth froze into a kind of sideways open oval shape, and my eyes, I'm sure, looked stunned, like I was caught in a lie. Once more I wondered—had my scheme been unnecessary? Would he have come to me without . . . ? No. It was the drug, I thought. He was a flirt, that I knew. And more than drunk, I assured myself. He didn't truly mean it.

"Well, youth," I said, trying to recover, though I was sure I was panting audible breaths.

"Nah," he said. And he pursed his lips in the flabby, flappy aspect of the severely inebriated.

I rolled, fluttered my eyes and shook my head all at once in what I imagined to be an extremely unflattering gesture. I was hit with a severe craving for a cigarette. Vlad looked at me with dopey, wavering intent.

"What," I asked.

"You wanted to escape." He pointed a waggling finger at me.

I shrugged, acting caught. "Of course I did."

"So you kidnapped me."

"What?" My breath was heavy in my mouth. I felt myself blinking rapidly, smiling an inane smile.

He nodded, his finger still pointed in my direction, as though he had found me out, but then a layer of awareness seemed to leave him, and the nodding turned internal, a negotiation with himself, his lips moving in an inaudible mumble. After what seemed like a lifetime of this he cocked his head and slurred, "I overdid it." Then his nodding turned to a shaking of the head, which went on for another interminable period, and the shaking took over his entire body, prompting a sort of wriggling in his spine, a twisting of his hands, a fluttering in his eyelids. It was as though he were performing a sinister dance—even drugged he had a kind of grace, a jittering Nijinsky—his bodily agitation romantic and terrifying. Finally, his movements slowed to a restless shifting back and forth. I tried to speak to him, but it was as though another layer of consciousness had been stripped away, and my heart felt practically seized with fear. Would I need to call 911? When I approached to check on him, as if in answer, he tried to rise out of the chair, knocking his drink and water glass to the floor, and I ran to him and placed my hands on his arms to try and still him, to get him to sit. Sweet boy, his arms were so strong and so firm and yet he clutched on to me so tightly to steady himself, like a child, he clutched me because he needed me, I felt cascades of tender thrills course through me as I led him back to his seat, using all my strength to steer him. On the first try we missed the chair, he fell to the floor on the side, and I had to plead, cajole, push, yank, and eventually slap him in order to hoist him up into the seat. I pushed my full weight against his incredible chest to keep him in position as he writhed. "You're all right, sweetheart, you're okay," I murmured repeatedly to him, pressing my body against his until he fully succumbed to the drug's physical force and slumped over on his left side, inert and fast asleep.

XV.

*I*nexperienced with pharmaceuticals as I was, I hadn't expected Vlad's reaction to the drug to be so visible and violent. I had thought, rather hazily, I admit, that he would drift off on the couch and I would unpack our provisions, lead him (somehow, I hadn't worked it out exactly) to my bed, and lie down beside him. Once there, I had hoped that the blunt forces of anatomical proximity and attraction, mixed with his still-intoxicated state, might take over. And after? I would have him away and to myself, he would be compromised, guilty, needing, ashamed, and, taking advantage of his inner conflict, I would heal him, help him, and thus create the space for the eternal, if physically fleeting, union of our souls.

I hadn't anticipated his physical struggle. His form lay twisted over the armrest of the chair at an evil angle. He looked the way Sid used to look as a toddler when she would fall asleep in her car seat, her body so completely collapsed that, if John was driving, I would climb into the back to hold her in place. There was work to do in the cabin, but I felt as though I couldn't leave him. I thought of a fact I had learned about preindustrial, agrarian times, and how in those times, some mothers would tie their babies to chairs with strips of cloth while they went about their duties around the house or in the fields. If I could only get him upright and secured, I felt he would be safe.

Considering Vlad's girth and solidity, I needed something stronger than fabric to effectively restrain him, and found a leftover pack of zip ties in the junk drawer that I had bought to tame the television wires. I squatted below where he was collapsed and used my back to push him upright, then inserted the plastic strip in a space between vertical slats at the back of the chair, threaded it around his right bicep, and pulled it tight, careful not to pinch his skin. For extra security I added another, higher on his arm. This seemed to work momentarily, he rested straight up, but then his body sagged in the other direction, falling over the side I had bound. I thought about binding his other arm, but I wanted him to be able to have use of at least one hand, that felt safer, kinder, what if he had to itch? I stared helplessly, the alcohol I had drunk that afternoon dulling my thoughts. Then I remembered the chain we used on the shed where we stored the kayaks. I hurried outside, opened the combination lock, and undid the length of metal that prevented the doors from springing open. I then returned to the house and wrapped the chain several times around his chest and torso, inserting three fingers in between the binding and his form so that I knew it wasn't too tight, and locked it in place. His head lolled, but that seemed all right; he had a strong pulse and was breathing normally and I now felt confident he wouldn't choke or otherwise injure himself.

After I finished I stepped back, regarding him, and a feeling of pleasure revved within me, like the acceleration of a motor. The sight of him, the fact of Vladimir's bound body, chained up in my hideaway cabin in the middle of nowhere, was fantastic and absurd. If someone were filming me, they might have seen me bite my palm in disbelief, cover my eyes, run my fingers through my hair, laugh, crouch, rise again, and put my hands over my face once more in shock at what I had done, at the spoils of my desire, the outcome of my obsession. I was playing up my reaction, for myself, like a child who wins a prize and can't stop emoting about it, reassuring myself of my perspective in the face of the extraordinary scene displayed before me. Then they might have seen me become quiet, approach the bound man, kneel before him and rest my head against his thigh, breathing in the metallic smell of his selvage jeans like incense at an altar.

I rested there for a few worshipful minutes, then roused and busied myself arranging the cabin, checking in on him occasionally like one would with a sleeping baby. I unpacked the groceries from the car, filled the drawers in the large bedroom with John's and my clothing. I put towels, washcloths, and bath mats in the bathroom. I unpacked the sheets and comforters from the Rubbermaid bins and after some wavering made up both beds. When he woke he should have the option to sleep in his own room. I dusted and swept and collected ant traps from the corners.

I wasn't sure what I was going to do with Vladimir when he woke up. I poured a large glass of wine and drank it as quickly as my stomach would allow to quash my nerves. It seemed to make no difference. I connected our phones to the Wi-Fi in case he or I received any desperate texts that would be better dealt with than ignored. It was early evening. I had a text from Sid that asked where I was, and I wrote her back saying I had gone on a little road trip and not to worry—I would update her. I had a text from John saying he found out that none of his accusers—none of the seven women who had written the complaints—would testify in person. I nearly wrote back, "They can do that?" but realized one text might prompt another. I told Sid to tell John I wasn't sure when I would be back. She texted, *Good for you*, and told me her time with Alexis was going well, though she physically felt "like shit" and she didn't understand why. She sent me the fingers-crossed emoji and a picture of a green face, and I sent a kiss and a heart in return.

Then I sat and looked at him, this heap of man, my prey, my prize, my Vladimir. Yes, he was mine. I decided I wouldn't make any decisions. I would be alive in the spontaneity of the moment. I didn't want to release him any time soon. It was for his safety, I told myself, though I also couldn't deny how pleased the sight of him made me feel. If he woke, I would trust that the right way forward would be revealed in the energy we exchanged. He might be upset or angry—nay, furious—but I would take that anger into my body, I would feel it, I would process it for him, and it would subside. He would be worried, but I would absorb his fear, so that it lifted from him like mist on a lake. He would hurl insults at me and I would catch and pocket them like a juggler catches and pockets floating scarves, knowing he did not understand what he said.

The main obstacle now, of course, was Cynthia. John and Sid would be satisfied by my text, whether they were angry or not, believing I was living some kind of Thelma-and-Louise-minus-Louise-style fantasy. They were absorbed by their troubles and lovers, they weren't thinking of me. Cynthia, however, was used to a good, dependable partner. I was sure she was used to being the one who was waited for, used to Vlad being the net that kept the family aloft, the one who kept Phee fed and on a sleep schedule. She might come home, pay the babysitter, and fall asleep tonight, but when the morning came and he wasn't there, I was concerned she might do something rash, like go to the police. An adult must be missing for seventy-two hours to file a report, was that right? Or was that simply some fact that they put in crime dramas to ratchet up tension? Furthermore, she absolutely knew that Vlad was going on this outing with me—he had texted her the babysitter information with my recommendation. If she went to John, well, I had to admit he knew me sometimes more than I knew myself, and I thought he might bring her straight here.

Then it came to me—of course, Cynthia and John. Vlad was with me, I knew about them, even if they didn't know I knew. What if I told him? Vlad might be enraged, he might need to take some time to think. He might need distance as he processed her betrayal. It would be childish on his part, perhaps, but understandable retribution. The question was only how to say it. I used his thumb to open his phone and read through the text thread between him and Cynthia. They were the texts of young parents—all about pickups, time expected home, meetings, therapy appointments, groceries, cute pictures of Phee, the occasional article link, the even more occasional note of love or gratitude. He was often reminding her to do things—go to the DMV, fill out paperwork, meet for this or that appointment. Neither of them seemed so inclined to text lengthy or soul-bearing missives to each other or participate in long text chains.

I sat with my own phone and texted drafts of the message to myself so that I could see how they looked when sent and received.

I found out about you and John. How could you do this to me? I am going away for a while to think. Please do not try to contact me. I will not reply.

It was appropriately terse but a shade too melodramatic.

Cynthia, you bitch.

No—Vlad was a respectful man, even in his anger he wouldn't resort to name-calling.

Cynthia. I know. Do not try to contact me. How could you do this to our family? After all you've put us through already?

While that might be the way I felt about it on behalf of Vlad, it was false as a message, and the vagaries and questions begged answering. Ideally I wanted as little follow-up communication as possible. Vlad began to snore slightly, a sweet, low purr. Why was I using her name? He wouldn't use her name.

I know about you and John. I can't think straight. I'm going on a trip. Do not contact me—I need some time. Use the babysitter as much as you want, we'll find a way to pay.

Better. There was something about addressing the daily concerns that felt more true to Vlad. It would be like him to set something up for her—like those suicide notes that talk about paying the gas bill—he wouldn't necessarily want to or know how to cut her off completely. Yes, that was the right tactic. I should enhance his caring aspect, even. I looked at his unmoving hands and thought of them lifting his daughter into the sky. I settled on the following:

I know about you and John. I can't think straight. I'm going away for a while. Do not contact me, please, I need time. Tell Phee I love her and will be back soon. Remember she has swim class this Wednesday. Use the babysitter, I'll find a way to pay.

I would wait to send it from his phone later tonight, with the hope that Cynthia might already be asleep. I had found the swim class information by looking at his phone calendar and seeing "Phee's 1st Swim Lesson" and thought it added a convincing touch.

Leaving the rest of the kitchen mess for later, I sat down across from Vladimir's sleeping form and opened the manuscript of my novel on my laptop. I found, however, that for the first time since I began the book, in this very cabin so many weeks ago, I felt an absence of momentum. I simply could not continue from my stopping point—a problem I had not yet encountered. I opened a new document and wrote a bit of auto-fiction, maybe even the start of a memoir—some paragraphs about old men and desire. But then I stopped after barely even a page. The stillness of the scene was too alluring to disturb it with deliberate thoughts and tapping fingers. For a while I simply looked at him—watching the light pass and fade on his form. Had I cursed myself by manifesting my desire? By shackling the engine of my ardor to a beer-hall chair? He was tied for his well-being, I reminded myself, not for my pleasure. Yet I couldn't deny how I felt, considering the pliability of his languid form, to have him all for myself, at the whim of my discrimination. But did I wish for the body of Vladimir, if it would even come to that, more than I wished for a finished book? Yes, no, in the moment I couldn't tell what was more noble—to submit to want and flesh, to give up everything for real person-to-person connection, or to forsake that entirely in favor of creating something lasting. And while I couldn't translate the experience into writing right now, perhaps later I could, later, having had the experience of resisting my timidity, my goodness, my incessant desire to please, all those (to use some academic verbosity) constructions of my femininity, I could call on this moment to give my writing real strength, real lived and felt power. And yet, I argued, I could also still find a way to get Vlad into my car and leave him at the entranceway of an emergency room, simplifying the entire situation, and return to the purity and productivity of unrequited longing.

The back-and-forth of my mind made me feel shaky and rattled. Like a mother who knows her child is not hateful, only hungry, I pushed those thoughts away—they were the thoughts of exhaustion. All the drinking of the day had left me headachy and restless. That was all, I said to myself, I simply needed some real food and to sleep—the excitement had taken too much out of this old girl.

Grateful for my foresight at having brought the groceries, I tore into the roasted chicken, and made a quick dinner of that with some pears and cheese and a premade broccoli slaw. I stood at the tap and drank several large glasses of water. I poured a tiny bit of bourbon into a juice glass and ate and drank at the kitchen counter. The bourbon proved soothing, so I poured some more, and then more again until I felt my hazy contentment give way to a sense of blurriness. Forcing my attention, I showered without wetting my hair and dressed in my most attractive nightgown (white, fitted and crocheted to the waist, then a billowing, full skirt) with a seamless nude bra underneath. I hoped the bra would not cut into my back flesh, but I have found that no matter how much one tries to prevent such mishaps—to ensure that one's pants don't pinch the waist, or that one's shapewear doesn't show through with an unsightly seam, some photograph will be taken in which you realize that you do, after all, look ridiculous: bulgy, baggy, and effortful.

Before retiring, I leaned against the door frame of the hallway that led to the bedrooms, letting my cheek rest on the smooth wooden wall, and gazed at Vladimir once more. I shut all the lights except for a small lamp; if he woke I didn't want him in total darkness. In the cast of the dim light he looked like a Francis Bacon painting—one of the artist's seated figures—constrained and exposed. I thought about the lore that George Dyer, Bacon's lover and frequent subject of his paintings, was a burglar, and they met because he had broken into the artist's home. I considered moving Vlad one more time, but then realized that even if I wanted to, I was too exhausted and bleary to complete the task. I slipped into bed with a novel that had recently won an award. It was a book Vladimir had suggested I read, and I hoped perhaps we could discuss it over coffee in the morning. The sheets were cool against my skin and I twisted my newly shaved legs luxuriously against the material. I masturbated, less out of urgency than habit, to keep my muscles alive and toned and to encourage lubrication. Unable to use Vladimir's image now that his physical presence was in the room next to me, I thought of some well-worn scenes from my distant past. I am amused at female masturbation scenes in films that show women on their stomachs, an uncomfortable position that does not allow for the full range of motion in the hand.

Returning to reading, and ruing my quitting of cigarettes, a truly foolish act, I made my way through the terse, enigmatic sentences, all of which seemed to be suggesting a dystopian situation. The writing was funny, but my attention lagged and drifted until I realized I was asleep with the book in my hand. I turned out the lights and lay in the darkness. At first it seemed like real sleep might elude me, but I eventually slid off. The air coming in from the open window was cool, the lake water lapping.

XVI.

*V*ladimir screamed at three in the morning. At first the sound was bestial; as it kept going I began to discern some words, mostly profanity. I gathered myself and took out his cell phone. I saw Cynthia had written a text telling him she was off to bed and not to wake her when he came home. I texted the preplanned message back to her, then dropped the phone in the glass of water on my nightstand and hid it under my bed.

When I walked into the living area, I saw him twisting forcibly against his restraints, pressing his feet to the ground in an attempt to lift the chair, using his left arm to claw at the zip ties, and then his teeth. He had wet himself, poor thing, there was a puddle on the floor. When he saw me, he lunged at me with the free parts of his body. If he had been loosed, I did not doubt he would have torn at my throat.

"What the fuck is happening? Get me out of here right now—you fucking lunatic, what the fuck is this?"

He was frightening. The anger of a gentle man is the most frightening kind of anger. His face was twisted and white with rage. Every vein I could perceive on his weight lifter's body was engorged and trembling against his skin. I could see the pulse in his neck beating as fast as a captured rabbit.

"Okay, okay, okay, okay, okay," I said to him.

"Shh, shh, shh, shh, shhhhhh," I said to him.

"Okay," I said.

And for some reason, something ancient and maternal, my soothing sounds worked. He stilled his body and took a deep breath. He emitted a sound that was nearly a laugh, with a quick inhale of panic following, and then began to breathe in and out rapidly, approaching hyperventilation.

"Shhhhh, shhhhhh, shhhhhhh," I said again.

"Breathe, sweetheart," I said, my tone firm, like a strict nurse.

He put his head down and forced himself to inhale slowly.

"In for five," I coached, "out for five, that's it."

I filled a glass of water for him and set it down on the left chair arm, hurrying away after I placed it in case he tried to grab me. But he kept his body quiet while he continued to breathe, and after a few cycles he took the glass of water and drank it.

"Thank you," he said after he had finished it.

Sweet man? Cunning man? I couldn't tell. He closed his eyes, sorting his thoughts, and then looked at me with some humor.

"So is this like that movie? That, um, you know that movie? That was a book? With the actress"—he corrected himself—"actor who's so good? I can't remember the name of the movie. She chains him to the bed and sledgehammers his legs?"

"*Misery*," I said, "Kathy Bates."

"Kathy Bates," he said. "She's so good." A wave of drowsiness swept over him and his head bobbed. Determined to stay awake, he shook himself.

"Do you want to kill me?" he asked, looking at me like a nervous child.

I felt filled with care at his pleading look, at the fear that I imagined was passing in waves over his chest and bowels. As I said, I hadn't fully thought through my plans after Vlad awoke, I hadn't decided what I was going to tell him, or how or if I was going to keep him. Yet as I looked at him, chained in the dim light, I felt aroused with a libidinous ingenuity. I focused on his hard, flat abdomen, secured against the chair, and allowed a story to arise and flow, as if I were setting it down on a page. Whenever I used to read about writers who "opened themselves to the voices" I used to roll my eyes, believing them sentimental and overly precious. But in this moment, whether it was adrenaline or the survival instinct, I found my front brain receded and a story emerged that came not so much from me as through me.

I told him that we had gotten quite drunk together in the cabin, and had, to my extreme mortification, become very flirtatious, although I knew, I said, that this was only the result of his intense intoxication. At this Vlad politely protested. Drunk as skunks, we were, I said, and in our drunkenness, he mentioned that he had, and again I told him I confessed this to him despite my extreme humiliation, always wanted to try some BSDM, and I rolled my eyes as I said the initials as though the letters hurt me to utter. At which point Vlad interrupted me and corrected the order of the letters, BDSM, with an understanding smile. I shrugged, flushed, nodded, and closed my eyes. He was listening, and I felt I had guessed correctly—that Vlad, patriarch, breadwinner, unwilling yet self-cherishing provider to his family, who (I remembered from what Cynthia told me in my office) was sexually distanced from his wife, would hold some fantasies of domination. What happened next, I said, was a blur for me, in and out, patches of vision here and there, but together we agreed that I would restrain him, playfully, that we would try it out for a bit of fun. I had zip-tied his arm, but he had asked for more, and so in our stupor we had agreed to restrain his chest.

"I don't remember any of this," he said.

"You were drinking at an alarming pace," I told him.

"And so what, did we—consummate, something?"

He looked down at his fly to check if it was open or closed.

"I don't know," I said, then looked at his expression and felt a rush of compassion. "I don't think so."

I told him that as mortified as I was to admit it, I must have blacked out as well. At some point in the night I remembered waking up on the floor in front of his chair and must have gotten myself changed and in bed without being fully conscious that he was still tied up. I was so sorry, I told him, this was by far the most absurd situation I had ever partaken in. I was not necessarily a dignified woman, I said, but I had never done anything like this. It must be all the stress—everything going on with the hearing. To my relief, he seemed to take it all in as truth.

"I didn't think I had it in me," he said.

"What?"

"Cheating," he said.

I told him there were extenuating circumstances. He asked like what, and I said, after much prevaricating, that I had told him some news. I hesitated, but he pressed upon me until I revealed that I had recently discovered that Cynthia and John were having an affair. I said that had I not been drunk I would not have told him, and I blamed the cachaça and said that I was sorry and that he should have found out from his wife, not from me.

His face crumpled. "Are you sure? I know John was helping Cyn with her memoir—they were doing a two-person writing group."

I responded quickly that I was absolutely sure, that I had caught them in flagrante delicto, practically, but a pocket of doubt opened up in my mind as I said it. Had they, in fact, been greeting in a friendly manner when I saw them? But no, I was sure I saw Cynthia grab him around the hip and pull him into her, I was sure I saw his hand run through her hair and the tilt of their heads toward each other. Besides, they couldn't have a writing group—John hadn't written for years.

Vlad was quiet again, then said, "I need to sleep." He looked at the puddle at his feet and said, "I'm sorry about the mess." I told him not to give it a second thought, that John had left some clothes here, that he could change and lie down in the guest room and after he rested we would get our bearings. He nodded like he had given up all agency, and then asked meekly if I wouldn't mind undoing the restraints. I acted shocked, as though I had forgotten they were even attached to his body. I kneeled between his legs (avoiding the urine) and undid the combination lock, unwrapped him, and then got a pair of kitchen scissors and slid the blade under the zip tie. I struggled a bit as the plastic was hard to cut and I didn't want to hurt him. I was thrillingly close to his body, and as I moved from the first zip tie to the second, he whispered, sadly it seemed, that I smelled good. I smiled and impulsively kissed him on the temple, like a mother, and then he took me with his left hand by the back of the neck, drew my face down to his, and kissed my mouth. I pulled away, surprised.

"I'm sorry," he said, but I said nothing and cut through the final tie. I led him to the guest room, and handed him a pair of John's pajama pants. Without waiting for me to leave, he started pulling off his sodden jeans and briefs. I looked away. When he finished changing I kicked the jeans out the doorway of the room and told him I would launder them. "They can't go in the dryer," he murmured, then took off his blazer, hung it over the back of a chair, and lay down on the bed. I stroked his face for a moment. He grabbed my wrist and pulled me toward him.

"Will you stay with me?" he asked. He was already dropping off, his pelvis shifting back and forth in an unconscious rhythm. I sat on the bed, gave his hand a squeeze, and told him that he would have a better sleep by himself. I drew the curtains in the room—it was nearly dawn, the dark was lifting.

I returned to my bedroom and arranged my pillows so that I was sitting up in bed. A sad and strange disappointment settled on my chest. I craved John and his cynicism and his massive form. I craved Sid and her body, still young, unfettered, and free enough to occasionally lay herself against me and gather succor from my warmth. I rose and looked in the mirror—scrunching my face so I could see every possible wrinkle. Vladimir's breath had smelled awful, but then again, mine probably did as well. My face hadn't melted from the bone when we kissed—I hadn't felt much of anything, though that may have been simply because I was so surprised. I couldn't tell from his weariness how much he believed me versus how much truth he intuited. Was the kiss, the invitation to lie down, a gesture of affection? Or was it a gesture of condescension, for the old, lame woman who didn't follow through on her kidnapping plans? Was it true that John was spending nights at his office helping Cynthia with her memoir and not pressing his lips against patches of her private skin? John had never read any of my manuscripts. When we were younger and I would ask him to look at something I wrote he would say he didn't want to interfere with my voice, that he didn't want to unduly influence my style. But I always knew that he was conflicted about my writing. Though he was slightly more august, and his publication and teaching style (affairs included) lent him a Harold Bloom–like gravitas and stature, he and I had the same job, were the same level of professor throughout our career, once junior, then associate, then senior. He had achieved some power when he became chair, and he was good at the business machinations of the college, but I never wanted that kind of influence. Meanwhile I managed to publish two novels along with my academic work. He did quite a bit of rereading of his own juvenilia but could never force himself to spit out enough poetry to fill even a small chapbook. I knew that every time he read my work he would have been battling against wanting to truly help me and wanting me to fail, if only to justify his own flaccid failure. Still, he could have saved me, I thought. He was a merciless critic, and my books, particularly my second, could have benefited from his slashing pen. Cynthia was already the better writer. If her book was a wild success, or even just a literary one, would I be able to withstand my jealousy?

Like moving the volume dial on the radio, I tuned my thoughts down to a low buzz and concentrated on the sounds of birds that were gathering fortitude with the rising sun. They must have built a nest somewhere close. I closed my eyes and slept for about an hour. The house was quiet when I woke. I thought perhaps that Vladimir had left, run for the hills, hitchhiked or stolen my car, done whatever he could to get away from me, the psycho bitch. But when I went to check the guest room, he was there, still asleep, the covers thrown off, his shirt shed, his rippled torso gleaming.

XVII.

He woke a little past noon. I heard him stirring in his room and packed the moka pot with espresso and started it on the stove. That morning I had taken the glass of water with his phone in it from beneath my bed, pulled out the waterlogged device, and put it in a bowl of rice. When he asked for it, I would tell him I had found it in the toilet and was trying to save it.

It was cold in the cabin. I wore wide-legged corduroy pants and a silk turtleneck beneath a fitted cambric work shirt topped with an oversized woolen cardigan. My hair was plaited and pinned on top of my head like a German. In the morning, when I realized Vlad would not be waking anytime soon, I spent an excessive amount of time applying my makeup so that it did not look like I was wearing makeup.

"Whoa," Vlad said as he entered the room. He wore his blazer over the pajama pants and his arms were crossed and shivering. I pointed to a sweater of John's I had selected for him—a lambswool pullover made for the coldest of winter days. He took off the blazer and put it on—it billowed and flowed girlishly around his hips.

"The coffee is almost ready," I said. He thanked me, then went to look out the glass doors that led to the lake. He seemed subdued, philosophical almost. I poured him the coffee, and not knowing how he took it and feeling too shy to ask, I filled a small pitcher with cream and made a tray with a bowl of sugar cubes. I placed it on the coffee table, and he turned toward the sound, sat down without speaking, and fixed his coffee with an obscene amount of milk and sugar. He looked bloodless and withered, a movie star playing a sick scene.

"This is so good," he said as he finished it, and I replenished his cup.

I waited for him to ask where his phone was, or suggest we leave right away, or propose some sort of plan that linked us with the outside world, but he drank his coffee and said nothing.

"Would you like some eggs?" I asked hesitantly.

"I will eat whatever you give me," he said.

I found the classical station on the radio and fixed him scrambled eggs, bacon, sausage links, raisin-bread toast, and a glass of orange juice in silence. Ravel's "Boléro" played, and he hummed along, staring into the middle distance.

When the food was ready he came to the kitchen table and ate with fixed intensity. It was like watching a time-lapse video of an invalid recovering strength. As he ate, in a steady rhythm, color returned to his gray face, and his limp limbs seemed to plump with renewed energy. When he finished, having consumed the meal in silence, he leaned back and ran his hands up and down the sides of his abdominals.

"Excuse me," he said, and walked very quickly to the bathroom, where he stayed for twenty minutes.

While he was engaged, I checked his phone, soaking in the rice, and confirmed that the screen was still warped and nonresponsive. Then I checked my own—another text from John came through, a picture of a platter of cherry tomatoes, basil, and fresh mozzarella on skewers. His message read, *The sovereign is called a tyrant who knows no laws but his own *caprese.** Pedant that he was, he followed it up with another text, *Voltaire, get it?* Then another: *This thing is a farce. I could resign now and end it. We'd save a fortune.*

I texted him back, *Why don't you?*

Civil suits. We didn't get all the evidence until the hearing started, Alexis and Sid are looking it over today.

Ok

Where are you? I'm worried. I miss you.

I missed him too, in a way. The thought of he and Sid and Alexis all working together, drinking beers and going over his evidence seemed fun and familial. I started and erased several messages to him, but then I heard the door handle of the bathroom turn and I clicked off my phone.

"Jesus," Vladimir said, "I feel like I was hit by a truck."

I asked him if he wanted some painkiller, but he said no, only water. I pointed him to the glasses. He asked if I had apple cider vinegar. I had bought some the day before, in fact, and he mixed in a tablespoon. "For belly bloat," he said, like a joke, though he meant it. As he was drinking, I pushed the bowl that contained his phone toward him.

"I found it in the toilet," I said. "I think it might have fallen out of your pocket."

"Nice one, Vlad," he said. "Thanks for rescuing it."

"Do you—want to see if it works?"

He shook his head. His lips were puffed with bitterness. "No."

"Do you want to—use mine?" His lassitude was confusing me.

"I want to take out a boat," he said. "Do you have boats?"

I pulled a kayak from the storage shed and brushed spiderwebs from the oar and the life jacket. I pushed him off, and he waved goodbye. Only when he was at a good distance out on the lake did I feel an erotic throb return, as I watched his shoulders undulate with the paddle, far from me. I went back inside the house and pulled the file of my book up on my laptop, hoping I had time to add an extra five hundred words before he returned. But instead I stared at the cursor blinking and wrote nothing.

What was he playing at? I couldn't understand. I understood that during the night, still under the effects of the sedative, he had only wanted to sleep, he couldn't think about the outside world, his wife, his daughter. But come this morning (or afternoon—I realized it was now after 2 p.m.), I had expected him to want to get back to that home and daughter as soon as possible. If he believed me about John and Cynthia, I would have expected him to be in more of a rage—ranting at me about my husband or fuming about his wife's betrayal. But never mind him, I also didn't understand my own mind. Did I wish to keep him here with me, in his docile, agreeable state? If he stayed, and we drank a bottle of wine or two, would it lead to our coupling? Last night, again, probably still under the influence, he had made it seem like that was a possibility. But I couldn't believe that was true. And besides, when he caught sight of my low breasts, my rumpled thighs, the loose skin of my stomach—

I thought of lying in the graveyard on the day David didn't come, the day we didn't run off together to Berlin. I thought of looking into the eyes of the cat who stepped over my body. At the time, I remembered, I had been hit with a deep, heartbreaking depression. There are no happy endings, I had thought. I was too old to be having the revelation at the time, but it pounded in my chest nonetheless, the dramatic words bringing dramatic tears to my eyes. I wondered though, now, what I would have done if David had come. Would we have even gotten to the airport before I myself turned back? Surely I would not have left my daughter, my shining pride, even if the gesture was supposed to be modeling a kind of female independence and pursuit of happiness I believed would serve her in the future.

Unable to withstand it any longer, I took a brisk two-mile walk to the gas station at the top of the road and bought myself a pack of cigarettes. As I returned, turning the corner toward the house, I once again expected to see my car gone, Vladimir fled. But the car was still parked where I left it, and when I entered the living room Vlad was sitting on the couch, wearing nothing but a towel, the space heater blasting his bare skin, reading an old lake house copy of *Lady Chatterley's Lover*. He rose when he saw me, gripping his meager covering.

"Sorry," he said. "I fell in the water. Then I came back and showered, then I picked this up, then I lost track of time."

"Let me get you some clothes."

"Thanks." He relaxed back on the couch and held up the book. "I forgot how good a writer Lawrence can be," he added.

"The beginning is very good," I said, my eyes locked on his face, trying not to notice that the towel had slipped quite low, so the V of his lower abdominals was visible. "But once the caretaker and Lady Chatterley actually get together it's nearly unreadable."

"The first paragraph—"

I made a sound of assent and interrupted, "'Ours is essentially a tragic age, so we refuse to take it tragically.'"

"Novels don't do that anymore," he said. "Big pronouncements about the way of life."

"He undercuts it though, doesn't he," I said. "He says something like, 'Or so Lady Chatterley thought.'"

"Good memory," he said.

"I don't know why I remember it," I said. "It struck me at the time, maybe."

I was backing out of the room as we spoke, wanting to get away from Vlad's aggressive state of undress as quickly as possible.

I came back with a pair of sweats and a shirt, put them on a chair (I found I could not hand them to him), told him to dress, and excused myself to the bathroom. In it I found his soaked and discarded clothes balled up in the tub, except for John's sweater, which hung over the shower bar. It would ruin the shape of the garment to dry like that. I put the clothes in the washing machine, avoiding crossing paths with Vladimir, then brought the sweater out to the deck, where I laid it flat on a cushion in the sun and did my best to reshape it.

Then I sat on the deck chair and lit a cigarette. I was smoking for less than a minute when Vladimir joined me. He was clothed, to my great relief.

"You bad girl. Can I have one?" he asked. "That looks divine." Something about the way he spoke—he could say the silliest word, *divine*, and make it sound like an artful, funny choice.

"I didn't know you smoked," I said, handing him one.

"Every once in a while," he said. "I quit when Phee was born, but I sneak one when I can."

And the tiniest pang of something passed over his face, the thought of his daughter, most probably.

But then he rolled his head, laid it on his shoulder, and raised his eyebrows at me. "I didn't know *you* smoked," he countered.

"I don't," I said, taking a drag.

And although I thought it might ruin whatever spell had come over him, I asked him what his plan was, and he said that before he answered he wanted to know mine.

I didn't have one, I told him. I had brought him to the cabin because I wanted to show him the space and offer it to him as a writing retreat once it was winterized, as a patron might, because I had enjoyed his book so much. I told him that we had obviously gotten off topic and out of hand. I said that as it was study week and I didn't have to teach, and I didn't necessarily want to be in the same house with John while the hearing was taking place, I had considered extending my time here, so long as the weather remained mild enough that space heaters during the day and blankets during the night would suffice. I said I could drive him back now or whenever he wanted, that he was welcome to stay.

He asked if there was any more wine, and I poured us two copper Moscow-mule mugs full of red and brought them back out on the porch.

"You live quite the designed life," he said when I handed him his cup.

"I'm just old," I said. "I've had enough time to get the right things and get rid of the wrong ones."

"You're not old," he said, and his voice was harsh in a way I hadn't heard before. "You're always saying that. Stop saying that."

My lower eyelids filled with tears, but I swallowed them down, smiled, and thanked him for reminding me.

He looked out to the lake. His profile was not as beautiful as his face full on—his nose looked more rounded and long, his neck extended diagonally from his chin.

"Do you know what happened to us in New York?" he asked.

I said I didn't. I wasn't sure what he was talking about.

"To Cynthia and me."

Ah. I said I knew what others had relayed, but not much more.

"I want to tell you what happened. I'm going to look at the lake and tell you the story."

For Cynthia it had started years and years ago—he began with that disclaimer. But for him, and for him and her, it all seemed to start when he sold his book. Before that they had been two adjuncts scraping by in New York City—carrying around jars of peanut butter in their bags to avoid buying food on the go, keeping credit cards in drawers, buying secondhand clothes, eating free pizza at student-oriented events, renting films from the libraries, going to open hours at the museums, seeing theater only if a friend got them free tickets. It was the way that they had lived since they were eighteen, thriftily and lightly. They took pride in spending so little and would challenge each other about who could get through the week on the lowest amount of money. It was simple and eco-conscious and freeing.

The book advance had been significant for him—it doubled his yearly income—but he was sensible enough to know it was not life changing. He didn't quit any of his adjunct teaching jobs. He and Cynthia went out for a fancy dinner, he bought a three-hundred-dollar pair of boots, they flew, rather than drove, to visit his parents in Florida. When they went out walking they bought six-dollar lattes without remonstrating themselves. They started shopping at the organic market. Cynthia, who had previously relied on the adequate therapists-in-training at the university where she worked, started psychoanalysis with a notorious practitioner who specialized in extreme trauma. There was a newfound ease and sense of possibility in their waking, working, everyday life.

They didn't consider the increase in taxes. They didn't consider the fact that because of his onetime burst of income the fee for their insurance plan would skyrocket. They got pregnant, mostly on purpose, but they weren't the kind to plan a baby by planning how much more money said baby would cost. By the time Phee was born they were already back to attempting to subsist off their monthly income. After she was born the great hemorrhaging began. Cynthia had two adjunct jobs at the time she got pregnant, and when she inquired about the maternity leave policies for non-tenured faculty, she was informed that they didn't have any—they replaced her immediately. Vlad started trying to find extra work wherever he could—editing other professors' papers, tutoring SAT students, mentoring senior projects and independent studies as well as teaching his own classes. Cynthia was home with the baby and getting restless—she needed babysitting, she needed to get out, she needed time to write—he could see she was fraying at the edges. He should have noticed how serious it was, but he was also fraying at the edges. The city was bearing down on him; everything was so expensive—babysitters were twenty dollars an hour, the psychoanalyst would see Cynthia three times a week or not at all (and he didn't accept insurance, so not at all), bills from the hospital and the midwife arrived with no seeming end. Cynthia had been sober when she and Vlad met at graduate school, her drinking and using had been something he knew about only from her writing, but then one night she came home from a walk with Phee with a bottle of white wine in the stroller caddy. That night had felt celebratory and bonding, they had fun, sloppy sex. Soon, however, the situation turned, as he should have known it would. They became enemies. When she drank she compared him to the litany of famous men who had left their wives when they had children for their own work, so that he could ascend while she floundered in obscurity. Bewildered, he told her to go to back to AA, and in response, she drank more. She refused to stop nursing, and Vlad was convinced Phee spit up more than an average baby, imbibing his wife's pickled breast milk. Their recycling clinked with glass bottles of hard liquor as she plummeted into a wrathful and impermeable depression.

One Sunday afternoon—he hadn't noted the date, and he should have; he constantly thought about what would have happened if he had remembered that it was April 22—he took Phee to the park. He had packed the diaper bag with care, bringing a blanket, the little neon tri-angle toy she loved, a change of clothes and diapers, bottles of pumped milk in freezer sleeves, a squeezy pouch of vegetables, a sandwich and a book for himself. He loaded up their stroller. He was so glad for the chance to escape her. Cynthia and the tyranny of her emotions. They were barely talking to each other at that time, out of deference to the oppressive tininess of their apartment and the fact that every discus-sion seemed to lead to an argument. That morning, however, she was buoyant, playful with Phee, and affectionate with him, calling him her handsome man and kissing him on the side of the mouth. He resisted her, assuming her lift in mood was only because he had promised to take the baby (and himself) away at 9 a.m. and return no earlier than 4 p.m. It was only because she felt guilty for sloughing Phee off on him that she was, for once, acting like a loving wife instead of a resentful cell mate.

She had been conscientious. Knowing how images can burn, she left a note outside the apartment door that said, "Please leave Phee in the high chair in the kitchen before you come into the bedroom."

He took that note as proof that she didn't fully mean it. If he had walked in with Phee and seen the bedroom door closed, he would have assumed she was communicating that she was still not in a place to see them. He would have assumed she was trying to let him know that she was finishing something. He would have left Phee in the stroller and lain down on the couch and tried to read the new short story in the *New Yorker*. He wouldn't have walked into the bedroom to find her foaming, moaning, and soiled, 911 already dialed on his phone.

After the hospital, the apologies, the forgiveness, the real sweet-ness after the crisis, she did what she had accused him of doing that first year. She ran away. She went to an inpatient facility in Pennsylvania geared toward the recuperation of severely depressed women for six months. She talked about her mother, started her memoir, and sold the first four chapters for much more of an advance than he had received. His parents gave them enough money so that he could hire a nanny on a salary for the year on the condition that he find them a better life and a stable job. His book appeared on some end-of-year lists, and he took the opportunity and wrote every contact he knew before he landed a tenure-track position at a small college in upstate New York. The Main Street looked like a town in New England. Cynthia had always wanted to live in New England.

He couldn't help but believe that it was all because of money—the having it and then the not having it. Yes, there was postpartum depression and the new-parent feeling of being caged inside one's home. Of course there was the psychologically resonant fact that she was now a mother, just like her own mother, who had committed suicide when she was ten years old. Of course it was the anniversary of her death. Of course there was her brain chemistry and the alcohol abuse and anti-depressant adjustments. Still it felt as though none of it would have happened if he had simply been able to keep them in the easy, bountiful style that had accompanied the first months after he sold the book. If they had continued feeling that optimism about the future of their lives together. If they hadn't lived in New York, among so many rich people, who sat in the playgrounds with Cynthia and him and told them about their private schools and tropical vacations in which someone else watched the baby. If he hadn't turned money cop and rejected requests for babysitters and cars and takeout and therapy. If he hadn't become her jailer just as much as the demanding, adorable Phee.

And now, with the possibility of owning a home, his secure position, the lower cost of childcare, the money Cynthia was making with her book, it seemed like they should be feeling carefree once again. But this time he was the one who felt trapped. He was so frightened of Cynthia, of what would happen should she relapse. The pressure of being a tenure-track professor meant he felt he always had to be doing more. He hadn't realized how much public transportation and the pedestrian lifestyle suited him—allowing him time to think, allowing him space between his work and his home. Reliance on the car depressed him.

Cynthia was only attracted to houses that were about one hundred to two hundred thousand dollars more than they could afford. Real estate conversations always ended in breakdowns. Now that Phee was in the college day care, it felt like he was running his ass to the ground while Cynthia had endless time to perfect her book. She even demanded she get to work nights while he put Phee to bed (he paused here to say that the possibility of the affair with John was nearly beside the point). They were stuck in a dynamic in which he couldn't refuse her anything—couldn't say that she had plenty of time to work given that her memoir-writing class qualified as less than part-time. Couldn't say that yes, she picked up Phee at three and watched her until he returned home at six, but those three hours were nothing when you considered he was waking up at five to keep his head above water, as well as not working on his new novel, the only thing in this world, other than his daughter, that meant something to him.

He let the words out in a torrent, not allowing time to interject or respond.

"So," he said when he finished, "is there more wine?"

I nodded and gestured inside. He told me he would come to the point when he returned, then went into the house. I almost asked him to find the mixed nuts and bring out a bowl, but then thought better of it. His wife, I'm sure, was an asker. I lit another cigarette, though I didn't want it.

When he returned, he used the arms of the chair to lift his feet from the ground, tucked and folded his legs into a yogic version of crisscross-applesauce, lowered himself into the seat, and continued.

"So I woke up this morning and thought, Cynthia got to run away."

I was surprised by his harshness. To call a suicide attempt "running away," that wasn't right. "You can't really call it that," I said. "She was in crisis."

"But the motivating factor of all of it was escaping. She wanted to escape. And she did. I had to stick around, and she read the complete works of Kawabata on a deck chair in some sanatorium that looked like Mann's *Magic Mountain*. Did she ask me before she decided to run? No. Did she prepare me? She did not. So." He shrugged, caustic and nonchalant.

"So you want to take revenge."

"Revenge? I don't know. Quid pro quo is more like it. Nothing extreme—just a few days to escape. Maybe I'll write, maybe I'll just clear enough space out that I could write. Or maybe I'll find something to write about." And he looked at me as if I might be his subject.

"Here?" I asked.

"Why not?"

"But," I protested, not understanding quite why I was protesting, for the sake of logic, maybe, or out of female solidarity, perhaps, or because as he had told his story I had felt a growing impatience and disdain for him that I could not yet comprehend or admit, "excuse me, but you, well, when she tried to—when she left, if that's the right word, you knew where she was. Maybe not emotionally, but physically. She doesn't know where you are."

"No, she does, well, basically she does."

"How?" I was confused. I had checked his phone when I returned from the gas station and it was still on the fritz. We had no landline at the cabin—he couldn't have called her.

"You told her."

My throat tightened and my heart pounded so thunderously it reverberated in my armpits. I felt the need to keep the appearance of eye contact with him and felt myself putting on a face of false surprise, squinting at his forehead, as though I were trying very hard to understand what he was saying.

"You wrote her that text message from my phone. About needing time."

"What?" My brow was still furrowed and my head was now shaking back and forth very quickly.

"I have my laptop in my bag. I can see my text messages on my computer."

I pushed words out of my mouth. "Well—drunk—you must have . . ."

"No, you wrote it. I didn't write that. I know that I didn't. It's okay," he said, smiling warmly at me. "It's interesting."

"Did she write back?"

"She did. We went back and forth a bit." He unfurled his legs from beneath him, lowered them to the deck, and used his heels to lift his buttocks up in a pelvic stretch. "She said I could have a few days."

"But do you want to stay a few days?"

"I do," he said, lifting his arms high and wide, his voice strangled from his stretch. "That is, if you'll have me."

"Did she—admit to—John?"

"No," he said casually. "But she'd be the first one to tell you she's a liar. So who knows."

He clasped his hands behind his head, looked over at me, and flashed his matinee idol grin, his teeth and lower lip stained purple from the wine.

"C'ai bum another cigarette?"

XVIII.

*W*e made thick coffee with cream and sugar to sober ourselves up and prepared dinner, listening to the cast album of *Sweeney Todd* with Patti LuPone and Michael Cerveris. I was Mrs. Lovett to his Sweeney. His easy acquiescence to the situation, and particularly to my deception, made me wary of him; every time our bodies were close I resisted the urge to spring away. Vlad made an herb frittata, I was assigned a salad, and together we assembled a plate of cheese and olives. He was a man who knew his way around the kitchen, slicing, peeling, chopping with alacrity. It was intimidating, after having mostly prepared food for my husband, whose only culinary contribution was the occasional placing of meat on top of fires. My hands felt clumsy as I dealt with the lettuce, and there wasn't a salad spinner so I used what felt like a conspicuous amount of paper towels to blot moisture from the leaves. I became self-consciously stymied about what a surprising but good combination of salad ingredients might be and went to the bathroom to search the internet until I came upon a lettuce, grape, walnut, and blue cheese salad. I sliced the grapes the wrong way, over-toasted the walnuts, and overcrumbled the blue cheese. When I told Vladimir what I was making he said something about how much he loved the vintage flavor mixtures of the early aughts, which I took, like nearly everything Vlad had said this afternoon, as both a reassurance and a slight.

I felt more comfortable around a cocktail, and once we finished our coffees I mixed us some manhattans. (The main tricks of a manhattan are good-quality cherries and getting it as cold as possible, nearly slushy, so that the bourbon is thick on the tongue.) We drank them while waiting for the frittata to finish in the oven. Our chatter was light and slightly forced—Vladimir kept bringing up "topics." At this moment, do you think the world is interested in the individual poetic voice? Which contemporary celebrated writers will be considered important fifty years from now? Is it possible to have literature that does not interface with identity without the presumption of a hegemony?

We set the table with cloth napkins, wineglasses, and a candle. Vlad told me that growing up and to this day, his mother exclusively uses disposable plastic dishes and cutlery that she throws out after each use. "She thinks she's gaming the system," he said. I was excited by the mention of his childhood: I wanted to know more, I wanted to picture his childhood bedroom, the posters he hung, the bedspread he chose. I wanted to know about his friends and influential teachers.

"I was a standard child of Russian immigrants," he told me. "Both my parents are scientists. They wanted me to be an engineer. I kept my head down and didn't tell anyone I wanted to be a writer. When I told my father I was majoring in comp lit at Yale he didn't speak to me for a month. I don't think they've read my book, but they keep it in a glass case inside of another glass case in a very peach room. The room would be good for a murder; everything is so puffy it would be soundproof. Floridian noir."

I asked if his parents got along with Cynthia. "They like her body," he replied, and the finality of his answer prevented me from asking anything more.

The magpies screamed outside the window as the light grayed. We opened a bottle of Sancerre for the meal. At the first taste of wine I knew that there was a strong current of intoxication already at work inside me, but I pushed through the glass, reckless, in search of a confidence that seemed elusive, no matter how much I drank. We ate sloppily and quickly. He held his fork with an overhand grip, which I couldn't tell if I found off-putting or alluring in a lusty *Tom Jones* kind of way. When we finished, Vlad asked if I knew how the hearing was going with John, and I said, "Let's text him and find out." Like two girls with a scheme to contact a clueless and unattainable crush, we sat close on the couch and huddled around my phone.

how did it go Today?

Thumbs down

what happened?

Same shit. They went through my rec letters.

Ugh.

Wilomena is not good at cross

Ugh.

Costing us so much money.

Right.

I may just resign.

Now?

Soon. So much money to lose.

Is that okay?

Sid says she thinks I'm okay.

To resign

Yeah. She went through evidence.
No good case for civil suits.

I thought of Sid reading through a flirtatious text exchange, a testimonial of an intimate act—

hello?

Was she okay with doing that?

Okay with what?

Looking through evidence

Fine

Ok

She says they have no case.

Ok

Only in BS academia.

Yeah.

so How are you?

Fine

Where are you?

. . .

hello?

I'm fine

When are you coming home?

. . .

hello?

. . .

what happened?

. . .

hello?

Vladimir lifted my hair. His mouth was a centimeter away from the space behind my ear. He brought his mouth against it, less a kiss, more a light smear. He reached his hand between my legs, but I pulled it out. Then he took my hand and pulled it toward his lap. I let it rest there, lifelessly, as I felt him stir underneath. I felt petrified, and annoyed at myself. Could I be any more idiotic? For the first time in what felt like my life I was getting exactly what I wanted, what I had fantasized and dreamed about, and I was reacting like a frigid spinster. I tried to relax as he pressed my hand against him harder and moved his mouth up and down my neck. Despite the terror that my skin was emanating wafts of Roquefort and garlic, I softened a little and let myself feel him through his thin cotton pants. His mouth was soft and dry. He worked his way up to my ear, then whispered.

"Professor," he said. "I didn't hand in my final exam. Am I in trouble?"

I reeled. I thought about the phrase "turned off" and how apt it was to sexual situations, because that was what I felt immediately at his words—as though the switch that controlled my arousal had been flicked to the off position. I went cold, and nausea rose in the back of my throat. Feeling as removed from sensation as a corpse might, I moved my hand from his lap and rose from the couch.

"What?" he asked. He had a grin on his face, like we were still playing a game.

"Sorry," I said. "I need some air."

He smoothed down his front and crossed his legs. "Okay." He laughed a little—half irritated, half self-conscious. He rubbed at his chin where a bit of stubble was beginning to grow and looked toward the wall opposite from where I stood.

The screen door was starting to come off its track and I made myself slowly lift and place it back into the groove so I didn't have some sort of hectic reaction and tear it down. I neglected to turn on the porch light and fumbled my way toward a seat. Scuttling sounds came from a nearby bush—nighttime feeding activity or fighting or mating.

My body collapsed in the chair, heavy with depression and self-mockery. Naturally it followed that any desire that Vlad had for me (if he had any, and wasn't simply acting out some inscrutable, self-destructive urge) belonged to a taxonomy that placed me in the category of pervy older-woman teacher and him in the category of a fresh-faced, innocent youth. I was a camp act for him. Some corny old fantasy from his adolescence.

And—this was the most embarrassing—I realized my fantasy had relied upon me being a sexy colleague, an attractive peer. I had imagined passion, something wordless and animal and back-brained. My feelings for Vladimir were beyond thought, and certainly beyond scenario. I had wanted him to allow me to forget who I was. I began to cry with disappointment, then laughed at myself for my tears. I had kidnapped him, essentially, I had drugged and deceived him, all because I wanted to satisfy my desire, and now I was finding fault with his perception of me. As if men who took advantage of women ever thought about how those women perceived them.

A tubby little raccoon waddled onto the porch. Its black doll-eyes stared at me. I held its gaze, wishing I could dissolve into a mammalian consciousness, abandon my thinking brain. The porch light clicked on and Vladimir appeared, holding my cigarettes. The raccoon, unhurried, toddled off the porch toward the forest. Vlad lit a cigarette, then tossed me the pack.

"Hey," he said, with a soft pleading to his voice. "Hey, I'm sorry."

I wanted to say that it was completely fine, that he had nothing to apologize for, but the words wouldn't come out of my mouth.

"I misread the situation, I think," he continued. He seemed actively concerned, and for a moment I considered what would happen if I decided to bring some departmental charges against him—suggesting he took advantage of me in a compromised state. Wouldn't that be a funny twist to the story. He was so modern and trained he would probably bow his head, apologize, resign, and run away.

But also people would laugh at how ridiculous it was that this specimen of man with his conventionally attractive wife would make a pass at a postmenopausal creature such as myself. I would be a joke. I remember how cruel we were about Monica Lewinsky, who we mocked as unworthy of an affair with Bill Clinton, though when I look back at old photographs I realize she was voluptuous and strong-featured and beautiful. Still, he was the most powerful man in the world at that time, and we shook our heads at him for not at least giving his attention to a nineties-style model or a film star. It made him seem soft and desperate.

"Are you okay?" he asked, and I realized I hadn't responded to him. I reassured him I was fine.

"I'm the one who's sorry," I said. "I didn't expect to react that way."

"I thought it was something you wanted," he said, contrite, and I understood that as a handsome man of his ilk, he knew his body as something he could give that might make someone else happy. A gift. And when I chained him, hadn't I wrapped him up and then opened him like a present?

"Have you," I searched for the right word, "transgressed, before?"

"No. Once, very early on. An old girlfriend from out of town."

"So why would you do it now?"

His voice lowered. "I have my reasons." I could feel him looking at me with half-lidded eyes.

"Oh, stop," I said. "Don't be stagey. Name one."

"I'm not—" he started, but then paused, arranging his phrasing. "I guess because I'm not doing it, am I. You are. I'm only acting out a part in some situation that I was placed in. You brought me here, you cast me in this role—I'm just playing it out for you."

"You don't have to. You can go, I'll drive you home." His words hurt me, like he was a marionette and I was an evil puppeteer. I felt the need to apologize. "I'm sorry about last night—everything got out of control."

"No, I like it, I'm glad you cast me. It's interesting."

Ah, I thought, so he had rationalized the situation so that he was in control of it—in control of the experience, of the part he was playing. Well, naturally he had that ability, it was the ability of the successful: to reseat themselves, no matter where they were, in a place of power. "Please don't patronize me," I said.

"No, no," he said. "I'm not. I like how we talk. I've thought about you. There have been a few moments in the past when the thought of kissing you has jumped into my mind."

"In a repulsive way?" I remembered a fellow cohort in my graduate program all those years ago—male and tall and reasonably attractive—who told me he pursued ugly women because he was fascinated by the grateful way they made love.

"Not at all," he said, then laughed a little and sucked in on his cigarette. The wildlife was quiet for a moment, I could hear the singeing of the paper as he inhaled.

A dry breeze blew against us, causing sparks from Vlad's ashes to fly in my direction like a small firework. The moment of quiet was enough for me to recognize how extremely tired I was, and the recognition of that tiredness released me, finally, to a place of matter-of-fact honesty.

"I'm writing a book," I told him. "It's almost done. I want to finish a draft while I'm up here."

"I can't wait to read it," he said.

"You don't have to say that. I want to get up early and work on it. You should write too, if you want to. We'll both write. We'll work in silence."

"Yes," he said. "I approve."

"So I'm going to go to bed."

I stood, then hesitated for a moment. I waited for him to say one more thing: to bless, condemn, or entice me, perhaps, or to wish me sweet dreams and a good night.

"Should I come with you?" he asked, staring at his hands, scowling.

"I don't know how to answer that," I said, in an affected tone, I admit, and yanked the stubborn screen door open, then closed it behind me, leaving Vlad and his cigarette alone on the porch to smolder.

He came into my bed around midnight. He crawled in beside me and wrapped his arms around me. He first rubbed my arm up and down, then my back, then my backside. I moved my hips in response and reached my hand back for his flank but did not turn toward him. He pulled my nightgown up and my underwear down and I kicked them off with my feet. He did not kiss me, but rested the top of his head against my shoulders. He pulled down his pajama pants and entered me. To my surprise, relief, and pleasure, I was not the least bit dry. His cock was long, slightly less than average thickness, and very hard. I thought of the word *lancing*. We moved together like that, not switching positions or adjusting limbs, as if to do so—to shift from our initial point of connection—would break a spell. Toward the end he reached a hand around to my front and I orgasmed immediately and silently. He kept it there and I orgasmed again, without effort or will or concentration. As he approached his own finish his intensity increased and he grabbed on to the backs of my shoulders and I orgasmed once more at the same time as him.

He kissed me on one shoulder and I patted him. He hung on for a while, breathing, but I could tell he was not sleeping. I told him he didn't have to stay and once he realized I meant it he thanked me and left, leaving a man-shaped imprint of sweat beside me.

XIX.

For the second night in a row I woke, this time from the sound of furniture—specifically the rickety mudroom table that nearly everyone knocked into—crashing to the ground, followed by the cursing of a low, rumbling voice I could tell was not Vladimir's and hands patting the wall to find the light switch.

Any rural area in the USA has its own River Styx of addicts, meth or opioids, half-souls floating amid the currents of daily life. They sit skinny on the stoops of general stores looking spent and expectant. They take their grandmother food shopping, or to the beach. They are sweet and thieving and skittering and fearful. We'd never had a break-in, but I had heard about several incidents of burglary happening in nearby lake houses. The vacation homes were assumed to belong to people who had money, and who left their properties unattended for months at a time. If my computer hadn't been in the living room I might have lain in my bed and let the thief take what he wanted. He needed it more than I did.

But my computer was there, sitting in full view on the table, the only existing copy of my novel saved as a file on the desktop. I cursed my stupidity—why had I not thought to save it to a flash drive or email it to myself? I thought about waking Vladimir, but I was afraid that the thief might hear our voices and run, my laptop in his arms. And so as quietly as I could, I took a large umbrella from the floor of the closet. I knew it was laughable, but I figured I could stab the trespasser if he tried to lunge at me, or open the umbrella to confound him. I walked lightly and slowly down the hall into the living room and flicked on the overhead light.

The refrigerator door was open, and the intruder was crouching in a way that blocked them from my view. I called out, loud, and he rose and hit his head on the bottom of the freezer door.

"Jesus Christ, woman," said my husband of almost thirty years, and I dropped my umbrella to the ground.

☙

"I didn't mean to scare you," John said, after I had yelped, cried a little, thoroughly berated him for the fright he'd given me, and fixed him a plate of leftover frittata and salad and a glass of wine.

"We have to move that table from the front," he said, rubbing his shins to signal he was injured. I sat down on the far side of the couch. I imagined Vladimir still behind me, his arms gripping me.

"What are you doing here?" I tried to ask the question kindly, with a smile.

"I wanted to see you. I didn't know if you were here or not, but I thought I'd try."

He said he missed me. That he'd been going over resigning with Sid and Alexis when he'd felt a gut punch of longing. The college was where we'd come together to start our mutual careers. We were a partnership, and his resignation didn't feel like a decision he should make on his own. He knew we were so distant these days, but he believed what we had was salvageable. He proposed we leave the college as a team. He could try and figure out some sort of consulting career—in advertising or corporate communications—some field in which nobody knew who he was. We could sell both houses and move to a small apartment in a city where we could spend the days going to museums, readings, theater. I could write if I wanted, or get another teaching position wherever we landed. Or we could relocate to Mexico, where our dollars would last forever, and live that yellow-dusted expatriate life, wearing linen and hats and crisping in the sun. We didn't need to stay shackled to this town of prudes and hypocrites.

I nodded, humoring him. He was addled and loud and uncharacteristically chatty. It felt like a matter of time until Vlad would hear the commotion and come into the living room and I didn't know how any of us would react. The more he spoke the more frustrated I became. It was so like John to come in with solutions without taking the time to see what I wanted or how I was feeling. He didn't ask, during his monologue, or even entertain the thought that I might want to stay at the college. He didn't ask how I wanted to live out my retirement, and if I might want to do it with him. It was assumption, always assumption that he could sweep in with some solution and I would simply go along with it.

I rose to pour myself some bourbon, then sat back down beside him as he went on about the cancerous strains of fascism that were infecting the academic campus. In the middle of his rant he interrupted himself. "I want you," he said, and lurched toward me, trying to kiss me with a wide, spread mouth.

I blocked him and turned away. "Stop it," I said. "You show up in the middle of the night, unannounced, what do you think you're doing?" He sat primly for a moment and apologized, but there was a slight bit of mirth in the way he sat, in the lift around his eyes. After everything, he was still funny, and I gave him a pursed-lip smile. He leaned toward me, and using the top of his head and the bristles of his hair, he rubbed up and down against my bared skin like an animal might, tickling and murmuring in a gravelly, playful baby voice he hadn't used with me for years. When he heard my breath catch he started using his hands, pinching and grabbing at parts of me he knew would make me shriek upon contact. I wriggled, leaning back on the couch. He took this as a sign of encouragement and began to pull up my nightgown. But no, I didn't want that, it was all too fast, I had not replaced my underwear after Vlad. I recoiled and yelled, louder than I intended.

I heard movement from the small bedroom and kneed John away from me, just as Vladimir Vladinski, junior professor and distinguished author of *negligible generalities*, emerged naked holding a lamp. After being kneed, John rose to his feet and stood there bemused, looking from Vlad to me for several seconds, until he sat down in the beer-hall chair (the chain still pooled on the floor around its feet) and began to laugh.

"Jesus," Vlad said, and immediately left the room. John kept laughing, putting on a big show with gasps and heaving breaths as I finished my bourbon, smoothed my skirt, patted at my hair, licked my fingers and ran them under my eyes in case of mascara drips. Vladimir returned wearing his T-shirt and the pair of John's pajama bottoms.

"Are those my pants?" John was wheezing and clutching his stomach. "I was wondering where those went. Sorry," he said, and started breathing as though to calm himself.

The whole display was so cynical. "Enough," I said. "Get it together." He pressed his palm to his sternum, closed his eyes and shook his head, then opened them and nodded at me with an artificial look of appreciation. "Nice work," he said, and to my surprise I glimpsed a trace of hurt in his expression.

Then he turned to Vladimir and said, "What's up, man?"

I intervened before he could reply. "Vladimir's in the guest room, John. He needed some space. We both did."

"Oh, okay," John said, nodding. "That explains it. I mean, it doesn't explain why you smell like another man's jizz—"

He could be so crass. I blushed to my forehead. Vladimir looked wounded.

"I do not—" I protested.

"Please." John gestured to interrupt me and smiled. "Who am I to judge."

"I didn't know you were here, Vlad," he continued. "It's truly a surprise. I love it, actually. I'm very infrequently surprised." His face was screwed up and mean.

I told him it was only fair. I felt unexpectedly moved, resentment swirling in my chest.

"Only fair?" He crossed his legs and leaned on his hand like Rodin's *Thinker*. God, he was so bellicose and pompous. "What do you mean?"

"You and Cynthia." Tears were hot against my eyes and I didn't understand why.

"Cynthia and me?" he said, and began laughing again, then repeated it several times in different intonations—"Cynthia and me, Me and Cynthia." He bobbled his head around, his double chin as bulbous as a frog's.

I snapped at him to stop. I felt like taking the chain from the floor and wrapping it around his fat neck.

"I saw you together." He wouldn't do this to me—shrug me off like a hysterical woman. He wouldn't turn me into the paranoid wife. I wouldn't let him.

"Oh, my friends," he said, dropping into a solemn register, "let me reassure you. Cynthia is far too far above my pay grade."

"No, I saw you." My face contorted, I leaned so far off the couch I was nearly standing.

"We're complicit, don't get me wrong. But not in a physical manner. Honestly." He held his hands up like a nabbed bandit. "Honestly."

Vladimir looked from me to John and back. "I thought you saw them 'in flagrante delicto.'"

"I don't know," I said, shrinking back in the couch, my bottom lip heavy.

"We write together," John said.

"*You're* writing?" I asked him.

"Yes," he said, snapping. "You're not the only one who writes."

"Writing what?" I was being cruel but I didn't care, for once I didn't feel an obligation to protect him.

"I don't like your tone."

"I don't like *you*." He was infuriating, talking to me like I was his child.

John stood and lurched from the room. "Where are you going?" I called after him.

"I have to piss," he said over his shoulder, and slammed the door to the bathroom.

Vladimir watched him go, then turned toward me. "I thought you caught them in something."

I assured him that I thought that I had. I explained to him what I had seen, and how surely he would have come to the same conclusion.

"You lied to me." He looked wounded, like a little boy who had been left out of a game.

"I thought it didn't matter to you, whether it was true or not." I was shivering. Ever since childhood, whenever I "got in trouble," my body would respond by dropping in temperature. I moved from the couch, turned on both space heaters, faced them toward each other, and crouched between them. Vladimir rose and stood over me.

"But I believed you. I wouldn't have—"

"How do you know that he's not lying?" I was vibrating with cold, my teeth were chattering. I turned both heaters up to full blast, they roared.

"I'm not lying," John said, emerging from the bathroom, wiping his wet hands on his pants. "I'm writing an epic poem and Cynthia's working on her memoir. We have a writing club. We do drugs, then we write. It's fun."

I think I looked to Vladimir to try and offer some words of peace-keeping or explanation, but before anyone could say anything, he lunged at John, tackling him to the ground, my husband falling like a scarecrow stuffed with wet sand. It was unfortunate, really, how mismatched they were. John barely struggled; he simply attempted to pull himself into the fetal position, trying to cover his face with his hands. My eyes rested on a scratched message on the medieval chair: "Death to Yuppies," written in script decorated with thorns. I found myself thinking about a time when yuppies were a thing we despised. What was a yuppie other than a young professional? What made them so objectionable? They were selfish, they had money, they were blind to societal ills. They liked nouveau cuisine and fitness. Was that it?

"You fuck," Vlad kept repeating, until he had John flattened out on the ground with two shins on his upper thighs and his hands pressed on John's biceps. I couldn't help but feel slightly stirred at the sight of Vlad on top of my husband, his knees spread wide, the fabric of his pants stretched against his rear.

"Do you have any idea what you're doing?" Vlad said, seething and trembling. "You give her drugs? Do you have any idea how fucked-up she could get? She's a mother. I have a kid. You might as well give her gasoline to light herself on fire."

He pounded on John's chest with his hands, more a shove than a blow, then rolled off and lay on the ground, staring at the ceiling.

"I don't give her drugs, son," John said in a weary voice. "She gives them to me." And he glanced at me to let me know this was true.

Vladimir sat up from the floor and twisted in my direction. "You have to take me home," he told me. "Right now."

Once again I felt annoyed at his paternalism. The whiff of the New England preacher that I had sensed early on in our acquaintance returned. His wife was a writer, entitled to her own process and troubles. If she wanted to do drugs (I assumed an amphetamine, possibly Adderall, though I wasn't sure), didn't that simply place her in the ranks of so many other writers, with complicated relationships to substances and work? Even if she was at risk, she was her own person, not his child. Didn't Sontag write all her books on speed, and Kerouac, and so many others? Coleridge? Sartre? Graham Greene? Just like a man to believe a woman had to keep her behavior in line while also churning out a work of genius.

"I've been drinking," I told him. "I can't drive you. We'll have to wait for the morning."

"She's probably on a bender right now," he said, rising to stand. "My child is not safe."

"She's not on a bender," John said. "I keep the drugs locked in my safe. She does a very little. She doesn't trust herself with more."

"She's trying," John added, and I saw that he cared for her, and was touched.

"She's an addict," Vlad said. He was now pacing back and forth. "You don't know. You said she gives you the drugs."

"She gets them from a student."

"So how do you know she doesn't have more?"

John rolled onto all fours, then used the arm of the couch to help himself upright, one heavy, trembling leg after another. "Because we talk. Because I know that all she wants is to get this book done so you can move out of that fucking condo and it can stop being about *you* all the time."

Vladimir stopped pacing, inhaled, and shook his head. John must have channeled something about Cynthia that he recognized, because the tension wilted from his body.

"When in my life has it ever been about me," he said softly. He looked away from us and mouthed something, some retort to Cynthia, I imagined. Then, head down, he held out his hand. "Gimme a cigarette."

"They're there," I told him, and pointed to the windowsill. He walked to them, looking hunched and beaten, put one between his lips and another behind his ear, and stood still, staring at the window for a long time. Eventually I realized he was looking at John and me, reflected in the glass. He lifted the lighter to the cigarette in his mouth.

"You can't smoke in here," I said quickly, and without acknowledging me he put the lighter in his pocket.

He moved toward the sliding door that led to the porch. Facing away from us, he said, "What is wrong with you guys," and shook his head. He struggled to pull the door open, then yanked it clear off the track so that it hung from the frame on a diagonal. John and I exchanged a look, and I put my hand up to stop him from saying anything, like Vlad was an angry teenager whose behavior we were trying to ignore.

We watched his back on the deck, his arm lifting and lowering the cigarette. When he finished he put it out in the coffee can full of water we'd been using as an ashtray (*plip*, in the silence) and walked to the lake. We heard the scraping of the gravel beach against the bottom of the kayak, then the splash and give of the water as he launched the boat.

"Wear a life jacket," John shouted toward his direction.

"You should go out and stop him. He shouldn't kayak at night." I went to the door and peered out, but I couldn't see past six feet in the dark.

"He's fine. What could happen?" John waved my concern away, then raised his eyebrows for a joke. "Ominous, no?"

I batted at his chest, telling him to hush. He reached his arm around me and I folded my head like a swan against his chest. We stood there for a while. He brushed my hair with his large hand.

John tinkered with the radio dial until he found the jazz station, which played something light and melodic as I cleaned the plates from the living room and tidied some refuse from dinner that I had been too tired to deal with earlier that evening. I made us chamomile tea, which we drank at the kitchen table. A comfortable, melancholic fatigue washed over us both, and when, in a recognition of nodding off, I jerked my head awake, I saw John, cheek on the table, asleep.

I crept into the bedroom, pulled back the wool camp blankets and the comforter, and stripped the linens, cold and sodden from the evening's earlier activities. I replaced them with an old set of flannel sheets printed with large sketched cats that Sid had loved when she was little. I remember walking into her room one night and finding her passionately wiping her face back and forth against one of the cat's faces—a seven-year-old's version of romance.

I woke John gently. "I can sleep out here," he said, but I told him I was too tired to bother with the pullout sofa, and he should just come to bed with me.

It was freezing in the bedroom, and the only way we could get warm was to wrap ourselves in and around each other, limb intersecting with limb. He rested his chin on top of my head and I nestled mine in the soft part of his neck.

Entwined, I saw from the bedside clock that it was after four in the morning.

"Are you going back to the college for the hearing tomorrow?" I asked.

"I don't know yet."

"Do you want me to set an alarm?"

"No."

He was emanating a kind of heat that calmed me at the core of my nervous system. *Security some men call the suburbs of hell.*

I was nearly gone when I remembered. "What's your poem about?"

"What?"

"The epic poem you're writing. What's it about?"

"Oh," he murmured. "It's about a modern-day Don Quixote. An old man who refuses to see the world as it is."

And huddled together like the babes in the wood, innocent and abandoned, we fell asleep.

XX.

The first time I wake I am surrounded by orange and smoke. Vladimir is pushing at me, shouting at me, but I can't understand his words. Colors and shadows. He half lifts me and I realize I am supposed to walk and I try to walk but I can't get my brain to speak correctly to my legs and so he mostly pulls me through the light, dark, cold, and heat out to the beach, where he puts my lower half in water and leaves again.

The second time I wake I am in a puke-yellow room with beige plastic molding on the ceiling. My body feels a pain I cannot countenance. I try to say hello. What comes from my throat sounds like a hum. Something, someone, appears in my vision and says, okay, okay, and then disappears. I strain to keep my eyes open as long as I can but then they close again.

The third time I wake I hear Sid's voice. Mom, she says, Mom, there you are. She sounds muffled and strangled. Her head appears before me, blurry, warped, but hers—blink twice if you can hear me, Mom—and I try to say, of course I can hear you, but all that comes out is a croaking sound and Sid gasps—just blink twice, Mom—she says, and so I do and she says I love you and I close my eyes once more.

XXI.

I am diagnosed with third-degree burns on 22 percent of my body. Mostly my legs, some on my neck and the lower part of my face.

John is diagnosed with third-degree burns on more than 30 percent of his body. His torso, up the back of his head, down the back of his legs, on his outer arms.

I am in the hospital for twenty days, rehabilitation for four months.

John is in the hospital for thirty-two days, rehabilitation for six months.

They patch our skin with the skin of a cadaver.

XXII.

*V*ladimir came back from his kayak ride and saw the conflagration inside. No phone to call 911, he dove into the lake water then ran into the house and dragged me out, then John, before running and knocking on neighboring lake houses until he found someone home. Much later I ask him how he chose who to save first. He didn't choose, really, he says, there was no time. But maybe, if he delved, there might have been the thought that he should save me first, if only because I am younger.

XXIII.

The day I transfer from the hospital to the rehabilitation center, Sid and Alexis come to settle me into my room. It is also yellow, and I make a joke about The Yellow Wallpaper, which is low-hanging fruit, but I am still on medication. We sit down, me on my twin bed with its faux polyester quilt, Sid in the armchair, Alexis behind her, her hand holding Sid's. They look like they are posing for a 1950s photograph of a corporate executive and his wife. "I'm pregnant," Sid tells me. "From the man on the train, do you remember, I told you about him?" Alexis squeezes her hand. "Are you happy?" I ask Alexis. "I am," she says. "We know nothing about him," Sid adds. "So it's like he doesn't exist," Alexis finishes.

XXIV.

The insurance assessment concludes that I neglected to turn off the space heaters.

My computer, containing the only draft of my book, is destroyed in the fire.

XXV.

*J*ohn arranges for Sid to drive him home from rehabilitation, but she is so pregnant and busy implanting herself into the infrastructure of her new job before she goes on maternity leave that I convince her to let me do it. We had gone to different facilities, at my request. I wanted to be as anonymous as possible while I healed, I didn't want to confront my relationship and repair my body at the same time and John felt the same way, I knew without asking. We haven't spoken since the hospital except for a few necessary administrative emails with Sid cc'd; otherwise we let her act as our go-between. Our silence isn't out of animosity, more a conservation of energy. We need the solitary time to reconcile ourselves with the new realities of our physical forms before we face each other.

I tell Sid not to tell him about the change of plans, that I'll come to him as a surprise. In the last few months a friend of Alexis's from law school had been working to procure an out-of-court settlement for us from the company that manufactured the space heaters, and the week of his release I receive the official amount of our remuneration. It is, as one might say in Victorian novels, a handsome sum, one that creates many possibilities (money is energy, an investment banker once told me), and I decide I will bring the news to him, to give us something to talk about, to frame our journey homeward, as it were. I even consider packing a picnic with cold chicken and sparkling lemonade, stopping in a wooded park on the way back, setting him up in a camp chair with a blanket on his knees, and recounting the happy news of our newfound inheritance.

But on the day of his release, it is sunless, cool, and spritzing rain, the final gasp of the dismal upstate New York spring giving way to summer. It is probably for the best, I tell myself. I don't know how either he or I will feel in the presence of each other, it would be a mistake to try and force us into some scene, I don't want to negotiate with the pressure of my own expectations, and besides all that, I don't know what the money means for us, for me, for us. A few days earlier a home health-aide service installed a bed on the ground floor, as John apparently still had some time before he could climb the stairs easily, and I'd spent hours since then arranging our knickknacks and furniture around it so that it felt somewhat coherent with the room. Two months after my release I am still physically compromised, and I break our Shiite mask and crack the glass on several pictures, unable to lift and move things properly. That morning I lug a heavy nightstand to the side of the bed and one of its legs cuts a long white gash in the wooden floor. I arrange the stand with a lamp and a bouquet of hyacinth I cut from our garden, then lay down for an hour to recover my strength.

His facility is two hours north of us, a wooded and rural area, populated mostly, as the signage would indicate, by a spread-out smattering of communes, hunting enthusiasts, eccentrics, and evangelicals. The final stretch I drive for thirty miles on a gravel road through dense forest, the spring flora—yellow, hot pink, lilac, ghost white—showing in patches through the green of the trees, the colors overbright and unsettling against the gray of the day. The entrance has imposing stone gates, followed by a long approach drive flanked by two low stone walls draped with ivy and edged by dripping, blooming forsythia. I feel momentarily jealous—my rehab place had been a new-construction building in suburbia—but when after some winding I arrive at the parking lot, I relent. The building itself is nothing to speak of: squat, brick 1980s architecture with disproportionately small windows spaced in awkward distance from each other, a few grubby benches in front, and a plastic gazebo I'm sure nobody ever uses tilting on an uneven patch of ground like an afterthought.

A young woman in pastel camouflage scrubs leads me to John's room. "He's a nice man," she says, and when I feebly joke that she probably says that about all the patients she smiles and tells me that she does, but with him she means it. At his door I close my eyes and take a few deep breaths to settle myself before knocking. Electra spends the entirety of Sophocles's play in a doorway, I say to my students, when we read his Theban trilogy in my Adaptations course. She is unable to return home and unable to venture into the world. Pay attention to doorways, to paths, to in-between spaces, I tell them, these are the places of transformation. The young woman in scrubs, who I don't realize is still standing behind me, misconstrues my hesitation and reaches around my waist, raps at the door, then turns the handle and pushes it ajar. "You're fine to go in," she says, encouraging me. "He's waiting."

I find him, bags packed, sitting in an armchair reading a newer translation of *Life Embitters* by the Catalan writer Josep Pla. He's lost about twenty-five pounds and his leanness suits him—he looks elegant and patrician. I didn't realize it until that moment, but I had expected, in line with some clichéd scene, to walk in on him numbly watching bad daytime television, smiling and drooling, his mind and spirit dampened. The fact that he is upright and reading, and reading something of substance, that he is still holding himself to a level of intellectual rigor even though he is injured and battered and dismissed from the world . . .

"Where's Sid?" he asks, in his style of abrasive fatherly concern. "Why are you here? Is she all right?"

I reassure him and explain my thinking. "We were going to see each other at home anyway," I say.

He nods, is still for a moment, and then, gripping the padded armrests tightly, he stands. I see that the hair from the back of his neck to the crown of his head is completely gone, replaced by a reddish-purple graft. He notices me looking and swivels his neck to reference it. "It will fade," he says. "I might be able to get plugs eventually, or so they tell me."

Later he tells me he was disturbed to see me, he had been thinking of the drive home as a spiritual enterprise, a journey he was trusting to gradually reacquaint himself with his old familiar world. "I pictured myself getting out of the car and touching the shrubs and hose on the side of the house and laying my hands against the siding," he says. "And then coming in through the back porch and finding you inside, bent over a magazine or puttering in the kitchen."

At that time, though, he offers no objections. He slowly bends down to retrieve an electric-blue sock cap from the corner of the chair. It is a fashionable and arresting color, and when he puts it on it conceals most of the back of his head, brings out his eyes, and, with his weight loss, makes him look like a weathered European longshoreman from a travel brochure.

"Your daughter bought it for me," he says, sheepish.

I nod my approval. "Shall we go?" I ask.

He agrees but doesn't move, and I realize one of his hands is still tightly wrapped on the arm of the chair for support. A cane rests against the wall, slightly out of his reach. I hand it to him and he takes it without looking at me. "We'll have to call someone for the bags I imagine," I say.

"Unless you can take them," he replies.

"I certainly can't," I say, and we both exhale a huff of something like laughter—a sound of shared resignation. I call the front desk and a teenaged boy arrives with a luggage rack. By the time he comes, I have taken John's other arm, the one not gripping the cane, and, not wanting to move for fear of faltering, we stand still, as though posing for a painting, and watch him work. "You guys are so cute together," the boy says, before pushing the cart out the door. John and I glance at each other in mock horror and follow him through the dim, blue-carpeted hallway.

The discharge process takes nearly two hours, so by the time we settle into the car, laden with pills and creams and printouts, we are both very hungry, and head directly to the nearest diner I find, which turns out to be a chrome-wrapped homage to some idea of the 1950s, with large spiral-bound plastic-coated menus.

Once we are seated, John reaches across the table and feels the silk scarf I have wrapped around my throat to cover my scarring.

I grew up with a picture of my mother's grandmother in my home. She was seated, wearing an elegant dress with a large bow on one side of her face. "See that bow," I remember my mother said once when she caught me looking at the photograph. "They didn't iodize salt when she was growing up. That bow is covering an enormous goiter." When I asked her how big, she said, "The size of an Idaho potato. At least."

Thanks to videos on the internet, I have, in the past two months since my discharge, become quite skilled at tying various fabrics in loopy configurations to conceal my damaged skin. I have never liked my neck, anyway.

"Can I see?" John asks, and I untie the loops to reveal the evidence of my burn that creeps up as high as the side of my chin. He reaches over and feels the bottom edge of my face.

"You don't need to cover it," he says. "It's rather pretty."

Later I'll remember what he said and become more emboldened to leave the scarf at home occasionally. Sometimes it will feel empowering, to lay myself bare to the furtive stares and averted eyes. Sometimes it will feel like old times, like when I put on a few pounds and would force myself to wear my tightest pants, no matter how they chafed or dug, as a form of punishment.

But that day in the diner I reply, "No thank you," and quickly redo my wrap before the waiter arrives to take our order.

We share a club sandwich and a garden salad and a plate of sweet potato fries, and then, because I want some ceremony to my announcement, I convince him to split a slice of coconut cake with me. When it arrives at our table, taller and larger than any piece of cake should ever be, I tell him about the settlement. He pauses, hearing the figure, blinks, and peers into his coffee, somber. I am anxious for him to respond. "What are you thinking?" I ask, an edge to my voice.

"I'm thinking . . ." He pauses. "I'm thinking . . ." He pauses again and I snap at him to please talk. "I'm thinking I should have ordered the lobster," he says, mournfully staring at his cup.

I choke on something between a groan and a laugh, making a far louder sound than I intend—so loud that the girl at the register starts toward me and I have to wave her off.

"Sorry," he says, smiling at his success, his eyes still cast down. He taps his fork against the cake plate in the "shave and a haircut" rhythm. "So you're not stuck with me after all. You could get your own place, I could get my own place, we could hire people to take care of us, the whole thing," he says.

Yes. I'd had the same thought—the money made separating simple. All the logistics that seemed so daunting could be handed off to someone else, someone who could be paid, whether it be selling the house or handling the medical bills or even buying us new homes in distinct and distant locations. "We could."

"I have some news to tell you, actually," he says. "The college is letting me keep my pension. Honorable discharge. They feel bad, I guess."

I congratulate him. Neither of us speaks for several minutes. I draw lines in the heaps of excess frosting we scraped from the cake.

"Dramatic irony, isn't it? We burned and we were burned. Very French, like Balzac," I say.

He smirks. "Heavy-handed, if you ask me."

I feel an old sardonic irritation tug at my chest. "Well, we were never so mighty, so our fall wasn't much to see. Besides, we got away with it," I say. "Mostly."

"You can't think about it like that," he says, his eyes dark and dismissive. "Getting away with something, not getting away with something, moral retribution. I don't matter, you don't matter. To think we do is just marketing. It's this cult of personality. You know that."

"I don't think that's a very popular argument right now."

"I'm not a very popular guy right now." He tilts his head and spreads his hands in the style of an old vaudeville performer.

"No, that's true, you're not," I say. And I imagine myself in an apartment, each space filled with the definitive and deliberate quiet of my own choices. A velvet sofa and bookshelves with a ladder. A cat, maybe, or maybe no cat, I had never craved pets. Then I picture John in his apartment, the leather club chairs from his office and faded red rugs bought by Sid (or me). A woman. There for the money, one way or another. Or as I look at him, his face framed by his new cap that Sid had surely procured from one of her fancy menswear stores, there for him. Does the woman bother me? Not really. It does all seem like a bit of a waste though, I think, to divide that energy, money, money, energy, when something simpler could be arranged.

Walking down the ramp of the restaurant, we stop and watch a small crew paste what appears to be an anti-evolution sign on a billboard across the road. It feels like a scene from a 1960s auteur film, the ugly poster rising against the dim sky, an old couple standing in the drizzle in front of the blinding silver building. I picture it being shot from above, the two of us small, arms linked, John's blue cap a vibrant beacon.

"Let's get the fuck out of here," he says, after we witness a panel featuring a crossed-out monkey silhouette erected and flattened on the frame.

Toward the end of the drive, his breathing is measured, his position in the seat pains him. Once home it requires a huge effort to help him to the bed, where he falls asleep on his side clutching a body pillow.

Please don't think I stay with him because of some Florence Nightingale syndrome, because he needs me and that gives me purpose and dominion or some tired story like that. The home health aide comes the very next day and cares for him until he is self-sufficient. I don't sacrifice my independence or interests; the following night, in fact, I attend a taped screening of a new, much-lauded opera at a movie theater in Albany. No, things work out because of the way they work out, because I open one door and then another, because I find that ease can be one of the greater forms of freedom.

XXVI.

John and I use some of the money to buy an apartment in the Washington Heights area of Manhattan. We sell the land the cabin stood on but keep our house in town—I still go upstate to teach two days a week during the academic year, though John mostly stays in the city. In our new lives, we watch the baby while Sid and Alexis work. We take him on slow walks in Fort Tryon Park and I look at all the bodies of all the people and concentrate on their beauty. We go to physical therapy. We go to the 92nd Street Y. We itch. We get memberships to Off-Broadway theaters. We rub prescription-strength cream on each other's hard-to-reach places. We become "friends" of museums. We go to film festivals at Lincoln Center. We complain of numbness. We plan a visit to Hungary. We get along, we're too frightened of what might happen if we didn't. We talk about art and ideas. Burns come with long-term complications. Of course, it sometimes hurts to move.

Vladimir writes a novel about a younger man's tender affair with an older woman. She dies in a fire in a cabin in the mountains. There are many descriptions, similes, and metaphors that concern the loosening quality of her skin. The book is deemed well-written but "bleak" and does not do well, though he is long-listed for a few awards.

Cynthia's book is a surprise national bestseller, a word-of-mouth hit that wins a National Book Critics Circle Award. She explains to me that "national bestseller" doesn't mean as much as it used to, now that nobody buys books. Vlad tells her that at least she recouped her advance, jealous but proud. She says, you will be next, baby, with generosity. It is like an ice floe has chipped off her, she is secure at last, or for now. They buy a renovated Victorian in the middle of town. When

I go on semiretirement, Cynthia is offered and accepts a tenure-track position.

John finishes his epic poem, submits it to a major poetry publication. They publish it, but it is immediately met with objection by young writers of the community, who deem the poem objectionable due to its sexual content and his history. John takes up pottery making. He likes the feeling of damp clay between his hands, soothing and cool.

After a year or so I begin to write once again. I email my work to myself after every session. The book is a painstakingly researched, fictionalized account of Sadie the Goat, a female pirate from the nineteenth century who wears her own pickled ear, bitten off years prior in a barroom brawl by Gallus Mag, enclosed in a locket around her neck. I write very slowly, and very little, every day. I am skeptical, now, of the flood. I am not nicer or more appreciative than I was before. But I am more measured. This is a kind of peace, or a warning.

Sid's baby is beautiful, and smiles all the time, a clear sign of intelligence. He lies on his mat and I read Shakespeare and Dickinson aloud so that he may absorb the benefits of their cadences. As a mother, Sid surprises me; she is natural, temperate, tender. I cannot think of any baby more lucky than he, having the parents he has.

So many systems disrupted. So many knots untangled, undone.

XXVII

One night when I'm upstate the front entrance bell rings. Once again, a visitor, unfamiliar with our town custom of entering through the back. When I open the door, a woman in her mid-thirties, ragged tissue in hand, introduces herself. I ask her in and pour her and myself a glass of wine, though since the fire and all the attendant bleariness that came with the healing process and medication, I barely ever drink anymore, wanting clarity above all else.

We sit in the living room. John and I moved most of our travel souvenirs to the apartment in Manhattan, so the space is spare. When I return (or visit, maybe, I no longer know which) from the cramped city, I like to be surrounded by luxurious expanses of empty floors and walls.

"He's not here, is he?" she asks. No, I tell her, he rarely returns to the house, he finds the long drive uncomfortable. She nods.

"I haven't seen him for more than ten years," she says. "I doubt he would recognize me. I've changed so much." She looks down sadly at her body, which is not to her liking.

She is young and beautiful. "You are beautiful," I say. "He would certainly know you."

She smiles and asks if I knew it was her.

"That you were one of the seven?" I ask. "Your name was on the list."

"No, that I started it. I got in contact with the other women. I organized the letter."

"You did," I say, my chest tightening. "Why?"

And I looked at her, this woman who had once been so formidable and impressive, charred, red, snakelike skin climbing up her sad, lined face. Once I asked John if she hated me, and he told me she didn't think about other people enough to hate them. I was sitting between his legs, and he was telling me how talented I was. I didn't ask, at what? I was blind at the time, reeling from the humiliation of high school, the scorn of my parents, the cruelty of the entitled young men who surrounded me at college. I had a volatile sense of self-regard, unable to befriend even the kindest girls my age while deeming professors my intimates, if only in my mind. "Talented at what?" I should have asked. Fucking, giving blow jobs, being desperate, he might have said.

    I was in my early thirties, sitting inside of a blue and gray cocoon of boredom, an ergonomic chair outside the office of a senior vice president of a national accounting firm. Cars, travel arrangements, coffee runs, meetings, schedules, IT departments. Fielding angry calls from his bosses. Enduring, liking maybe, the moments he leaned over my shoulder to look at what I was working on. The smell of his upper-management cologne. Tabs of master's degree programs saved on the desktop, for which I was too deadened, at the end of the day, to address. Weekends drinking and doing yoga, trying to recover a sense of self one way or another. The money wasn't even that great. My only question was "Why did I think I was better than this?"

    When I think of my mental state in college, I think of the Drunk Toddler video on the internet. In the video, a toddler dressed in a midriff top, her baby chub pressing against the confines of her clothes, lumbers from mini table to mini table chugging drinks that her parents have made to look like little alcohol bottles. She knocks over chairs, throws plates, stumbling with delirious confidence. She smears food all over her face. She is delighted with herself, unaware of the mess she is making, the sight she looks, the implications of her movements.

    He should have seen it. He should have seen how young I was inside, how little I knew about what I wanted, about what was good for me. He should have thrown me out of his office, told me to take a cold shower, to grow up, to find friends or a boyfriend my own age. I was of age, but I was a child. He had complimented me, praised me, made me feel as though I had something to offer the world, but that was only courtship, I finally realized. I had taken it as truth.

    As I sat at my desk, highlighting receipts, or on hold with the billing department, I started to wonder if there were other women like me, stumbling around in their late twenties and early thirties, wasting their lives, unable to find purpose. Other women who were so confused about what they were worth. I felt infused with an energy I hadn't experienced for years, since before college, a sense that what I was doing was right, that it needed to be done. The college was supposed to steer me through the transition from adolescence to adulthood, and instead, it had knocked me completely off course. I reached out to alumni. It wasn't difficult to find other women. We didn't deserve to be treated so casually. Casually. That was the word. At an age when every moment was important, when we were forming our conceptions of who we were, we had been used and passed off without care.

Perhaps that is what she thinks. Or perhaps that is what I imagine the young woman, sitting across from me in the same seat as Vladimir sat on the night of our first meeting, *might* think.

"There were long-term psychological effects," she says at one point in the evening. "I was so young," she says at another. "I didn't know what it meant," she says, "and I didn't realize, until much later, what it did to me."

I take it all in. She wants me to bear witness and I am happy to comply. "Are you better now?" I ask.

"Mostly," she replies.

She diverts the conversation frequently, telling me about fellow classmates and their outcomes, or reflecting on the changes in the town and student body since she graduated.

When we part, I touch her shoulder and say, "Everything is still in front of you." Her eyes fill with tears and she thanks me. I don't mind saying it. I believe it, and she needs to hear it.

Dazzling, explosive, pitch-dark and blinding light, like a steamroller, like a humming bird, in the body, in the atmosphere, in the currents of our blood, on the street corners, hidden in melodies, in smells and dropping temperatures and rising speed. In rooms we forgot we've inhabited, clothing we forgot we owned, touch we forgot we felt.

Oh, Shame.

Acknowledgments

*T*he translation of the epigraph is by Anne Carson.

Thanks to David Rogers for early reading and advice. Thanks to Anna Stein—I feel so lucky that this book and I found our way to you. Thanks to Lauren Wein for artful and inspired editing and conversation. Thank you to Julie Flanagan, Lucy Luck, Claire Nozieres, Grace Robinson, and Will Watkins. Thanks to Ravi Mirchandani and Roshani Moorjani. Thank you to the Avid Reader cohort, especially Jessica Chin, Amy Guay, Jordan Rodman, and Meredith Vilarello.

Thanks to Hannah Cabell and Ryan King, Jennie and Chris Jonas, Janet and Rachel Kleinman, Miriam Silverman and Adam Green. Thanks to Steve Coats for scenic inspiration. Thanks to Hannah Heller for letting me use her joke and more. Endless thanks to Kallan Dana for her multiple reads, constant discussion, friendship, and life support.

Thanks to my parents. Thank you to Ruth, my star, and Archie, my good luck charm. And thank you, Adam, my first reader, thoughtful editor, biggest advocate, best audience, and truest friend.